No Gold on Boothill

A Western Trio

No Gold on Boothill

A Western Trio

DAN CUSHMAN

Five Star • Waterville, Maine

"Buckaroos of the Big Die" first appeared in *The Pecos Kid Western* (6/51). Copyright © 1951 by Popular Publications, Inc. Copyright © renewed 1979 by Dan Cushman. Copyright © 2001 by Dan Cushman for restored material.

"The Conestoga Pirate" first appeared in *Frontier Stories* (Winter, 44). Copyright © 1944 by Fiction House, Inc. Copyright © renewed 1972 by Dan Cushman. Copyright © 2001 by Dan Cushman for restored material.

"No Gold on Boothill" first appeared in *Action Stories* (Summer, 45). Copyright © 1945 by Fiction House, Inc. Copyright © renewed 1973 by Dan Cushman. Copyright © 2001 by Dan Cushman for restored material.

Five Star First Edition Western Series.

Published in 2001 in conjunction with Golden West Literary Agency.

Set in 11 pt. Plantin by Al Chase.

Printed in the United States on permanent paper.

Library of Congress Cataloging-in-Publication Data

Cushman, Dan.
   No gold on Boothill : a western trio / by Dan Cushman.
—1st ed.
     p. cm.
   Contents: Buckaroos of the Big Die—The conestoga pirate—No gold on Boothill.
    ISBN 0-7862-2735-4 (hc : alk. paper)
    1. Western stories. I. Title.
PS3553.U738 N55 2001
813'.54—dc21   2001023677

Table of Contents

Buckaroos of the Big Die

The Pecos Kid Western, initiated by Popular Publications, Inc., with the first issue dated July, 1950, was essentially a hero pulp magazine, like *The Masked Rider Western* or *The Rio Kid Western*, magazines published by the competing Standard Magazines, *The Pecos Kid Western* featured a long short novel in every issue about the Pecos Kid, but unlike most of the Western hero pulp magazines all of these stories were written by a single author, Dan Cushman, who had created the character especially for *The Pecos Kid Western*. The year 1950 was not an auspicious time to be creating a new pulp magazine, since pulp magazines were being replaced on newsstands by paperback books. Despite the hostile market in 1950, *The Pecos Kid Western* did continue publication for five issues, concluding with the issue dated June, 1951. The stories about the Pecos Kid that Dan Cushman wrote for this magazine have not otherwise been available since their first publication. THE PECOS KID (Five Star Westerns, 1999) contains the first two short novels. THE PECOS KID RETURNS (Five Star Westerns, 2000) contains the third and fourth stories. This is the final Pecos Kid story.

I

"Trouble at Ridley Landing"

The three men had ridden hard, and they had ridden a long way. Now it was sunset, and they reined in at the rim of the Missouri River with Fort Benton, Montana Territory, spread out on the flats below.

William Calhoun Warren, better known as the Pecos Kid, unlimbered his lean body, spat alkali dust from his lips, and spoke: "Well, there she is, boys. I only wish we could stay a while."

One of his companions was huge, blunt-faced Jim Swing; the other was Butch, the mixed blood whose name was Hernandez Pedro Gonzales y Fuente Jesús María Flanagan.

Pecos's words made Hernandez jerk erect and stop fondling the guitar tied back of his saddle. "Eh? Why have we been riding night and day eef not to stop a while, *señor?* Do you not know what thees town is? Thees is Fort Benton, the Paris of the prairies, the Madrid of the Beeg Muddy . . . Fort Benton weeth its peetfalls of pleasure all filled to the second story weeth beautiful women all waiting for Hernandez." He drove the heel of his palm to the cantle of his saddle for emphasis. "*Señor,* no! Your Hernandez will not break the heart of one single woman after she has waited for him so long."

"Women, women!" Big Jim said in a voice that was so high-pitched it came as a surprise even for those long acquainted with him. "All you think about is women. What I need is a swim in the river, a barbershop shave, and a big steak with apple pie."

"Was it for Hernandez the two old maid seesters in Miles City pulled out each other's hair in that disgraceful spectacle, or was . . . ?"

"Sure, I like women. A couple or three of 'em, but I know when to quit."

A grin relaxed the lines in the Pecos Kid's face, He took off his hat and fingered some reddish hair away from his forehead. His hair had sweated and dried again, leaving it stiff. He was good-looking when he smiled. It transformed his face, wiping away the hard lines that had been placed there by three years of civil war and ten of the frontier all before reaching the age of thirty.

"Well, maybe we can stay."

"Maybe, *señor?* You believe all this they tell you in Helena, that big Jawn Ridley is up again from being dead and shooting hell out of your friends? In Chihuahua every summer do half of my friends shoot hell out of the other half of my friends, and do I ride from here to there trying to save them? And eef they did, what would they do to me but toss me in prison for my debts? I say to hell weeth all thees. Eef there is a fight, let it come looking for me. All I want is to sing songs and make love."

Pecos said: "The point of it is, boys, we had a hand in that ruckus one time, and I hate to leave anything half finished."

Hernandez said: "Hah!" He scraped alkali off his tongue and spat. "Another day of thees and I tell you who will be feenished . . . your poor *amigo,* Hernandez, and, when I am buried on the lonesome prairie, who then will comfort the weeping women from Milk River to Río Concho, all tearing out their hair like farmers pulling carrots?"

Jim said: "The only ones that'll pull out their hair when you die, Butch, are the ones you owe money."

"Ha! My creditors are all bald-headed already."

"I'm not bald-headed."

Pecos said: "You will be before you collect two bits of the money Butch owes you."

Hernandez cursed him in choice Spanish, English, and Apache while riding down the freight road to Fort Benton's main street. It was a gee-hawing welter of freight outfits, all trying to find space at the Stephens Company docks where the sternwheeler *Red Cloud* was unloading.

"You wait here," Pecos said, and dismounted in front of the stage office. "I'll inquire. Then we'll know where we stand."

Hernandez, with a handsome flash of teeth against mahogany-tanned skin, cried: "*Sí,* I will wait for you inside that saloon!"

"Like hell! You take on a load of liquor before I find out what's what and I'll drain it out of you through a Forty-Four caliber hole."

Hernandez challenged him to a duel, but he did it in a tired voice, through a sense of duty. Pecos was inside only a couple minutes. Seeing the jaw-locked look on his face as he came back through the door, Hernandez, with a deep sigh, said: "Farewell, Fort Benson, gem of the Gros Ventre country, pearl of the prairies. Farewell, you peetfalls of pleasure. Tonight your Hernandez is not there. Tonight your Hernandez rides weeth that madman from Texas, the Pecos Kid."

"Yeah," Pecos said. "We got to pick up some oats. A little grub. Get a sack of beer if you want to, Butch, but we'll have to drink it along the way. That fellow in Last Chance was right about Jawn Ridley. He's up and cutting loose again."

11

"Let heem cut loose! Nobody has cut loose at your Hernandez seence that enraged father in Coeur d'Alene one month ago."

"Well, it isn't just that. You recollect old Gus Hyslop? Mighty nice old fellow . . . for a Yankee. He's in Ridley Landing, waiting to be hanged. Know what for? For killing Carris Garde. *And I killed Carris Garde myself.*"

"*¡Madre de Dios!*" whispered Hernandez. "We will not then waste time on beer. He is to be hanged where?"

"He was alive three days ago when that sternwheeler, *Red Cloud*, left the landing. The U.S. commissioner stayed his execution pending an appeal to the territorial governor. An appeal was just a formality, though. The governor won't buck Jawn Ridley. Not for anybody as unimportant as old Gus. So it depends on when the governor's decision gets there."

"Perhaps they have hanged heem already. Forgive me, Pecos, but we must theenk of thees things."

"Yeah." He said it through tight lips, his narrow, pale-blue eyes looking toward bluff-lined prairie rims to the east. "Yeah. You know what'd be worse'n getting there a week too late? It'd be getting there five minutes too late."

They crossed the rickety wagon bridge, and climbed slowly to the prairie rim. It was growing dark. In the far distance they could see the break between ranges of mountains where the Missouri River dug its gorge. The Arrow and the Judith flowed in there. Farther, beyond vision, lay the Musselshell, and a hard day's ride after that was their goal, Ridley Landing, headquarters for big Jawn Ridley's cattle empire. They had worked for Jawn once and had fought with him once, and now they were going back.

They rode all night and stopped at a deserted line shack to swap saddles.

"Three sleeps. Maybe *two*. We'll make better time by

riding through the cool hours and taking one rest from noon to four. We won't worry about the stock. I got a couple hundred dollars yet. We'll trade our stock and money to boot when we get to Dykeman's over on the Judith. He always has a big herd rounded up for the remount buyers this time of year. We got to get to Ridley Landing. We got to get there if it kills us and the horses both."

They rode toward Arrow River, slept through the hot hours, fried bacon and pan bread on a tiny sagebrush fire, and pushed on. They crossed the Arrow at night, and the Judith at night, and swapped for fresh horses at Dykeman's at dawn. They rode through badlands, prairie hills, and badlands again to Musselshell Landing.

The French-Cree proprietor of the trading post awoke and thumped forward in his chair when they walked tired, sweaty, and alkali-coated through the door. He shrugged and gave them a yellow-toothed grin when asked about the fate of Hyslop at Ridley Landing, thirty miles to the east.

"Perhaps they hang him yesterday, *m'shus*. Ridley Landing is a long ride for one hanging, unless, of course, it is someone in a man's own family. He is your papa, perhaps?"

"Just a friend."

"Eh, it will teach people to stay away from Ridley Landing and come to me, a good store." He stood in the door and shouted after them: "Tell them that! In four years since I bought the store, the sheriff has not visited once."

It was early, with the sun just beginning to show a pinkish glow over the summits of the Wolftone Hills. Ridley Landing, a cluster of log shacks, lay below on a shoulder of land separating Big Muddy Creek from the Missouri. It might have been a ghost town. There was no movement anywhere, no rigs or horses at the wagon yard, no sign of life at the big ice house that served as a jail.

Hernandez, resting one leg around the saddle horn, said: "It looks like no hanging today."

Pecos said through tight lips: "How about a hanging *yesterday?*"

It was seldom that he used spurs on a horse, but he did now, and rode down the bluff through a cloud of dust. He held a steady trot across the bottoms where sage grew high enough to slap his stirrups, forded the shallow breadth of the Big Muddy, and drew up by a shack where smoke drifted from the chimney.

A shaggy, greasy man came to the door. Pecos recognized him to be an old wolfer called Belly River George.

George spat tobacco juice, wiped his whiskers with the back of his hand, and said: "Well, damn me, if it ain't the Pecos Kid, back looking for his chunk of hang rope, too. And there's the Mex and the big fellow. Say, you do have a gun, don't you? . . . comin' back here after everything, ready to spit right in Jawn Ridley's eye."

"What happened to Gus Hyslop?"

"Now there's a question! You tell me. . . ."

"Is he alive?"

"Far as I'm concerned, he's alive, but I wouldn't wager on him being alive too long. I'll wager he'd have been alive longer if he'd stayed inside the skookum house, instead of busting loose and getting. . . ."

Pecos shouted: "Stop talking in circles!"

Belly River George let his eyes rove to the gun at Pecos's hip and back to his face. "Don't get ringy. I. . . ."

"What happened?"

"Why, they had him in jail, the old ice house yonder, one they always used, and he caved in the skull of that deppity U.S.

14

marshal they sent up from Helena, and got away. He. . . ."

"When was this?"

"Last night. Couldn't've been later than ten o'clock. I don't own a watch, but I was over at. . . ."

"Who's after him?"

"Everybody that was in town. Fifteen, eighteen men under Bill Oriet. He's the deppity from Threesleep. Two-gun deppity with a mustache, gut full of twelve-year-old bourbon and Havana cigar ash all over his vest. Fanciest damned deppity. . . ."

Hernandez said: "Hyslop kill the marshal? Hyslop never killed so much as a chicken."

"All right, don't get angry with me. I ain't fighting you nor Jawn Ridley. I'm just a poor damned trapper. I was here, fixing to cook some doughgods for breakfast, not bothering anybody, when you. . . ."

"Sorry, George." Pecos relaxed and managed a grin. His eyes roved the town, and the hills beyond. Hyslop had escaped over those hills, he supposed, heading back to the homesteaders' community on the Sage and Horn Creek. The posse would run him down. Perhaps the posse had already run him down. Jawn Ridley's posse.

He quieted Hernandez, who was beside him asking questions, and said: "Go ahead, George. Tell the whole story."

"Like I said, they had him in the ice house. Built a special log wall down the middle. Made it half cell and half a sort of office where a shotgun guard could sit. Hyslop had been there better'n a month, ever since they found him holed up in the badlands, and he never made any more move than a rabbit. Well, they were getting ready to hang him day after tomorrow, when this Deppity U.S. Marshal McGraw showed up from Helena. Heard he had a ruckus with Bill Oriet and Ridley, but I don't know anything about that. All I know is the marshal was guarding him last night. He must have been asleep in his chair, and Hyslop wrenched an iron leg off his cot and hit him on the head with it. Reached out through the little window they'd made in the door to shove grub through. Caved in the marshal's skull like he'd had a twelve-pound sledge. Got away. Stole Joe Echol's horse. They trailed him east of town up the ridge by the lugs that Joe had in the horse-shoes. I don't know how much farther. Hell, nobody needs to tell me where he's headed. He's headed for that outlaw town at Bull Sink."

"How did he get out of the cell? Did he smash in the door?"

It was plain that Belly River George had already given thought to the question and still wasn't sure of the answer. "No-o, he unlocked it. They figure he reached out with a piece of the bed, and got hold of the key after the marshal was dead. I don't know. As I said, I'm just a trapper, mindin' my own business, not wanting to get caught in the ruckus."

Pecos gave him a dollar, saying—"Buy a drink."—and rode on at a lope, dismounting, limping on languid legs inside the jail.

The marshal's overturned chair was there, and a blood-stain. The plank door to the cell stood open. Pecos supposed it was possible that someone could retrieve a key from a fallen man outside, although it was hard to see just how.

Hernandez, standing behind him, said: "That old man, Hyslop, did not kill him, no more than he killed Carris Garde. Ridley did not dare hang him for fear of the G.A.R. in Helena. Perhaps he will not fear the G.A.R. so much now that he can say this poor old man has killed the United States mar-shal, eh?"

Jim said: "You mean Ridley would kill a United States marshal?"

"I mean he will win if he has to kill the very governor of the territory."

The bloodstain had made Pecos a trifle sick. He turned and limped into the early daylight, pulling his Levi's down from the insides of his legs. He kept looking at the yellow clay ridge over which the posse, some hours earlier, had trailed the escaping man. Trailed him in the dark. It didn't seem reasonable. It was more likely that someone had watched him escape, and now they'd be following him from a safe distance, giving him the chance to hole up at one of the homestead camps. From the start it had seemed ridiculous that Jawn Ridley would go to so much trouble framing harmless old Gus Hyslop to a hangman's rope. But Hyslop, the murderer of a United States marshal, protected by those Yankee farmers, would be something he could sink his fangs into.

Pecos said: "We'll ride. We'll go straight to Harry Layne's. I don't think they've caught Gus and hanged him yet. They're looking for a bigger fight than that. They're trying to crowd those Yankees into the position of fighting for an escaped murderer." He laughed. "I guess there'll be time and cards enough so we can deal ourselves a hand in that game."

"Eh, so." Hernandez hitched his gun around with its butt pointed toward his right hand from the exact middle of his abdomen. "For many months we have had trouble weeth no one. But now thees buttermilk times of peace have ended. We will not feenish the job we should have feenished before leaving for Idaho last year. You know, Keed, what your Hernandez would do? He would ride up the freight road to the home ranch of Jawn Ridley, straight to the door of his Citadel, his castle on the hill, and there he would settle with the king himself."

The edge was back in Pecos's voice. "Shooting it out with Ridley, seh, will be my last resort."

"Nevertheless, one day it will be you or Jawn Ridley on the ground and the other standing over him with a smoking Colt. But thees is your country. You are citizen here, no matter how you fought in the War between the States to prevent it. I am only visitor from south of the border. You Yankees have many strange customs I do not understand."

"I'm not a Yankee, seh."

"Now, eef this were Chihuahua, the land of my birth, I will tell you what I, Hernandez Pedro Gonzales y Fuente Jesús María Flanagan, would deal with this man. I would ride to his door and cry . . . 'Come out, you peeg, that I may fight you a duel with seex-guns.' Then we could all ride back to Fort Benton and make love to women with our faces shaved and good whisky in our stomachs. Behold, like thees I would kill him!"

Hernandez pivoted, handled his Colt in a deft cross draw, and fired. His target was a beer bottle crowning a heap of rubbish thirty yards away. It crumpled with a *zing* of flying glass. He fired twice more pounding a bottle on each side of it, then, his temper relieved, he showed his white teeth in a wide smile while he poked smoking cartridge cases from the gun.

He said: "For twenty days I have been weethout practice, and now you would fling me into a range war. Eh, so, who worries about keeling poor Hernandez?"

Big Jim said in his piping tone: "That was good shootin', Butch."

"Pah! What *peon* could not shoot bottles from an ash heap? Thees is the kind of shooting I did when first learning as a boy seex years old with my first gun. Sometime I will tell you of my uncle, General Ramón Telesforo Julio y Aldasoro de Santillo Fuente, *caballero de la libertad*, weeth medal from the fingers of Bolivar. We call him Ray for short. Well, one day in a contest with the *bandido* chief, Miguel Ortiz, my uncle fired

18

first into the target a bullet from a caliber Thirty-Two, and after that one time a Navy Thirty-Six, and after that one from a Colt Forty-Five, each one straight on the other so that all three bullets became a single piece of lead and in the target was one hole, the Forty-Five. That was good shooting, no? But Ray could not do it from horseback, so let me tell you about my other uncle, General Carlos Augusto Don José de Santiago. . . ."

Jim said: "That sounds sort of far-fetched to me, Butch."

"Eh, well someday, eef it were not for my debts, I would return with you to Chihuahua and you could see for yourself." He took hold of Pecos's arm. "But, come. Let us ride to help that poor old man. And eef they have already keelled him, then I myself, Hernandez, will ride to The Citadel to settle the score."

II

"Range War"

The posse's hoof tracks lay deeply in the soft badlands clay. After following a coulée, the tracks climbed steeply to one of the innumerable sharp hogbacks that cut down from the Medicine Ridge and, following that, reached the Medicine itself. There Pecos and his two companions drew up to breathe their horses.

To the south, on a stream flowing from the pine-studded Medicine Ridge, they could see The Citadel, headquarters of the Ridley cattle empire. It had a mile or more of corrals, sheds, and bunkhouses sprawled on both sides of the stream. Farther on, surrounded by the dark green of the gardens, was the house itself, standing white and sharply defined in the early sun. Looking in the other direction, they could see the Missouri, the freight road to Milk River, one hundred and twelve miles away, and a side road leading to the Stinchfield home ranch in the deep coulée at Fifty Springs.

Hernandez came close to Pecos and said: "You are theenking of her, eh? That girl? That red rose of the prairie, Letty Stinchfield. You are a fool, Keed. Once you have parted from a woman, you should never come back."

"You wouldn't know about that, Butch."

"I, Hernandez Pedro Gonzales y Fuente Flanagan, would not know about women? That is like telling Sam Colt he does not know about bullets. Why, I remember. . . ."

20

"Anyhow, she's not the one who brought me back. She's married to Al Ridley by this time."

"He, that poet? That rabbit? I theenk, once we have rescued our old friend, Hyslop, from those killers, I will pay a visit to Letty Stinchfield."

"If she's married to Al, you'll leave her alone."

"Eh? Then I will see heem. I will give heem some advice about women for old time's sake."

They rode on. The sun in their faces grew hot. They lost the trail on some water-sodden beaver meadows and picked it up again. It led to the bench lands of the river and became hard to follow. Cattle had crossed and re-crossed it on their way to water.

At noon, Pecos remounted after a long period of close trailing and said: "This is too slow. Anyhow, it looks like the posse split up. We'll have to make a guess on it. He might have a hide-out in the badlands, or he headed for some homestead shanty."

Hernandez said: "Or that rustler town at Bull Sink?"

"Gus has nothing in common with Jack Kansas and those longriders. I'd think our best bet is Horn Creek."

They crossed Big Sage Creek and reached the prairie rims. From there a vast sweep of prairie was visible with, here and there, a homesteader's shack or a bright green rectangle of wheat or oats, growing well after the May rains.

Big Jim said: "Why does Ridley get so stirred up about 'em? They haven't plowed one mile out of a hundred thousand. Even so, these sodbusters wouldn't have done him harm if he hadn't forced them into it. Owning the landing and the store, every pound of grain they raised could go through his hands, and he'd profit on it."

Pecos said: "It's not a matter of money, it's a matter of pride. He was an officer with the Confederacy. He never left the war behind. And these being Union veterans . . . why, if they'd been old Rebs, or Red River 'breeds, or Swedes from Minnesota even, Jawn Ridley might have made a tolerable neighbor." He pointed off across the big hedge of prairie, eight miles in extent, that separated the Sage from Horn Creek. "Harry Layne lives yonder. Gus should know better than to head there, but I'd lay dollars against one of Hernandez Flanagan's I.O.U.s that's just what he did."

They rode to the Layne place and found it deserted, chickens scratching by the house, two mongrel milch cows in the shade of some dwarfed box elder trees. Nearby, Horn Creek ran knee-deep and warm as blood. On the western bank, where the road crossed, the ruts were still slightly damp. A wagon had crossed, dripping water in that direction, but it had been at least two hours before.

"They headed back toward Rutledge's?" Jim asked.

"No. We'd have seen 'em if they'd gone that way."

From somewhere, at a great distance, came the flat, hand-clap sound of gunshots. They listened, and the sounds came again. Through heat-deadened air they were more like the echo of shots than the shots themselves.

"That's from the river side," Pecos said. "Say, Gus's shanty is down there. You don't suppose he'd be fool enough to go straight home? No, he wouldn't. He'd have no reason to."

Jim said: "He'd go there if he had his gun cached out."

"He had the marshal's gun."

"You know how an old badger like Gus is about a gun. What if he used an old Henry? A gun gets so it's a part of a man."

"How about the Laynes, here? Somebody must have warned 'em."

"Visiting."

Hernandez, his hands filled with cold biscuits from the shack, said: "No, there is bread rising and going sour. No woman visits weeth her bread going sour. They got out in one beeg hurry, taking their keeds."

Two brothers named Duckett had taken up land downstream, but the shooting was down farther off than that. Their place was also deserted. So was Hyslop's—it stood bleached and abandoned, pigweed growing in front of the door, the fence to the garden plot broken down by roving range cattle.

There had been no shooting for an hour. They rode down warily to the stream and watered their horses, and then turned eastward and climbed the gently terraced benches that separated Horn and Bull Creeks. From the bottom of Bull Creek a pillar of smoke rose almost vertically in the pale summer air.

"Whose place is *that?*" Jim asked, and neither of the other two could answer.

They got there two hours later. The sun had set, leaving the bottoms of Bull Creek in shadows. Below were two glowing rectangles where a homesteader's shack and shed had stood. No movement anywhere.

The road dropped evenly down cutbacks and snaked back and forth through sage belly-deep to a horse. Here and there the sunset glinted on a heavy cartridge case. Without dismounting, Hernandez picked up one of them and sniffed the blackened end.

"Thees afternoon. Forty-Four caliber. Rifle . . . see the mark of the firing pin?"

A gun sent up a puff of smoke from a gully across the bottoms, and a bullet, falling short, hit and hummed away, both sounds chased by the *ka-whack* of explosion.

Hernandez, by reflex, bent, stripped his Winchester from

his scabbard, and had it to his shoulder. There Pecos stopped him.

"No! That's not one of Ridley's. Those are *gunmen* he hires. No gunman would take a shot like that."

They watched the dark gully long after the gunsmoke had drifted away. Then, saying—"Wait here."—Pecos rode forward at a slow jog with his hand lifted in the air.

He reached the muddy trickle of Bull Creek without incident and climbed the other side. A dead man lay on his back just beyond some pole corrals that had escaped the fire. Someone had placed a battered old hat over his face.

Pecos was then no more than one hundred and fifty yards from the gully. He dismounted, took off his six-shooter, hung it over the saddle horn, and walked on, over the hummocky grass clumps, in his crippled, cowboy manner. He glimpsed movement and called: "Hey, up there! This is Pecos! This is the Pecos Kid."

The man then skulked into sight. He was short, quite heavy, garbed in the sort of clothes you might pick up on the town dump down in Fort Benton or Miles City.

"Pecos?" he said with suspicions.

Pecos recognized him then as the one of the Duckett brothers, although which one he didn't know.

"Hello, Duckett."

"Oh, what you doin' back in the country?"

"What happened?"

"You can see. Burned 'em out. They killed Jimmy."

"That your brother?"

He said—"Yes."—in an empty voice. "I'm Wils Duckett. We were holed up in the shed, but they sneaked up by way of the crick and got the hay shed on fire. We hung on for half an hour, I guess, but the fire kept coming, and we made a run for it. That's where they got him. In the back." He started to cry

24

and curse. He called them every name he could think of.

"How long ago was that?"

"Couple, three hours. I don't know. Everybody else left, but I wouldn't. I didn't want to leave Jimmy layin' there. I thought maybe I'd get a chance and kill some of 'em. They didn't show themselves, though. Just sneaked up on their bellies like snakes and burned the shack. Afterward they headed off yonder." He motioned up the creek. "I heard some shooting about an hour ago."

"This your place?" Duckett seemed to be stunned, and so Pecos repeated himself. "You move over here from the Horn?"

"No. This is Calahan's. We got warning from young Wilbert Cassman that Ridley had his killers on the loose. He'd heard about Hyslop and thought he might use it as an excuse to make trouble. Good Lord, I never expected he'd go on the kill like this."

"Where's Gus?"

"I don't know."

Pecos jerked his head at the smoldering remnants of the house and asked: "Calahan has a woman and kids . . . where did they go?"

"Took the rig and drove to Brodenbach's just before noon. Ought to be there by now. That's what was decided on at the spring meeting in case of trouble. I guess 'most all the women and kids will be there."

Duckett estimated the posse at eight men. That meant there were at least ten groups. He was not certain which way they'd ridden except that he'd seen somebody out yonder, and pointed up the creek.

There were more gunshots then. Pecos listened. These were sharper, but still at a considerable distance. Then, up the Horn, more smoke appeared in the sky.

"Who's got the next homestead?"

Duckett said: "*You* ought to know that."

Pecos nodded. It was the Parker relinquishment they had taken over last summer while on the payroll of Jawn Ridley. "Who's living there?"

"Nobody."

Hernandez and Big Jim rode down at a gallop with word about the gunfire.

Pecos nodded that he'd heard it and said to Duckett: "You're welcome to the pack horse if you'd like to ride along."

"I got to bury Jimmy," he said. "I won't leave him just lying here."

The trio rode upstream. Box elders and cottonwoods grew here and there, now deep in shadow. Some big, hard-faced banks that had been pinkish with sunset were turning gray. The shooting had stopped. In all there had been no more than fifteen shots. A cool wind drifted along the bottoms, carrying the creek odors of poplar and horse mint—and then the raw smell of smoke.

From a flank of the valley they saw the Parker shack shrunken to a heap of coals and nobody about.

Big Jim said: "Figure the shooting was here?"

"No. It was a far piece, 'way yonder. You're not in those Idaho woods now. This is Montana. This is where you can hear things. I don't know this is a fact, but I've been told that on a clear quiet Sunday at Fortyrod you can hear the new church bell at Fort Benton, and that's better'n twenty-three miles."

"Someday," said Hernandez, "I will tell you about the church bells of Santa Rosalia, a mission of my country, that one hears on clear nights, reenging sharp and clear across mountain and desert, although the mission and bells have all been destroyed one hundred years ago."

"Oh, hell," said Big Jim.

"Eet is true, you profaner of Santa Rosalia!"

Pecos said: "No telling where they went, or where the other end of that so-called posse went. We'd better ride to Brodenbach's."

Night and the night silence settled as they rode. Once, listening from a hump of prairie, they heard voices, but at a distance that could have been two miles or ten. And once there was the peculiar, stuttering noise of a gunshot mixed with echo, far, far away.

III

"Hoeman Army"

It was long past midnight, but still there was no sight of dawn when they reached the creek hills overlooking Brodenbach's farm. Brodenbach was perhaps the most prosperous of the settlers, and he had accumulated a sprawling assortment of sheds and corrals. The outlines and back shadows of several rigs could be seen in the yard.

Pecos dismounted, groaning from fatigue. He rolled a cigarette and lighted it in the concealment of his hat.

Hernandez said: "They would perhaps have hot coffee down there."

"They'd have some lead biscuits for us, too. And some beds to sleep in. Six feet deep. I'd rather ride into Fort Worth givin' three cheers for General Sherman than I would ride down on a houseful of women with scatter-guns. Take a Winchester, a man either ducks it or he don't. They can sight six feet wide with one of those old cylinder-bore doubles and still that number two buck will cut you up like beef in a Chinese restaurant. I reckon it wouldn't hurt to light for a while."

They slept on the prairie and awoke at dawn. A man, crippled but with a rifle across his arm, shaded his eyes to see as they rode down. It was Cassman, stove up from a hip break he had suffered in a runaway the fall before.

"We heard you were in the country!" he shouted from a

distance. "My boy was lyin' low at the Layne place and saw you ride past. He was scared you were back working for Ridley, but I knew that wasn't so." He climbed a pitch of ground from the corrals, breathing hard through his nostrils. "I told him you wouldn't let that pretty Stinchfield gal marry Al Ridley without doing something about it."

Pecos let a smile soften his weathered face and said: "Oh, hell, Cassman!"

"Wouldn't it bowl Jawn Ridley over if you carried her off on your horse like that fellow in McGUFFY'S READER?"

Smoke rose from the stone chimney, and soon there was a smell of frying pork and fritters. It made Pecos dizzy from hunger.

He asked: "All the women and kids here?"

"Some of 'em went to Dehon's."

"Where are the men?"

"Laws, I don't know. They figured on making a fight at Calahan's, but they got jumped before Rutledge or Deitz or any of those fellows got there. I understand they killed both the Duckett boys."

"Only Jimmy. We just came from there."

They ate and rode northwestward to the Wagonhammer Springs where Ridley maintained a winter camp to keep his cattle from drifting over on the blizzard-swept Threesleep range. There they found three men hanged to the limb of a box elder. One of the men was a filthy old wolfer and reputed horse thief from Bull Sink. The second was a young stranger. The third, still wearing his tan bulldog toed shoes, was Gus Hyslop.

Fatigue and anger made the Pecos Kid lose control of himself. He wasn't sure what he said, and the knuckles on his right hand were skinned from beating against the tree, but once the rage was burned out of him, he felt better.

Hernandez said: "Now perhaps we will ride to The Citadel and keel him, eh?"

"I don't know. My God, I don't know."

They had nothing to dig with. They buried the three men by laying them beneath an undercut bank and caving in the dirt over them. Hernandez spoke prayers in Spanish, then they rode on down gullies to Soda Coulée, and from there back to Harry Layne's, thus completing in slightly more than twenty-four hours their big circle of the country.

This time there were horses in the corral and men moving around. A sentry showed, and they rode down beneath the guns of two men in the lower sheds.

"Why, it's Pecos, Big Jim, and the Spaniard," somebody said.

A spidery, peaked faced man named Clayton Forsler advanced with an old Henry rifle over his arm and told them to stop.

"They're all right!" Layne called to him.

"I'm not so sure of that. They worked for Ridley once, didn't they? If Ridley could hire 'em once, he could hire 'em again."

Pecos said: "Ridley couldn't hire me, and neither could you. You save some of that fight for later on. I guess you'll get your chance to use it."

Pecos walked on, ignoring the rifle, and looked around the farmyard. There were eight men, and they had been quarreling. He could see the signs. He said: "They hung old Gus. We just buried him, a wolfer, and some stranger that looked like a cowboy." The news made them uncomfortable and sick, but it didn't come as a surprise. He asked: "Or did you know?"

Layne, a short man with pinkish skin, said: "We asked him not to go. Begged him not to. He went anyhow. Fought his way, almost. He said it was him they were after. Said he'd give himself up and then maybe they'd leave us alone."

Forsler cried: "Well, maybe they will! They got no quarrel with us . . . the law hasn't, anyhow. I'm sorry as anybody about Gus, but he shouldn't have come here."

Pecos said: "Forsler, do you think he killed that deputy and escaped? They left the door open. They wanted him to walk out, and he did. They wanted him to run to you for only one reason . . . so they could claim you were harboring a murderer. Who were those two others they hung?"

None of them knew. Pecos walked to the house, found some coffee steeping on the grounds, and poured it. "It's up to you boys," he said. "I'm not butting in where I'm not wanted. But we'll be three more guns if you can use 'em."

Layne cried: "And damned good guns!"

He knew what the answer would be. Even Forsler, trying to act reluctant, felt an unfathomable relief at their arrival.

"You have any plans?" Pecos asked.

"There's nothing we can do," Layne said. "A man can't protect his place. They'll ride up and shoot hell out of him. On the other hand, they won't come in where we're all ganged up together. There's no answer to it."

"Where are the others? Where's Calahan, Hood, and Zollar?"

"Down at Dehon's, I guess. Hood was burned out. I saw smoke coming from thataway."

Forsler said: "Of course, he was burned out. Hood's was the first place they came to. Wilbert said it was six men under that gunman, Joe Livingstone. Livingstone gave Hood and his woman fifteen minutes to take what they could and get out. They were killing the lambs that Hood brought over from Paxton's last fall . . . that's what the shooting was."

Hernandez said: "A man would raise those steenking

31

sheep and then wonder why trouble comes hees way?"

"It's a free country. We raise what we like."

Hernandez turned his back and said: "Keed! Jeem! Listen to what I say. There is only one thing to do. Let us borrow fresh horses and ride to The Citadel. How many are there? Two or three of his gunmen? Let us settle with the king himself, and then we could ride back to Fort Benton where those women are waiting for us."

Pecos drank his coffee and tossed away the thick heel. "I wouldn't lay too much money on us finding any Ridley to shoot at. But this game of burn-out can be played by both sides. I say, let's all of us ride over there."

The idea of challenging Ridley at his stronghold, The Citadel, shocked the group to silence. They had thought of Ridley as being all-powerful for too long. Layne's hand trembled a little as he reached up to scratch the week's growth of whiskers on his cheeks. "Well . . . I don't know."

"His men can't be two places at the same time."

"If we make open war. . . ."

Pecos cried in angry exasperation: "What do you call it when he hangs old Gus, kills one of the Duckett boys, and rides through the country burning your shacks and shooting your stock?"

"We attack him and there wouldn't be anything to stop him," Layne burst out. "Damn it, don't look at me that way! You fellows aren't married. You got nothing to lose. I felt the same one time myself, when I was a young buck. It makes a difference when you got three kids to think of. I'm no coward, but I tell you I'd crawl out of this country on my belly before I'd let anything happen to those kids."

"That, seh, is up to you. Of course, there's this to think of, too. You crawl in front of Ridley, and he'll get just that much tougher. You bare your teeth and turn on him and maybe he'd see that he could get hurt, too. You ever see a cat stand up in front of a hound? You give me a good standing-up tomcat, and I'll go through Texas scaring off all the hound dogs back to Arkansas."

Tall, meek-looking Sophus Briggs said: "I'll ride with you, Pecos. And I got me some kids, too. Come to think of it, I got *seven* kids."

They saddled and started out. It was a scabby-looking crew. The homesteaders were poorly mounted and poorly armed. Some of them had no saddles; some used the blind bridles from their work harnesses. Although they all had rifles, one was a single-shot Sharps, one a single-shot Army Springfield, two were Henry rifles. Some of the men had no arms at all. Layne carried a cap and ball revolver dating to the war, and Forsler had at his side an old double horse pistol loaded with buckshot.

Hernandez kept laughing under his breath as they rode up the creek bottoms. "Such guns! I would be ashamed to trade for wolf hides to the Indians. Did you see the old Henry that Briggs is carrying? I tell you, you could drop a bullet through the barrel of that old rimfire and never touch one side. And that horse pistol filled with buckshot! What good will all these *peon* guns do us in a fight?"

Pecos laughed and said: "If Forsler ever gets 'em close up in front of that old horse pistol, the war'll be over."

They rode in a strung-out column following the flat-bottomed coulée. On both sides were low cutbanks dissected by little gullies. There was no cover save for some clumps of bluish bullberry thorns, and sometimes the cut-in bed of the creek.

It was Pecos's horse that gave him warning. He glanced around. There was a glint of gun shine in one of the gullies. They had ridden within a hundred and fifty yards of it. He recognized the ambush without showing alarm. He said: "Don't look around, boys. You hear me? Keep hold of yourselves. They're ambushed here, and we're in it. They aim to get us in the narrows."

Forsler spoke in an anguished treble: "What are we doing? Let's get out of here."

"Keep riding another fifty yards. Then I'll give you the sign. We'll ride for it at once. Yonder. West bank. See, that space between the gullies?"

They rode in a breathless tenseness for ten or twelve yards when Judson, a heavy-set, middle-aged man, riding with a blanket and surcingle substituting for a saddle, cried out: "I ain't ridin' any deeper into their trap!"

He pull-hauled his old Henry rifle from the tie strings that held it to the surcingle and, flanking his work horse to get him into a heavy-legged gallop, wheeled and rode into the creek, and up again, and across a sage-dotted flat. A gun cracked driving him back on the horse's rump. He was hit, but not badly enough to shock the reflexes out of him, and he made a wild forward grab, losing the rifle but getting the surcingle. He rode off with the horse lunging in a series of long crowhops, one leg on each side of the animal's rump, his shirt tail out and flapping. His battered old hat had somehow become lodged to the horse's hind hoof. Under other circumstances it would have been a comic spectacle.

By that time they were all at a gallop. Gunsmoke spurted up from six or seven locations, in the gully behind them, from the cutbank narrows ahead. Pecos rode to the streambed and turned to follow it. He intended to reach the cover of one of its undercut banks and drive back the upstream flank of the attack, but the burn of a high-velocity bullet told him that Ridley's killers had him in their crossfire.

Now, at least, he knew where everyone was placed. He dismounted on the wrong side of his horse, dragging the Winchester from its scabbard and digging his boot heels to a stop. On one knee, with the bridle reins in his left hand, he got the rifle up and fired. His bullet sent up a geyser of dirt on the crest of the bank that protected the main nest of ambushers. The horse kept dragging him.

Lying on his side, he got one bridle string cinched to a thick sage trunk. A bullet hit and blinded him with dirt. He slid around the horse, went halfway to his boot tops in sand, kept going. A bullet splashed water in his face. He fell forward, caught himself on his elbows, swung his rifle to his shoulder, and fired as fast as he could lever the cartridges.

The carbine was hot in his hands. The action had a tendency to stick. He spit on it while getting cartridges from his belt and feeding them through the spring opening. He stopped with the magazine half filled and fired it dry again.

He doubted that he had hit anyone. He doubted he had even come close. He just went on the theory that no hired gunman wanted to get killed for eighty a month, and that his volley of lead would keep them down long enough to let the hoe men escape.

He stopped. His mouth was gritty from dirt. He spit and reloaded. Hernandez, creeping up behind him, said: "Keed, we are in a worse spot than my uncle, *el general* Ramón Telesforo Julio y Aldasoro de Santillo Fuente, when he captured the prison at Ciudad Matamoros in the revolution of Poco Pepe and found heemself locked inside. Now I say we have laid down our young lives for those *peones,* and I will wager *doblóns del oro* against *gringo* dollars that they will not quit running until sundown."

Pecos said: "You're getting soft, Butch. I've seen the time when you needed this much action to whet your appetite for breakfast."

"Eh, yes. But some peeg has shot a bullet hole through my guitar. Do you know thees is the fourth guitar I have lost in two years?"

In moving forward, Hernandez rose too high and a bullet chased him down again.

"Where's Jim?" Pecos asked.

"Here I am," Big Jim said through a lull in the shooting. He was muck from head to foot from crawling through the creek. "You got us in a hell of a spot, Pecos. These sodbusters won't stand and fight. Why, they got nothing to fight with."

Some of the sodbusters appeared about four hundred yards down the creek and crossed from the east bank to the west, finding new positions. The shooting died, and broke out with new fury.

"You're wrong about 'em," Pecos said, laughing. "Those sodbusters are back in business."

Now it was the main group of Ridley's men in a crossfire. One of them, hit, went sprawling over and over down a cutbank. He was hung up in sagebrush at the bottom. He got free and, holding his thigh, lunged away, hopping high on his good leg.

Hernandez laughed through his teeth. He reloaded, aimed again. "The third notch! Eet is just right! Come, some more of you *gringos!* You would learn the taste of lead from Hernandez? Ha! The boot is on the other foot now that you fight with *un caballero de libertad* instead of some poor Yankee sheepherders!" He fired. "*That's* for shooting a hole through the guitar of Hernandez. And *that* for the hole in my feefty dollar hat."

Pecos, loading, said: "That hole, seh, was shot in your hat by an enraged father down in Coeur d'Alene."

There was no sign of anyone, now. The shooting petered out. On the air was a mingled odor of bruised sage, clay dust, and gunsmoke. From a distance, horses were galloping.

A man shouted: "Curly! Curly, bring your men here."

Pecos said: "Curly who? Curly Forbes, you suppose?"

"Eh, perhaps. Curly Forbes weeth five notches in his guns. Put to flight by *peones*. Thus, *señores,* weeth men who carve notches in the butts of guns. You show me a man who carves notches for these he has killed, and I will show you a shoots-in-the-back coward."

IV

"Fire the Citadel"

Half an hour later, with look-outs posted on both cutbanks, they boiled creek water and treated Judson's wounded hip. The bone was broken, and he had lost blood. After a long powwow, three men went back to Layne's for a buckboard and a mattress. They ran into trouble, and the look-outs were of the opinion that Ridley's men had swung around toward the lower Sage, so it was decided to take Judson eight miles across the prairie to Brodenbach's where the women could care for him. Forsler and Briggs drove him, reducing their number to eight as they headed up rising ground toward the rocky escarpment of the Medicine Ridge.

The smell of pines was good after the long dryness, and once over the first ridge it was damp and green like another world. Grass grew to the knees of their horses. In the bottoms, a creek ran, cold and clear, filled with the gray, darting shapes of trout.

Layne asked—"Why in hell is he fighting for a country like ours when he has this?"—and didn't get an answer.

The sun set. They rode through twilight, and it was dark when they stopped to look down on The Citadel. Lights burned here and there in the big house and, downstream, in one of the bunkhouses.

"We won't cut loose at the big house," Pecos said. "We

wouldn't get the one we wanted. Things don't work out that way. He might not even be there. We'd probably kill his wife, or one of those poor Chinamen that work for him." He pointed out the various buildings, the foreman's house where Mike Coffey lived, the blacksmith shop and food sheds, the bunkhouses. "Those sheds are tied together, and this time of year they're mostly empty. They'll burn like gunpowder in Dodge City." He tested the wind. "That's from the river. We'll come up from that way, and, if everything goes right, we'll have our bonfire started before anybody raises a shout. Don't shoot until you get shot at. There's a lot of honest, hard-working cowboys here, and it's not helping us any to kill 'em."

In tense silence they rode on a circle of the ranch and came down a little-used trail. The slope was quite barren, and a moon just breaking the horizon put them sharply in view.

A man's startled voice said—"Hey there!"—as they reached the creek.

"Hello," Pecos said, still riding easily. "Who is it?"

"Who in hell are *you?*"

The Pecos Kid kept coming with his hands wide of his body and said: "It's all right. Where's Jawn Ridley?"

"I don't know where he is."

Pecos saw him then. He stood by a corner of a corral about fifteen steps up the bank of the creek. He was gangling and slope-shouldered. Pecos remembered him from the year before—he was called Missou, and he was one of the gunmen Ridley had brought up from Miles City. He had a Winchester across his arm and a brace of Colt pistols strapped around his waist.

Pecos said with an easy laugh: "Missou, you hadn't better fall in the crick with all that ballast or Jawn will need hoisting equipment to salvage you."

Missou for the fist time realized who this was. He whispered—"The Pecos Kid."—and it was apparent that it had unnerved him. Then he saw Hernandez swinging to Pecos's left and Big Jim to his right. He realized he could not keep all of them covered and started back toward the corner of the corral. It was too far away. He must have thought Jim was going for his gun. He started around with his rifle.

Hernandez spoke a sharp warning. He drew in the cross-draw Spanish-style with an opposite half twist of his body, fired across the saddle horn. The bullet, grazing Missou's body, struck his arm near the elbow and knocked him spinning. His feet popped out from under him. He lay with one shoulder propped against the bottom corral pole, momentarily stunned from bullet shock.

Men, alarmed by the shot, ran from the bunkhouse with a thudding of boots. "It's by the lower corral!" somebody shouted. The men were about one hundred paces away.

Pecos rode across the creek, disarmed Missou, and tossed the guns to Jim. "Here, give these to the boys. I'll go around this way and double back. Tell 'em to wait by the creek."

Still riding, he skirted the corrals. Hernandez was behind him. He turned and said: "Open that corral gate and start the saddle stock running. There's a hay shed yonder, but I wouldn't want to burn a horse."

Hernandez opened the gate, and the horses, already spooked by the gunshot, ran in one thunderous, wall-eyed circle and found freedom.

"Hey, what's going on?" a cowboy shouted.

Hernandez said: "You like to live a while? Then stay back."

"Who in hell are you?"

"Hernandez Pedro Gonzales y Fuente Jesús María Flanagan."

"It's them!" a man was shouting. "It's Pecos and the Spik-Mick and their hoe-man army."

"The Pecos Kid! He's in Idaho."

"The hell he is. He's out there."

There was movement in many quarters. A gun cracked, lacing white flame through the night. The bullet cut splinters from a corral pole and droned away. There were more shots, all of them wild.

Pecos was then behind the hay shed. He struck a match, leaned through the window, and dropped the match inside. The flame caught and spread rapidly.

With an armload of hay he moved on. He set a second fire against the back of a storage shed. A voice he recognized to be that of Mike Coffey, the foreman, was bellowing, trying to find out what was wrong.

Pecos met Hernandez coming around the hay shed from the other direction. "Get hold of Big Jim and those hoe men and bring them up through the creek as far as the box elders. They can command the whole yard from there, and still be clear to ride off."

He ran on toward the foreman's house that stood on a shelf of ground overlooking bunkhouses, storehouses, and corrals. Coffey had left in a hurry, the lamp was lighted, the door open.

Pecos had a look around. "Mike?" he said, knowing well enough there would be no answer. He walked through the house to make certain it was empty. The kerosene lamp stood on an oilcloth-covered table. A rose plush rocking chair was pulled up beside it, and a newspaper laid where Coffey had dropped it beside the chair. It was a Cheyenne paper. Pecos folded it, put it in his pocket, and without further ado smashed the lamp on the floor. Seconds after, flames were racing across the floor.

He ran back to his horse. Flames bursting through the rear openings of the hay shed lighted his way. There was shouting among the corrals and response from the creek bottoms. Over it he could hear the braying, cursing voice of Missou: "Come and get me, damn you. Come and get me before I bleed to death."

Pecos returned to the box elders, saying his name at every interval in the gunfire so he wouldn't be mistaken for one of Ridley's gunmen. "Save your shots," he said. "Powder flame will just mark where we're going."

He led them down the creek for fifty yards where a trail crossed, and they followed the trail toward a notch in the eastern ridge. There was pursuit that they fought back. Below, the fire had half consumed one hay shed and had spread to another. Coffey's house still locked in the flames, but all its windows glowed smoky red. The lights had gone out in Ridleys mansion.

Pecos took off his hat and wiped sweat from his forehead. "That's a hell of a thing," he said.

Hernandez said: "He brought it upon heemself."

"Sure, and he's earned a lot more. But still it's a hell of a thing."

They waited at Harry Layne's through the night, and through the next day, wondering what Jawn Ridley's response would be. There were no more burnings. Young Tommy Dehon rode over the next morning with the report that Mead Shaeffer, a trapper from the badlands, had been at the landing the day before where Joe Livingstone, Curly Forbes, and the rest of Ridley's gunmen were off on a big spree. Furthermore, Bill Oriet, the deputy sheriff, had returned to Threesleep, so it looked like the trouble, for the time being, was over.

About two hours after Tommy's arrival, several riders appeared on the crest of the cutbanks and, without dismounting, watched the house. Finally one of them, a tall and powerfully built man, rode down alone, with a white handkerchief tied on the muzzle of his rifle.

"That's Mike Coffey," the Pecos Kid said. "Take it easy with the guns. Mike may be a tough old lobo, but he's square enough. I guess maybe Jawn Ridley sent him for just that reason. I'll go yonder and talk."

They met across the creek and shook hands.

"So you came back," Coffey said. "I always heard that a grudge meant more to you than money."

"I harbor no grudge against Ridley, seh. I want you to be straight about that. I hate his yellow insides. But that's not why I came back. I came back because I felt responsible for what's happened to them." He waved his hand, indicating the men in the house. "By the way, how's everything at your place?"

Coffey laughed with a bitter jerk of his head. "You know how they are. You burned me out. There were some things that meant an awful lot to me in that house."

"Why, some of the boys here say the same thing. That's why it all seems so foolish."

"You sure *we* burned them out?"

"This is a silly argument, Mike. We all know who's behind it."

Coffey made an exasperated gesture. "I didn't come to argue. Pecos, we each got in a wallop at the other, and that makes it even, so. . . ."

"I'd guess you got in a couple more wallops than we did. You hung poor old Gus Hyslop. I'm going to have a hard time forgetting that."

"He was a cattle thief, Kid. I'm not telling you that for

43

Ridley. I'm telling you personal, from me to you. He was a
rustler and so were those two from Bull Sink that were hung
with him. Hyslop didn't kill Garde, of course. You know it,
and everybody knows it. We had to hold him on some sort of
charge while we run down those others. They confessed.
They confessed to the whole thing. No, we're not apologizing
on account of Hyslop. You've been drifting along the frontier
long enough to know what happens to rustlers."

"Did you kill the deputy U.S. marshal, too?"

"I didn't come here to talk about this stuff, and I'm not
going to. Some things happened that I'm sorry did happen,
but it's too late. It's all water down the creek. I came here to
talk about *now*. Jawn Ridley is willing to call it quits. He won't
send another rider inside the lines of these nesters' claims,
and you stay away from the Medicine . . . the freight road . . . I
reckon it'll make a good enough deadline . . . and so help me,
don't any of you ever try to ride across it."

An uneasy truce hung over the range. There were house
raisings and barn raisings with parties afterward as one after
another of the burned-out places was rebuilt, but a feeling of
tension always lay close under the surface, and no man ever
ventured far alone, or without a gun near at hand.

There was rain during early June, the grain was good, but
the only available steamboat landing was closed to them, so
there was no conceivable way of getting their crops to a
market.

Toward the final days of June, Pecos, Hernandez, and Big
Jim returned from a trip to Miles City with word that the
Northern Pacific railway, after being long stranded in Bis-
marck, North Dakota, due to the failure of the Jay Cooke
Company, was once more on the way. Its rails were past
Dickenson, the timbers for its big bridge already on the

ground at Medora, and a land boom was under way at Glendive where it would make its first juncture with the Yellowstone, a river it was to follow for the next three hundred and fifty miles.

Pecos had with him a Department of the Interior survey map that he spread out on a table in Layne's shack.

"The N.P. will never help us," Layne said. "It's too far. It's one hundred and sixty miles from Threesleep, and Threesleep's fifty-five miles, figured as the snow flies."

"Look at the map. The old freight road went straight south because it wasn't aimed at the Yellowstone, but for the shortest route to the Union Pacific and Cheyenne. But striking southeast we could reach the railroad in eighty miles. Hell, you could drive a wagon across the prairie any place, if it weren't for Deserter Coulée. We'll have to dig a road across the coulée, is all. Get fifteen men together with horses, plows, and that scraper I saw in Brodenbach's yard. I'll ride south again and talk to the engineering crew that's in advance of the rail line. In Dakota, the N.P. even built some leader roads themselves, that's how anxious they are for farm tonnage. I'll talk 'em out of a ton of giant powder, free for nothing. We'll open this country up, Jawn Ridley and his steamboat monopoly be damned."

V

"Letty's Wedding"

Jawn Ridley heard about the proposed road by a roundabout way through the Northern Pacific promotional officer at the territorial capital in Helena. He made no attempt to stop the blasting of a switchback through Deserter Coulée, and for a space of three weeks he made no apparent countermove. Then one day several hundred lean trail-herd cattle made their appearance and had to be driven back from some fenced fields. More hundreds came. The numbers mounted, until it was a good estimate that ten thousand head were spreading across the Sage and Horn Creek range. They picked off the range grass, and it became a night and day fight for homesteaders to keep them from crashing down fences and overrunning them.

A cowboy following Deserter Coulée, from Miles City to the new Poplar River range, stopped for supper and a night's camp with the road crew and told how a representative for Ridley was living at the Western Hotel in Miles, buying every hoof of unassigned trail-herd cattle that arrived from the south, and next morning, after an all night ride, young Tommy Dehon got there with news that already a fourth of the wheat and oat crop had been destroyed.

Pecos left Hernandez and Jim with the road crew and rode back. He stopped at Judson's where the fences were down and the fields laid waste. Judson, a bachelor, was still laid up with his broken hip, and, because he couldn't watch it, his farm was the first victim. A longhorn steer had even crowded inside his shack and, unable to fit its horns once again through the door, was chomping around, wall-eyed, turning the place into a shambles.

Pecos managed to get the animal outside. He rammed the door shut, although there was nothing to save. Then, hearing gunshots at a distance, he followed the creek down to Hood's place that only a month before had been rebuilt during a house-raising party.

Hood, a grizzled, disreputable-looking farmer, stood squinting against the sun to watch Pecos ride up. He had a rifle in his hands. Eighteen or nineteen steers lay dead at distances ranging from a hundred yards to a quarter mile.

"What's up?" Pecos asked.

Hood's voice was strained and bitter. "I'll show you what's up!" A steer approached, following the fence of his spud patch. He tossed the rifle to his shoulder, beaded down, and fired. The steer, hit, went to its knees. It stayed upright for almost half a minute before rolling loosely to its side. Hood snapped the lever, sending the empty cartridge flying, and said: "*That!* There's a critter Jawn Ridley will never fatten on my grain."

"Seven dollars," Pecos said.

"What?"

"That's what he cost. Bone-bag trail-herd price. Ridley has a man in Miles buying 'em by the thousand. That critter wasn't even from Texas. He was Mex stock. Seven dollars on the hoof."

Mrs. Hood, faded and beat out, came from the door with a couple of scared kids hanging to her and said: "Don't, Paw! It's no use. Cartridges cost a nickel apiece. Jawn Ridley can afford more steers than we can bullets."

47

Cursing, Hood levered the gun and shot and levered it and shot again. A dozen or so of the critters had stopped just beyond his range, and it infuriated him. He shot the gun dry. "What can we do? You should have shot him that day you went up there to his Citadel instead of just burning some sheds. That's the only answer to it . . . shoot *him!*"

"Maybe we could get all the men together and drive 'em into the badlands."

"They won't stay in the badlands. It's all hot rock and sword grass down there. They'll lay in the shade for a day and come back. Maybe Jawn Ridley has men driving 'em back. Anyhow, once these critters get the smell of green oat grass and wheat, nothing can stop 'em. They belly under the fences, jump over 'em, pile up twenty deep until down goes a section, posts and all."

"What are the other farmers doing?"

"Killing 'em. Wils Duckett has killed more'n two hundred. Had up to yesterday. More'n that today, if he got back from Threesleep with more cartridges."

Pecos bent one knee around the saddle horn and rubbed his head as though the news made his eyes ache. "Ever think what'll happen in a couple or three days when those carcasses start to swell up and bust?"

"Huh?" Hood looked startled.

"You'll move out, that's what. I remember what it used to be like down in Wyoming when the buffalo hunters went through. Town named Deerhorn that everybody had to move out of. Just picked up and left. That stench is something no man can stand."

Mrs. Hood cried: "Paw, you should have shot 'em farther from the house!"

"Shut up to me, woman!" he shouted back. "You thought it was a good idea when you heard Duckett was doing it."

★ ★ ★ ★ ★

Pecos met with the farmers at Brodenbach's the following night and listened to hours of pointless talk, of men giving vent to their anger. It tired him and irked him. He wasn't their kind, and he had never got over his cowboy's contempt for a sodbuster. Finally he said: "There's only one thing that might stop Ridley. He's upsetting an old agreement with the Stinchfield outfit when he floods the range. By next fall you'll look at this country and think it's been sheeped out, and the Stinchfields won't like it. Maybe they don't know what's going on. I'll go over and let 'em know."

He rode toward Ridley Landing through afternoon heat intending to cross by means of the ferry, but as he climbed the hump of the lower Medicine, he saw a double-seated top buggy make the turn to The Citadel. There were either three or four persons in the buggy. A shine of white led him to think that at least one was a woman, but at two miles, with heat waves dancing in the air, it was impossible to be sure. He kept thinking about it all the way to the river, and there curiosity made him turn back and head for The Citadel that he sighted just as night settled.

Every window in the big house was ablaze, the fountain was torchlit on four sides, and Chinese lanterns had been strung along the curving driveway. Several rigs were un-hitched in the carriage yard. The guest corral was filled with horses. As he watched, people came and went from the big house.

The air, as always in the evening, had a cool fragrance, sounds traveled well, and he could hear the babble of voices, both men and women, and then the waltz music of a violin and harp. Once each year it was Jawn Ridley's custom to stage a grand ball, even chartering a special boat to carry guests to his ranch from Fort Benton and the landings along

49

the way, and such an occasion, he decided, was this.

He rode downhill, not so much through curiosity as because he enjoyed the clear, sweet sound of music. Not until he was quite close did he realize that something was wrong.

From somewhere in the region of the bunkhouses Jawn Ridley was issuing orders. His voice was controlled, but his Army training revealed itself, and it carried well. He sent two men riding, conferred briefly with one who had just returned, and sent him off, too. Pecos then saw Ridley, powerful and firm-striding, climbing the path to the grounds.

Women, gathered in a gossiping group near the fountain, changed the tone of their conversation as he approached. Men who stood around in twos and threes, their positions marked by their lighted cigars and cigarettes, took note of his approach, also. It was quiet, so quiet Pecos could hear the crunch of Ridley's boots on the gravel path. He strode past the groups of men and women without looking to right or left, and went inside the house.

Pecos's curiosity took him closer than he had intended. He crossed the wagon road to the hedge surrounding the grounds. He lighted a cigarette. No one paid the slightest attention to him. He amused himself with the thought that he might go in and have a few words with Ridley, appearing like a skeleton at the feast, but he dismissed it. Hernandez. yes, but not him. He lacked the dramatic flair for such things. Something made him wonder about Al Ridley, Jawn's son. He had always liked Al—liked him and sympathized with him, a misfit, a boy who belonged in the polite drawing rooms of the East instead of in this rough, raw country, trying to pretend he was the man his father wanted him to be.

Then he glimpsed a movement that jolted him, and for a few seconds his pulse quickened. It was the Stinchfield girl, Letty. She had appeared briefly beneath one of the lanterns and through some mannerism—her firm way of walking, the high set of her shoulders—had revealed her identity to him. She came in sight again beneath the large, half-round portico of the house. She was dressed in a lacy, starchy white dress. Then she disappeared inside with the screen door slapping shut after her.

He had a sudden, uncontrollable desire to talk to her. He threw away his cigarette. He walked to the carriage path. He would have gone straight on and entered one of the side doors to the house itself, but he glimpsed her again, leaving by the back way. Somehow, in the brief space of three or four minutes she had changed to a riding costume. A hostler was near the carriage house, holding a horse by the bridle.

Pecos ran around the sheds, stumbling over the discarded remains of carts and wagons, and stopped in the middle of the road. She had mounted and spurred to a gallop. She almost rode him down.

"What do you want?" she cried in an angry whisper. Then she saw who he was.

She reined around, holding the horse so tightly it was forced back to its haunches. It reared and fought the bit. She didn't notice that. She was a fine horsewoman and kept in the saddle as though stuck in it.

"You," she whispered. "Pecos."

He walked up, took the bridle, and held the horse with a sure grip as he looked in her face.

In the months that had passed he had almost forgotten that she was so beautiful. Taken by themselves, none of her features was exceptional. Her face was rather too broad across the eyes, her mouth was too large, her nose too small, yet put together they gave her a striking beauty, a beauty with fire and color. She sat a horse very erect. It was a stamp of her character. She didn't bend to the horse's movement. She

51

rode with her head high, her shoulders back, her abdomen drawn in, her boots rammed out hard against the stirrups.

"Letty." It had been long since he'd used her name, and it didn't fit his tongue any more. "Hello, Letty. I was just going to see you. I didn't think you'd be leaving the party already."

"Don't laugh at me!"

He thought for a moment she would cut at him with the quirt she held in her left hand. "Hold on. I'm not laughing at you." Something occurred to him that had an unsteadying effect. The lacy dress she'd been wearing was the sort that brides wore. "What was going on down there?"

"You mean you really don't know?"

"Of course not. I was headed for the landing when. . . ."

She said with a mirthless jerk of her slim shoulders: "Why, this is my wedding night."

"Who'd you marry?"

"Al Ridley, of course."

"Oh, Al."

"Why don't you laugh like everyone else?"

The defiance suddenly went out of her. He thought she was going to cry. The horse had quieted under Pecos's grasp and now allowed itself to be led from the path to the cover of some scrub pine. The shadows hid them from anyone approaching around the carriage shed, but he could still see her face, how tight her lips were, how hard she bit down on her lower lip.

He moved over to help her dismount. She swung from the stirrup and kept hanging onto him. She held tightly to his shirt and pressed her eyes against his shoulder.

"Oh, Pecos. Pecos, why did you ever go away?"

"Now, kid. Let's not go into that again. You don't care anything about me. I'm just a no-good saddle tramp."

She clung to him harder than ever. "Pecos, take me away.

Please. I don't want to ever face anybody here again. Listen, I have a little money in the bank at Fort Benton. We'll take it and buy coach fare to Salt Lake City. We can go farther. So far nobody will ever know who I am, or care."

"Is that the only reason . . . because you're ashamed to face them?"

"No. You know it isn't. I'd have left with you last summer, but you never asked. You just rode away. . . ." She stopped and said in a changed voice: "Was it because of Jack Kansas?"

Kansas was the leader of those horse rustlers at Bull Sink. She had visited Kansas the summer before, and Pecos had found them together. It still put a knife of jealousy through him when he remembered it.

She said: "I never was in love with Jack Kansas. It was just an adventure. It gave me a silly thrill to think I was doing something, for once in my life, that Gramp, or Uncle Dennis, or Jawn Ridley didn't tell me to. I know what you think after finding us there that night, but it's not true."

He took her by the shoulders and with commanding strength held her away from him. "I know. I overheard enough that night to know. You're a good kid, Letty. You're an honest kid. You're a little bit wild, and a little bit crazy, like a blooded colt that never got the training it should, but you're honest. It'd never do for us to run off. If you married Al Ridley, the thing to do is go back to him."

"To him! Don't you know what happened?"

"I'm still wondering."

"He ran away. He was supposed to take me to the landing in the surrey. We were to catch the steam launch to Fort Benton, and from there go to Helena on our honeymoon. I waited for him in the surrey. Waited there, with Uncle Joe, the Negro coachman, dressed up in a top hat with a white rose in his buttonhole, ready to drive us off. I waited and waited, with everyone watching, and he never came. *He never came!*"

"You mean Al just ran off?"

"Yes! I was there for half an hour. Finally Jawn came and said Al had been taken sick. But that wasn't true. Everyone knew it wasn't true. He had taken a horse and left. I don't know where. I don't care. I never want to see him again. I never want to see any of them again."

"Honey, the thing for you to do is to go back there and tell those cackling females to go to hell."

She wouldn't look at him. She kept talking. "I was there in the surrey. I heard some of the men talking. They'd had too much to drink, and I could hear them. . . ."

"I'll walk back with you, Letty. I'll guarantee nobody'll make any remarks."

"He'd kill you, Pecos."

"Jawn? No, Jawn wouldn't kill me."

"I don't want to, Pecos." She seemed very tired. "Take me some place. If we could just sit for a while out under the trees, where I couldn't see the house, or hear the music. . . ."

He sat with her until long in the night, then together they rode to the ferry and roused old Good-Eye, the boatman, from his tiny six-by-ten shack. Good-Eye blinked when he saw them together, but he refrained from commenting and took them across on his leaky cable boat.

"Wait for you?" Good-Eye asked at the far bank.

Pecos said—"Yes."—and rode with Letty to the Stinchfield home ranch. It was only three miles, and he was back within the hour.

"True what they say about Al Ridley lighting out after the ceremony?" Good-Eye asked. He chuckled and spat tobacco juice at the Missouri's muddy current. "I took the Maxtons across about three hours ago, and I couldn't help overhearing what they said."

"What *did* they say?"

"That Al had run off right after the ceremony." He cast a glance around, squinting his one good eye, although they were nearing midstream and no one could possibly hear them.

He had something else troubling him, and Pecos guessed what it was—he had an idea where Al had run to. "I always liked Al," Pecos said. "I do yet. I'd sure like to talk to him."

"Yah," said Good-Eye. "Well, I'll tell you. I hauled him and his horse across on this ferry just about half an hour after sundown."

"Then turn your tackle around. I'm going back to look for him."

He rode up the Milk River road, unfamiliar with the country, and with no idea where Al would go. He slept in the bunk of a line shack and about noon rode up to Stinchfield's big, wandering log ranch house.

Dennis Stinchfield, looking pouchy and ill after a bad night with the bottle, came out buttoning his white, ruffled shirt. He was about forty, good-looking, and the possessor of a reputation that extended throughout the honky-tonks of the territory.

He shook hands with Pecos and said: "Come in and have a drink." Inside, pouring from a decanter, he went on: "I heard you were in the country. Jawn Ridley was telling me. You haven't taken up my land over there on Sage Creek, have you? No? Guess you're not eligible. Fought in the wrong army or something."

He was taking his dig, but it was hard not to like Dennis, and Pecos laughed it off. He had a drink that hit hard on his hungry stomach. He refused a second and said: "Yeah. I'm

the general of an army that'd make John Brown and his Aboli-
tionists look like Queen Victoria's Buckingham guards. But,
hell, Dennis, I was never a man to count the number of fleas
on a dog when I saw him getting kicked around. Maybe that's
why I'm never more'n one horse and an old applehorn saddle
away from bankruptcy. You and me both, when this year is
over."

"What do you mean?"

"I have my mind on the ten or twenty thousand head of
bone-bag steers, the hungriest steers ever to wet their bellies
in the Río Grande heading nawth. They'll rake the grass in
the Wolftones and the Medicine Ridge next. And then. . . ."

"They're Ridley's worry. I got a river between me and
them."

"How'll that river be in December? Froze solid, and
they'll be around visiting. Hell, a man can wade the Missouri
along in August. They won't wait till winter."

"If you came here with an idea that you could turn me
against Ridley. . . ."

"I'd hoped . . . but to hell with it. No, there was something
else. I was thinking you knew where Al Ridley was."

"Well, think again, because I don't. He didn't come here.
If he did, I'd break his neck." He cursed and laughed a little.
"What a silly trick. Running off like that. You know, Kid, he
was in love with Letty. He always has been. I can't figure it
out. What do you want of him?"

"He's a friend of mine. I thought maybe I could help him."

He looked long in Pecos's eyes. "Say, I think you mean it. I
think you *do* mean it. If I see him, I'll get in touch with you."

Pecos thanked him. He asked about Letty, heard she was
still asleep, and left.

VI

"Maverick Bridegroom"

Four days later, Al Ridley found Pecos at the road camp in Deserter Coulée. Ridley remained on his horse while the Pecos Kid walked around him through the dust kicked up by a team and scraper. Ridley was tall and gave the appearance of being ashamed of it. He was twenty-one or twenty-two, which made him as old as the average 'puncher who came, saddle-tough and worldly, up the long trail from Texas, but still he seemed immature.

"I heard you were looking for me," Al said after fumbling a handshake.

"Why, yes." Pecos rubbed a two-day growth on his jaw. "I wanted to talk with you. I thought maybe I could help you out."

Al said: "If you're going to tell me what to do about Letty, you don't need to waste your time. I don't have to explain this to anybody."

Pecos asked softly: "Not even to her?"

"No, not even to her!"

"All right, Al. That's up to you. You can run out on her, and on *them,* but you'll have to travel a long way before you can get away from yourself."

"I'm not getting out for good. I just need some time. I got to think things over."

"About Letty? Don't think too long, kid. You'll come back

57

and she won't be there."

"I got to be away from my father for a while. You don't know what it's like to be around him. You don't know what he does to you. Not only to me, but to men like Mike Coffey and to a gunman like Joe Livingstone, even. You want to fight against him, but you can't."

Pecos got hold of the bridle. "Get down, Al. It's almost suppertime. Have some coffee and doughgod with us."

"I can't stay here and eat their grub. Not after what us Ridleys have done to 'em."

"We're having something besides doughgod. We're having Ridley beef stew. The *entrée* . . . isn't that what they call it in those Union Pacific rest-a-rawnts?"

Al dismounted and washed in the trickle of water that flowed down Deserter Coulée, and he still refused supper.

Pecos said: "Your dad's not the only one you're afraid of. You're afraid of Letty, too."

"Why should I be?"

"Maybe you've heard stories about Jack Kansas. Maybe you think she's comparing you with Kansas and laughing behind your back." He knew by the shot expression on Al's face that he'd hit it on the head. "Well, maybe you are doing right by going yonder, hitting the trail, proving to yourself that you're a man. But let me tell you something . . . you're wrong about Kansas. I happen to know you're wrong about Kansas."

He fixed a grub bundle for Al Ridley, asked if he had any money, and lent him a five-dollar gold piece.

"You got any destination?" he asked. "Or are you just riding?"

"I had it in mind to go south and get a job on the N.P. I heard you had some friends down there, working on a surveying crew."

Pecos gave him a note for a crew boss named Ralph Chambers, and bid him good bye. Next day, with the crossing completed, Pecos returned with most of the others to Brodenbach's, and rode on toward Layne's with Jim and Hernandez.

August had arrived with the hottest days of the year. A southwest wind blew like the blast from a furnace, and now, added to it, was the stench of rotting carcasses. It grew stronger. Sometimes, intensified by a shift in the wind, it was enough to stop a man cold and take the air from his lungs. Horn Creek had diminished to a thin trickle of water from one pothole to the next. Pecos, Jim, and Hernandez dismounted, soaked their kerchiefs in water and mud, and, breathing through them, rode on.

Layne's house stood abandoned with corral poles nailed across the doors and windows. The place had been made uninhabitable by the gas of rotting carcasses.

Hernandez, his words muffled by the kerchief, said: "Thees is sometime called poetic justice, Keed."

"It'd be poetic justice if these bone-bag cattle stamped Ridley and his so-called Citadel into the ground."

They rode and found pure air on a prairie summit to the south. A stench more fearful even than before arose from Duckett's.

Pecos laughed and said: "Yeah, Duckett was the champ. *He* had to go to Threesleep for more cartridges."

The Laynes and Zollars had moved in with the Dehons whose house, somewhat removed in the coulée, was still habitable.

At a meeting two nights later it was decided to send Dehon and Sophus Briggs to Helena to seek help at the territorial headquarters of the G.A.R.

Days passed. Calahan gave up trying to patrol his fences, packed his family and his poor possessions in an ancient Conestoga wagon, and became the first to use the new Deserter road when he struck out for Medora, hoping to find work on the N.P. His departure was a disturbing influence, and a few days later Wils Duckett left, too, but he returned later with word that the N.P., bountifully supplied with labor from the depression-stricken East, was laying off men rather than putting them on.

Dehon and Briggs returned from Helena with no particular hope that their journey had netted the slightest result. Some wheat, corn, and garden truck that escaped the marauding thousands were harvested in the middle of August. A month had passed without rain, drying up the last potholes along Sage Creek, and then the Horn, although Bull Creek still ran a trickle. Of all the homesteaders, only Brodenbach could boast a good year, and a change had taken place in him. He was no longer cordial in greeting his less successful neighbors. When Big Jim rode to his place with the suggestion that he and his neighbors pool their resources to face the winter, he found that Brodenbach was already hauling his grass to the N.P. feed buyers at Glendive.

"I'll pool my share," he told Big Jim, but a week later it was noticed that Brodenbach was loading not only his grain, but all his household furnishings as well. Advised of this, a group of farmers rode up from Sophus Briggs's place, but saddle horses bearing the Rocking R Ridley brand were tied to the porch railing, and Ridley cowboys watched them from the corrals.

As Briggs and his companions stopped to look, big Mike Coffey came from the house and gestured to them.

Briggs cupped his hands and shouted: "Where's Brodenbach?"

One of Ridley's men laughed and said: "We planted him to see if he'd grow."

"Keep quiet, Shorty," Mike Coffey said. He left his gun behind and walked across the bare-beaten yard. "We bought him out. We paid him a fair price. We'll pay you a fair price, too. If you haven't proved up, we'll pay for your relinquishment."

"How much?" Briggs said.

"Hundred dollars each, and you can take anything with you you're able to haul away."

"How much did you pay Brodenbach?"

"That has nothing to do with it."

"Where is he? We'd like to talk with him."

"By now he should be halfway to the Yellowstone."

No deals were made, although at that moment one hundred dollars loomed large to some of them. At a powwow that night Briggs brought up the point that Ridley would not be willing to buy even at that figure unless his hand was being forced.

Hood said: "You think the G.A.R. is making it tough on him?"

"I don't know, but *I* sure as hell won't sell until I find out."

Briggs and Dehon again left for the territorial capital. Others worked at Dehon's and at Calahan's whose farm had been chosen as winter headquarters.

It was the last week in August. Pecos, after helping at the Rutledge place, rode southward following the bottoms of the Big Sage. Here, in the shade of box elders and bullberries, were longhorn cattle, all hide bone and tendon from the trail. A sidehill spring at Judson's old place had been trampled to half an acre of black sand, and cattle continually muzzled from one deep track to another for the few drops of seepage water they contained.

61

Pecos stopped to roll a cigarette. It was then he became aware of someone following him. He finished rolling the cigarette and lighted it. He turned casually in the saddle to look upstream, but there was no one. Not wishing to be trapped between the creek sides, he started around the broken fence that enclosed Judson's spud patch. A man then appeared on the horizon and came that way.

At a quarter mile, through the heat that rose like waves from the top of a cook stove, the man seemed to be twenty feet high, and the animal he rode might have been a giraffe. When they shrank to proportion, he could see that the giraffe was a small sorrel broncho, and the man was a stranger, short, powerful, and black-whiskered. He had a Winchester out, its butt resting on the pommel of his saddle. He slowed from a trot to a walk, and, when Pecos drew his Winchester, he stopped altogether.

Two other riders had now come in sight, one from the bottoms, one from a dry wash that bounded the far side of the spud patch. Recognizing the odds, Pecos slid his Winchester back in the scabbard. The rider from the bottoms then spurred to a short gallop. He was a gangling, slope-shouldered man with one side of his mouth bulged from tobacco. His face was familiar, but Pecos couldn't place it.

"Hello, Pecos. I'm Joe Livingstone. Maybe you remember me."

"I've heard of you."

Livingstone was the Utah gunman Ridley had chosen to replace Carris Garde. There were stories that he had outdrawn and killed Johnny Six-Spot, and there were other stories that he had caught Johnny without his guns and shot him down without giving him a chance.

Livingstone said: "We traveled a long way since Mescalero."

"Oh, yes." Pecos remembered him then, except under a different name. "You haven't been back there lately, have you?"

"Not lately, but I will sometime. I'm not afraid of those stranglers. They got no proof that I was in on any cattle stealing. I was hired to ride with a gun, just like you, and Jim and that shifty Mex. Only I made a mistake of picking out the losing side." He grinned harder than ever, showing his dirty teeth. "Things have changed, though. I picked out the *good* side this time."

Pecos asked: "You riding for cattle? I've been noticing a few strays drifted across Mike Coffey's deadline."

"We came looking for you."

"What do you want with me?"

"Now I don't want you at all. Jawn Ridley does, though. And when Jawn wants somebody, he comes."

The black-whiskered man jogged up with the rifle in both hands, his thumb hooked over the hammer. The third man, a young, freckled, cold-eyed kid, had slid his rump beyond the cantle of his saddle and had his right hand closed on the butt of his Colt revolver.

Pecos, looking around with one eye squinted against the smoke of his cigarette, said: "Thanks for the compliment. I must be a real ring-tailed ripper that Jawn sends three of his gunmen to get me. That's exactly two more'n I'd send to get you, Livingstone."

"It's two men more'n we need to get you, too, only we had orders to bring you in *alive*."

VII

"Talk—or Else"

He rode with them cross-country, up the Medicine Ridge down to The Citadel. Until then, moved by bravado, Joe Livingstone had not disarmed him. He did so now, however, explaining that the boss might like him better unarmed.

"You keep on the good side of him, Kid," he said with a nasty, loose-mouthed grin. "I know you were mighty dear friends at one time, drank together, smoked those thick Havana cigars . . . but those days are gone. When you go in there, you answer everything he says. Say 'yes, sir,' and 'no, sir.' This advice is all free, on account of what we went through together down in Mescalero . . . and because sometime I'm going to have the privilege of walking up to you, outdrawing you, and shooting you right between the eyes."

Pecos laughed in his easy, tired way and said: "Between the eyes, or between the shoulders like you shot Johnny Six-Spot?"

Livingstone froze and said through his teeth: "Don't push that stuff too far, Kid, or you'll never get inside the house."

They rode up the carriage path. The lawn, once carefully tended, looked dry, and all around the edgings the grass had gone to seed. The shrubs that Ridley had brought by stage and steamboat all the way from the Dutch nurseries in Pennsylvania and New York were unclipped, and some of them were dead. The house, in some indefinable manner, also seemed beat and neglected. They dismounted, and clanked their spurs across the porch. A Chinaman, hearing them, came to the door and promptly took off.

"Take your spurs off," Livingstone said, his right-hand Colt now unholstered, rammed against the Pecos Kid's back. "Have you shacked up with the sodbusters so long you've forgotten how the other half lives?" He glanced around and said: "Blackie, you get inside. In the big room. See to it nothing happens. Lennie, you stay by the door."

Pecos pulled off his spurs and went inside. The house held the stale odor of shut-in tobacco smoke. The shades had been pulled against the afternoon sun, and he had to grope his way through the entry hall to the door of the big room.

"All right, Joe," the voice of Jawn Ridley said. "You can wait in the entry. I don't think Pecos will cause too much trouble."

Pecos waited for the flicker of sun brightness to leave his eyes, and at last the things around him took shape. Jawn Ridley was seated behind a mahogany table, an uncorked bottle of brandy at his left, a pearl-handled Remington six-shooter at his right. He was a big man, big in every way, tall, and broad, and thick through. He was probably in his early forties. His face was rather narrow, of a type generally referred to as aristocratic, with high cheek bones and a good jaw. His hair was dark brown and just starting to show an edge of gray. Pecos had never noticed the gray before. It needed the attention of a barber, too, as did his mustache.

"Well, Major," Ridley said. There was a sharp edge of sarcasm in his words. Both of them had served as officers in the Army of the Confederacy during the war, and it was quite obvious that Pecos, to Ridley's eyes, had disgraced himself.

"How are things with you and your new-found friends, the Yankees?"

"Not very well, seh. I guess you've just about succeeded in running 'em out."

"Did you have any doubt that I'd end up winner?"

He gave it his consideration. "I'm still a little bit in doubt. You got fifteen, twenty thousand extra cattle on your hands now. Even at seven dollars a head you've got a lot of cattle."

"Are you explaining my business to me?"

"I wouldn't attempt to do that, Jawn. I'm just pointing out your problem. You'll have to carry 'em through without digging your range up by the roots. After all, there's nothing so important to a cattleman as his grass."

Ridley grinned, showing his powerful teeth. "I can see you, sitting in one of those shacks with our nester friends, waiting for Jawn Ridley to destroy his range and put himself out of business. But it's all a dream, Major. It won't happen. I've thought of everything. I still have grass in the Wolftones and the Medicine Ridge. I'll bring them through the winter, then I'll move north. I'll dump them on the Milk River range. I'll put weight on them up there and let this grass come back. A couple of years from now and you'll be able to see the wind blow waves in this range again."

"King of the country."

"I'm not a braggart, Major. I'll just state a matter of fact. I win! That's how I play the game. *I win!*"

Pecos took off his hat and fingered sweaty hair away from his forehead. He said: "You remind me of an old fellow I knew down in Texas when I was a boy. He was so ornery even his own friends didn't like him."

"When a man has accumulated what I have, he has no friends. All his old friends hate him through jealousy, and all his new friends only worship him for his power. You're telling me nothing I don't know when you say there isn't a man in the country that wouldn't kick me if they ever got me down. But I didn't get you here to howl like a wolf over a fallen adversary. I got you here for one reason only. I want to know where to find my son."

There was a commotion on the stairs, a thump of boot heels, and Joe Livingstone saying: "No, ma'am. I got orders not to let anybody in there."

A woman cried shrilly: "Don't touch me! Don't touch me, do you hear?"

He recognized the voice of Lynn Ridley—Jawn Ridley's wife—a woman who once claimed to be an invalid.

She got the door open despite Joe Livingstone's attempts to stop her. She saw Pecos and cried: "Don't tell him where my boy is. He wants to kill my boy!"

Ridley said: "Get her out of here!"

She had fallen halfway through the door. The black-whiskered gunman who had been lurking unobserved in a far corner of the room now started forward.

"Get back!" Ridley said. "Livingstone can handle this. Get her out of here. I don't care how you do it, get her out of here."

She was Ridley's age, although she looked much older. Her hair was so white it seemed almost bluish. She was a skeleton with skin hanging on it. And yet, at one time, she had probably been beautiful. She was on hands and knees. Joe Livingstone, half lifting her, tried to urge her to her feet.

Jawn Ridley roared: "Carry her upstairs!"

The scene had unnerved Ridley. Sweat glistened below his hairline. He exhaled, poured a drink, and downed it. He had been pouring too many drinks lately and it showed in the looseness of the skin under his eyes and around the side of his jaw.

67

Dan Cushman

Pecos said: "You speak of being a Southerner. Officer of the Confederacy. In the South you'd be killed for that, seh."

Ridley got to his feet with a sudden straightening of his powerful legs. He flung the glass with all his strength at Pecos's face. It *zinged* past so close Pecos could feel a damp spatter of liquor.

"Shut up! You hear me, you yella Yank turncoat, shut up! This is The Citadel. Here *I* ask the questions. Here I call the tune. You answer when you're spoken to, because I could have you killed at a snap of my finger. Do you realize that?"

Pecos wiped drops of brandy from his cheek, laughed without humor, and said: "Yes, seh."

"Where is my son?" Ridley shouted.

"I have no way of knowing where your son is."

"He went to you. Don't deny it. He went to you. You were at that road camp, and he went to you."

"He borrowed five dollars from me, and rode south."

Ridley rammed a hand deeply in his pocket. He found a five dollar gold piece. He hurled it, as he had the glass, with all his strength. "There's your money. Now, where is he?"

"I don't know."

"You're a liar. You're a yella Yank liar. You tried to turn him against me from the first day you saw him. As soon as you came back, he started sneaking away to see you."

"That's not true."

Ridley started around the table. Pecos, turning to face him, was brought to a stop when Livingstone's gun rammed his spine. He stopped with a quick gasp of pain, his hands wide of his body.

Ridley swung his open hand. The blow caught him across his neck and the base of the jaw. It sent him reeling off the edge of the table, across a chair. He saw Ridley striding after him. He started up with doubled fists and was clubbed from

68

behind. He was on hands and knees. He tried to get up. He was hit again. He brought his eyes into focus, and this time he was seated with one leg bent under him, his forearms resting on the chair. He passed his hand across his face and looked at it. It was smeared with blood.

"Where is he?" Ridley asked. He had control of his voice again. It was raw and hoarse. He asked the question without relaxing his clenched teeth. "Where is he?"

"He went south." Pecos's mind was functioning again. He had to convince Ridley that he didn't at that moment know where the boy was, but that he had the means of finding out. "You damned fool. If you'd have come to my camp peacefully and asked, I'd have been able to tell you where he is, or at least where he *was* ten or twelve days ago. I got a letter from him."

"Where was it from?"

"He gave no address."

"There must have been a post office stamp."

"Maybe. I didn't pay any attention. It's in my war bag."

Pecos got to his feet. He had been struck across the ridge of the nose, and blood still flowed from his nostrils. Each turn of his head seemed to split it down the middle, but the dizziness was going away.

Ridley, after breathing deeply, went back around the table. The release of his anger had done him good. He acted more like the Ridley of a year before. He sat down, fiddled with his heavy linked watch chain, and, looking at Pecos, he jerked his big shoulders in a laugh. "You're a sight. Do you get nosebleeds often? Maybe it's the altitude. You ought to see a good sawbones and have him give you a quinine tonic."

"You're supposed to laugh," Pecos said, turning to Livingstone.

Ridley said: "Give and take, Major. And so far you've

given as well as you've taken. Now, you know, I could find out where that boy is. I could beat it out of you. I don't like to do those things, so you'd better tell me where I can reach him."

"Why don't you leave the kid alone?"

"I don't need your advice."

"The kid thought he should go out and earn his own way for a while. He wanted time to make up his mind what to do."

"About what?"

"About you. About Letty."

"He's made me. . . ." He checked himself. He motioned to Livingstone and the other gunman. "Go outside. I can handle this fellow all right." He waited, drumming his thick, excellently formed fingers on the table until the men were gone and the door closed. "He's made me the laughingstock of the county. Me, Jawn Ridley, the king of Landers County. They've made up a poem about it. They were singing it in my own bunkhouse." Ridley waved his hand at the view through his front windows. "Do you think I built all that for myself? I wanted a son. A real son. A son that could carry it on the way it should be carried on. And what did I get? *Him!* He took after his mother. Piano, a poet, all the noble qualities he'd need to be a spinster. I should have found a woman worthy of me, worthy of this country. I should have found a woman for me like I found for him. Letty. *She* wouldn't have come through that door screaming and making a sight of herself. No, if she was convinced I needed stopping, she'd have stopped me with a gun. They could give me the son I want, he and Letty."

"You can't force the boy to be someone he isn't."

"I'll make a man of him." He drove his fist onto the table. "I'll make a man of him like they made one of me, in the

Army. They use no soft gloves there. They make a man of you or they kill you."

"I've been in the Army, too."

"Yes. You were in a damned good Army. You served under Tully. I can't understand how *this* ever happened to you. Lining up with a bunch of damn' Yankee sodbusters, fighting your own kind, trying to chop the country up with wire like they did east in Kansas, trying to turn it grass-side under."

Using his kerchief, Pecos got his face cleaned off. The pain was leaving his head. He could move his neck now without having it seem to split in two. He looked down on Ridley and said: "You really believe you're running some kind of a crusade, don't you?"

"I know *I'm right*. I'm as right ridding the country of those hoe men as I'd be in ridding a dog of fleas. I can't understand you. I've tried to, but I can't. I can't see why you'd turn against me. I offered you everything. I'd have made you a big man in this country. I've had it in my mind to move to the capital, open a bank, finance a north-south railroad. I'd have left the ranch with you and Al to run as you saw fit. That's what my dream was after I first got to know you, Warren. Then you stabbed me in the back. And now my own son!"

Pecos looked at him, trying to understand him, trying to put himself in Ridley's shoes.

Ridley went on. "There's something about ingratitude. . . . Oh, to hell with it. To hell with *you*. It's like I said. If I ever went down, there isn't a man but would take a kick at me. But I'm not going down. When spring comes, there'll be only me, and I'll hold this country all the way from Threesleep to Milk River. Then maybe you'll come back, Warren. Maybe you and Al will both come back where you belong."

71

"You mean you'd take me back on the old proposition in spite of everything?"

"I'd take you back on my terms. From the first day I've disliked your guts, but I've sort of admired you. You and that stubborn Texas pride. Standing against the avalanche with a tin shovel. Sticking up for that poor, unfortunate, demented woman that the law says is my wife. Taking a beating rather than break your word to Al. Can't you see? You're the South. You're the reason she fought, you're the reason she was magnificent, and you're the reason she was licked. You're like me. And I suppose that's why, someday, I'll have to kill you."

"Why not today?" Pecos asked.

"No, not today. Get out, damn you. Get out of my sight. You were lying about that letter. You know where he is. I could get it out of you, but I'd have to kill you. I don't want to kill you. Not today. I want you to be around to see what the end product of all this is. Next winter, next spring, next fall. . . ."

VIII

"The Big Die"

The hot days continued until well into September. The equinoctial storms common in that country did not arrive. There were cold days and windy days, but rain was limited to a few fine spatters and some snow that edged the evergreens on the higher slopes of the Medicine Ridge. The range was gray; the grass clumps were hard nodules eaten to the roots by foraging cattle. Only in the Wolftones and in the Medicine Ridge was there grass, and Ridley's cowboys stayed on constant patrol, driving the herds away, saving it as a reserve for the cold days of winter.

Rain came in October, soaking the parched ground, starting the streams again. The rain changed to snow, the snow melted off, and for a few days it was like spring again with a bright tinge of green showing across the prairie. Dehon and Layne rolled up the new road with a wagonload of provisions from Glendive, half paid for and half bought on credit from the merchants of that rosily optimistic community.

The women picked chokeberries and bullberries for jelly and wine. In early November came the great flight of ducks from the north. They settled on the river by the hundreds of thousands. Taking flight, their number almost blackened the sky. Ducks were shot by wagonloads and hauled in to be salted and smoked and stored away for winter. Later, when the thermometer dropped each night to below the freezing point, they were hung inside the cache houses, those window-less cabins on stilts where food was kept dark, frozen, and safe from marauding skunks until the warm days of spring. Aside from Hood, who decided to return to his own place, the farmers formed a large community at Dehon's where, through sharing, the worst hardships could be softened.

At Dehon's, Hernandez Pedro Gonzales y Fuente Jesús María Flanagan appeared one morning with a homemade desk, an armload of books, his guitar and a buggy whip, and announced that school was in session. His curriculum in-cluded reading and song in almost equal proportions that he explained by examples from his little black book of which he was inordinately proud. "Weeth thees book," he would say, "could your schoolmaster be a great banker like Jay Cooke, eef only the sums in it were owing to him instead of by me. Always you should keep books on your transactions, for a debt is a theeng of honor that you should never forget owing to the last day of time. Behold, your schoolmaster at any time can tell to the last *centavo* how much money he owes all the way from Chihuahua. Now, leafing to the last page, I read the sum of feefty-two thousand, seex hundred, forty-one dollars, and seex beets!"

Bringing up the subject to the Pecos Kid, Harry Layne asked: "Is it possible for a man to get to owing that much money?"

"Oh, hell, that's all talk," Pecos said. "He don't remember to put down all his debts. He owes *that* much money to Big Jim and me alone."

The great blizzard came in December. It started gently with a warm wind from a bullet-colored sky. There were big flakes of snow that melted as they fell. It turned to rain, and the rain froze. Short-cropped tufts of grass were turned to radial clusters of spiny ice. The thermometer on Dehon's rear porch stood at twenty degrees above zero. Snow blew in little drifts.

In the barn, conditioned after a fashion for cold weather, Hernandez suddenly increased in popularity as men were driven inside. There was singing and square dancing and a sampling of chokeberry wine. The blizzard mounted. For three days and nights it howled down, drifting hills of snow over the edge of the coulée, then the sun came out brilliantly over an infinity of white.

With teams and horses a road was broken to the spring hole in the coulée and, on succeeding days, across the ten miles of badland rims to the Hood place. For a week it was clear and cold, with the thermometer touching ten or fifteen below at dawn, rising a few degrees above zero in the afternoon. Then the day turned bullet-colored, and a wind came, cold but from the southwest.

Jean Folette, a French half-breed trapper who had found hospitality for the night, sniffed the wind and said: "It is well, *m'shus,* that you build shack on side hill and not in coulée bottom, for thees is a chinook and by night thees coulée will be one beeg rivaire."

That night, however, after shrinking the snow to a third of its previous thickness, there was an unpredictable shift in the wind, and in the short space of an hour the thermometer dropped from forty above to ten below. Drifts that had been feather-soft became a brittle honeycomb of ice.

The cold held. Already the farmers had to start feeding their store of cornstalk and oat-straw hay. Range cattle wandered the prairie. Those native to the country tried to dig for food, but the Texas and Mexican trailers were mystified by the misfortune that had befallen them, and started massing in the coulées.

Ridley's men, fifty strong, made a sweep of the range first in one direction and then in the other, driving part of the herd to the Wolftones and the rest to the Medicine Ridge. A second blizzard came to heap snow on iced-over range. The thermometer stood at twenty below zero on the Twentieth day of December, and twenty-five below on the Twenty-Fifth as Hernandez presented his pupils in his Christmas program. Men joked about the cold, assuming it would touch thirty-one on the last day of the month, and rise to a warm one below on the first day of the year.

However, it was thirty-five below on the Thirty-First of December, and forty-two below on New Year's Day. For a week it clung within five degrees of the forty mark, and then plunged to the fifties. At that temperature it was impossible to heat any building except the main house, and, as there was not room for everyone, it was turned over to the women and smaller children, with the men in their felt boots and Mackinaws hugging the stove in Hernandez's barn schoolhouse. Frost lay thickly over the windowpanes so one had to dig through a quarter inch of it to peep outside. It formed on the rafters and the ceiling boards and down the walls, each day whiter and thicker until the cabin's interior had the appearance of a crystal cave. A man entering from outside was instantly surrounded by a white cloud of mist—mist that as quickly disappeared when the door was closed. Moisture from the many occupants of the room distilled on the door and ran down in droplets that froze to ice where the draft from outside found entrance around the edges, so that it was a daily task with a rude ice pick to keep the door in working order.

Outside, the extreme temperature made life more difficult in many ways. The snow was harsh and abusive to a horse's hoofs. Sleds were harder to pull with the snow fragments hanging to the runners like resinous, abrasive points. It creaked underfoot, and a man could be heard walking through the still cold at a quarter mile. It affected the air as well, giving it a new resistance. Smoke rose from chimneys and hung stagnated for hours, white against the darker sky. A rifle bullet flying through such air sent back a crack like splitting wood, and dropped off so rapidly that what had once been point-blank range was now the first step of a rear sight's elevation.

On the Thirteenth of January the thermometer dropped below fifty-five which was the lowest it would register. Next afternoon two of Ridley's cowboys rode up half frozen and were welcomed inside. Neither was much more than twenty-one, and both were range riders as distinguished from the eighty-a-month gunmen led by Joe Livingstone. It had been sixty-one below that morning in Ridley Landing. A year ago the same day, one of them remembered, the prairie had been clear of snow and it was warm enough for a swim in the river.

Drinking coffee, warming their feet before the fire, they told of days of riding, of camping in the open between two fires, of shelter in dugouts and line shacks, driving cattle back from the bleak expanses of prairies, of breaking up concentrations in coulées, of chopping water holes that froze new crusts of ice as they chopped. Five hundred cattle had died already, but that was nothing to what might be expected later on. Even native cattle in the Wolftones and the Medicine Ridge were wearing out their hoofs digging for food through snow and ice.

One of them said with serious belief: "Blanche Yellowtail . . . Big George's squaw at the Landing . . . she says we're due for a change in the moon, and it'll bring a chinook. It'll be just in time. They're piling up at the head of Thirty-

Eight Mile Coulée, just piling up, trompin' one another to death."

Pecos said: "What if Blanche is wrong?"

"Why, then, it'll be too bad for Ridley. It'll be too bad for everybody. It'll be the worst thing that ever hit the country."

The new moon came, cold and bluish, riding very small in the sky. The cold held. From the north a current of air jiggled a few still spines of grass that protruded from the crusted snow. Each day wolves, skulking the coulée, came closer to the house, gray shapes, sensing the warmth that was denied them.

The cottonwood fuel that had been considered sufficient for the winter was almost gone. Crews with sleds cleared the coulée of its few remaining trees, a shed came next, and then one of the less-needed corrals.

The Pecos Kid, hating the cold with all his Texas heritage, rode back from a scouting trip to the badlands, his horse's front covered with frost, icicles frozen to the hairs of his own nostrils. His feet, despite moccasins and thick wrappings of wool rags, had been nipped, so they itched like fire once he had thawed himself in the kitchen.

"I was all the way to Bull Sink," he said. "Jack Kansas and his longriders have pulled out, just like I said they would. Only four or five wolfers down there. Plenty of fuel in those river bottoms a couple or three miles from town. We got to move, and there's no point in waiting another hour."

It was a day's travel to Bull Sink, and a day's haul back again. Moving took a week.

The strong cold kept its grip. Of the skinny trail-herd cattle, only a fraction was left. The rest were piled up in the coulées, frozen to stiff masses, covered deeper each day by a powder of snow. Cowboys, stopping at Bull Sink, reported that Ridley had already lost between eighteen and twenty thousand. The 66 and Square and Compass outfits to the west had been equally hard hit. Three weeks more without chinook would mean the finish of every outfit between Dakota and the Musselshell.

Word came that Ridley had traveled to Miles City. He returned and got his men together, and in a last, desperate move to save his whole herd he attempted to drive across the river to some badland coulées around Redstone where, due to some trick in the wind, the bitter cold had not touched, and good grass lay beneath a feather-light cover of snow.

The river had frozen, and moved, and frozen again. It was a jagged mass of ice blocks, upended, thrust one over the other. A wind flowed from the northeast, following the riverbed. It cut like wire, and no man could face it. Riders, swinging rope goads, managed to drive part of the herd to mid-river. There they turned back in a slip-sliding, terrified stampede. Ridley, following in a cutter, cursed his men and kept ordering them on.

After more than twenty-four hours, only a handful of cattle had crossed the river; the rest were scattered along the bottoms or, tails in the wind, climbed through deep snow up the coulées. Then, as if anything more were necessary, the wind increased. At Bull Sink, protected in its badlands pocket, it was only an eddy that swirled the ground snow into new drifts, and Hernandez held school as usual, but along the river and across the high prairie it swept as a final destroyer, freezing everything in front of it.

Two days later, the thermometer rose until it stood at eight below zero, and it seemed almost warm. In mid-February, four of Ridley's cowboys came to Bull Sink, repaired one of the shacks, and holed up till spring. They had rebelled at Ridley's abuse, and he had discharged them. Attracted to Hernandez's school, they sat around all day, feeding wood to the stove, inserting an occasional comment generally in regard to an arithmetic problem that they always asked to be stated in various quantities of bones—if Ridley had fifty tons of bones, at three dollars a ton, and the Square and Compass had twice as many bones at two dollars a ton, how many . . . ? The bone-picker's joke was the standard of that dismal season.

One afternoon they had an unexpected visitor in the person of Dennis Stinchfield. He drove up in a team and cutter, wrapped to the top of his head in a ratskin coat, his legs buried in buffalo robes, only his eyes, nose, and frost-covered mustache exposed to the cold. With such protection he was jovial and able to joke about the weather. He paid one of the Briggs kids fifty cents to take care of his team and found the Pecos Kid playing two-handed euchre with Jean Folette in what had once been Dinny's Chicago Bar.

"I've wintered all right," Dennis said with his good smile. "We even got cattle left. Bet your life! Forty head in that coulée behind the house. You haven't got a drink to warm a man's gullet up, have you?"

Pecos informed him that the last liquor had been consumed a month ago. Dennis, he noticed, had lost some of his softness. He looked rugged and younger, bearing a certain resemblance to Letty that had never been apparent before.

"How's Letty?" Pecos asked.

"I sent her to Benton, and she came back again. Wouldn't that blast you? One of the coldest days, about a month ago, here she came riding in on an Army horse. She'd taken the mail sled to Fort Wells. A good girl, Pecos. It sure broke her up to see those cattle turned to stone in the coulées." His cigar had frozen, and now, holding it over the stove, he thawed it out. "Hasn't this been hell? Pecos, I saw the damnedest thing up on the bench. It was right on top of the ridge, and all the snow had blowed away, and there stood this cow. I watched for a long time, and finally I rode up there. There she was, standing up, frozen solid with her legs sort of braced out, head down, eyes still open. It gave me the creeps. It gets a man to feeling like everything in the world is going to freeze up solid, and there never will be any warmth again, ever."

Folette said in his French-Cree accent: "But under the rivaire, deep in the mud, the catfeesh sleep, and snug in his hole the badger. Eh, I theenk men and cows are damn' fool or they would not stand on top of thees country."

Pecos, playing a card, said: "We're doing the same thing here as far as that goes, holing up for winter. What brings you out, Dennis?"

Dennis looked at the wolfer and said: "I hate to interrupt your game. . . ."

"Hell, two-handed euchre is no game, anyhow," Pecos said. "It's plain robbery the way the French play it." He tossed the trapper two bits and walked with Dennis to the front of the room.

Dennis said: "I know how you feel about Jawn Ridley, Kid, but things have been a little bad for him. He used his credit at the wrong time, and now he's wiped out, cleaned. He's finished."

"Well, I didn't lick him. He was too tough for me. He was so tough nobody could lick him except himself."

"He's been hitting the bottle."

"Where's his wife?"

"She's there. Just the two of them, all alone in that big, old house. It's hell."

Pecos turned from the window, saying: "I can't tell you how sorry I've always felt for that woman."

"Me, too. That's why I'm here. I thought maybe you could tell me where to find Al."

The last Pecos had heard, Al was working as chainman on an N.P. surveying crew. He told him that and added: "They won't be driving stakes in this kind of weather, though. The crew is probably back in Bismarck."

"You don't hear from him?"

"I told Jawn once that I'd received a letter. That was a lie, when I was trying to save myself from getting killed. Dehon was at Glendive, loading supplies this fall, and heard about him working with the surveyors."

"That damned yella kid!" Dennis Stinchfield had never forgiven him for running out on his niece after their wedding.

"You're not going 'way down there looking for him?"

"I'll go to Fort Wells. I'll get a message through from there on the Army telegraph. They have a line following the Yellowstone now. A message should find him somewhere along the way."

IX

"Al Ridley Comes Home"

Al Ridley was in Medora, sitting out the days in a little tar-paper shack heated by an alcohol stove. His only duty was to go outside each hour or so to peer through the eyepiece of a transit and make certain that the bridge crew was bringing each new section into level. Actually he could have spent his entire day indoors, for cold weather had brought the timber work to a virtual standstill, and the lens of the transit each time misted over from the moisture of his eye before he could accurately find his point through the cross-hairs.

Al Ridley was as thin as ever, and he still had a stooped habit of carrying himself, but the months had done something to him. He seemed more sure of himself. The responsibility of command had been thrust upon him. He had learned to give orders, and it ceased to surprise him when they were obeyed.

It was about three in the afternoon, and he was reading an old copy of the *Northwestern Gazette*, when he heard the creak and clatter of a handcar and, looking from the window, saw that a couple of Bohunks had pumped the telegraph operator over the temporary tracks from O'Fallen. He was carrying a message scrawled on company communication paper.

"This is for you, Al," he said, coming inside. "It came through from the Bozeman operator, attention all stations, so

83

I thought I'd better run it out to you. I hope there's nothing wrong . . . that line about your mother."

Al read the message and closed it in his hand to fight down the sudden jumpiness that seized him. "She's been . . . sick for along time."

Although he wanted to be alone to think about the message, he had to invite the operator in for a smoke and a pot of coffee. He read the message several times. It was signed **Dennis** and said that **many things** at home needed his attention. It would be **especially good** for his mother if he would return without delay.

He wired Bismarck for a relief man and waited three days for his arrival. It was another two-day wait for the bobsled stage that took him across the Montana line to Beaver Creek. He stayed an afternoon and night in a tiny, log stage station, and spent still another day reaching Glendive.

At Glendive he found that the stage that ordinarily ran once a week to Threesleep had been discontinued because of the cold. A search of the livery stables found no one willing to gamble his stock on a journey to Ridley Landing, so he was forced to spend his savings for a team and cutter and set out, wrapped in buffalo robes, the rear of the box filled with oats, food, and a small sack of first-class mail that he had consented to deliver in Threesleep.

He drove to Flatwillow in one day, to Threesleep the next, and made the long haul to The Citadel between dawn and midnight of the third. The weather had been a sharp, clear twenty-below with a whisper of north wind that died as the sun set. Aside from an occasional wolf or coyote, he saw no living thing until he turned up Ridley Creek where a few winter-lank cattle were in the brush muzzling through the ground cover. At first glance even The Citadel looked lifeless with drifts banked up even with the eaves of bunkhouses, the snow in the corrals undisturbed, but as he approached, a dog commenced barking, and there was a creak and drag as a bunkhouse door opened.

It was Joe Livingstone. He came out in sheepskin mocks, with a long, rat-skin coat on over his underwear, and a .45 thrust in the pocket of the coat.

"Well, I'll be damned," he said with a twist of contempt on his mouth, "if it isn't the son and heir. Say, your dad was looking for you. Didn't you know you were supposed to ride off in a coach and four with a whole damned paddleboat to take you to hell or wherever?"

Al ignored the smirking remark and asked: "Where's my dad now?"

"At the house, I guess."

There was no sign of smoke from the front chimneys.

"My mother all right?"

Grinning with his rabbit teeth, Livingstone said: "Well, she's the same as ever."

The remark made Al unsteady and reckless from anger. An uncontrollable impulse swept over him, and he grabbed the whip from its socket and swung its butt with all his strength at the gunman's head.

Livingstone had time to take half a step backward and break the force of the blow with upflung hands. A discarded wagon tongue beneath the snow caught his heel, making him spill backward. He caught himself on his elbows and grabbed for the six-shooter. It was rammed deeply in his pocket. Its hammer caught, and he had to pull several times before freeing it. Al Ridley could have grabbed the Sharps carbine in the seat beside him. Instead, he leaped out and drove the instep of his boot to Livingstone's hand. He kicked again and again until he was sure the gun was gone. Livingstone, swapping ends in the snow, got out of reach. Cursing, with his sleeves and drawers cold from snow, he backed toward the bunkhouse.

In the door, Curly Forbes with a Winchester in his hands shouted: "Joe! Joe, who is it?"

"That chippy Al Ridley."

Al kicked through the snow, felt the solid weight of the .45, and picked it up. It had been warm from the bunkhouse, and a cake of snow was already freezing solidly around it.

"You forgot your gun," Al said, and hurled it after him. It missed Livingstone's head by no more than ten inches and kept going to clump against the logs by the door. Curly Forbes did not make a move to use his rifle, or say a word.

Al drove on to the carriage house. He knocked to arouse the hostler who usually slept in a room in front. He was not there. He had to open the doors and put the team up himself. A light shone dimly through the deeply frosted windows on the far side of the house. He went inside and found his father, seated behind his desk with a bottle in front of him.

Big Jawn Ridley stared at him without moving. His face had a resigned truculence. He showed no surprise, no pleasure, no anger. He merely looked. "So you came back," he said.

"Where's Mother?"

"I don't know. I suppose she's upstairs."

"Is she asleep?"

"How in hell do I know if she's asleep?"

Al started away, and his father got to his feet. "*I'm* fine!" he said bitterly. "The ranch is fine. All of the cattle are fine. I knew you'd want to know about those things."

"Sorry. I guess it's been tough."

Jawn walked around the desk not taking his eyes off him. "I know why you came back. You come to kick me like the rest. Like Mike Coffey. Ten years on my payroll, eating my grub, taking trips to Helena and Saint Louis at my expense. And now where is he? Gone. All of them gone. All except those two gunmen down there. The worst of the bunch, but they stuck with me."

"I told you I was sorry. I meant it."

"Where you been?"

"At Medora. Working on the N.P."

"You figure on staying a while? Or are you going back?"

"I'll stay."

Jawn Ridley looked at him for a long five seconds. He jerked his big shoulders and said: "Oh." It could have meant anything. There was no anger in him. He was tired, bitter, and savage. The tone of his—"Oh."—showed all of those things. He poured himself a drink. "You want a shot?"

"I'm going up to see Mother."

His mother was like a skeleton in the cold room. She got up and clutched him to her breast. She shivered and wept and said: "Thank God, you've come. He tried to drive me away from here, but I wouldn't go without you. I knew you'd come back here, and, if I wasn't here, he could do with you as he wanted."

He kept reassuring her, telling her that they would go away together, all the while knowing it would be impossible until spring. At last he got her back beneath the deep coverlets of her bed.

It was almost dawn when he went back downstairs. Jawn Ridley still sat in his office. The fire was down to a tiny clutch of coals. The air was so cold one could see the misty whiteness of his breath.

"You think I'm licked. *They* think I'm licked. I'll live to kick them all in the teeth, those worthless 'punchers, those Yankee squatters with their G.A.R. paper, the Pecos Kid and his saddlebag tramps, and Mike Coffey. I'll meet Mike sometime, some place, and I'll kill him. I'll kill him with my fists. No, I'm not finished. I'll put cattle on this range next year. Maybe the Square and Compass is finished. If it is, I'll put cattle on their old range, too. I'll hold this country from Musselshell to Dakota." He laughed, the force of it bounding off the walls, echoing harder because of the cold. "King of the country. I'll show them whether I'm through or not!"

Al said: "Mother isn't so well. She ought to have some heat up there."

"Oh," he muttered. Al couldn't be sure he had even heard his words. "I'll carry the Stinchfields like I always have. All in the family, Son. All in the family. She's a real woman, and she's still your wife. She came back from Helena. She's been driving cattle everyday. The Stinchfields will have some of that good Missouri she-stock left for next year, and every head of it was saved by her, not by that worthless old Dennis. She's a woman, Son. She's a Ridley. By the gods, she's a *real* Ridley."

"I can't face her, Dad."

Jawn spun on him. He bore down on him in long strides. "You will face her. You'll face her and make a real wife of her, do you understand? You'll raise children by her. You'll give me the kind of children I had a right to expect from that woman up there."

Al made an attempt to answer, but something tied his tongue in knots, and the old fear of his father lay in his eyes.

Ridley walked past him, through the door to the big room, shouting for the Chinese cook. "Wing! Wing, where are you?"

A short, moon-faced Chinaman came running in, still buttoning his shirt, saying: "Yes, boss!"

"Clean up the rig. Get a fire going in the stove. In the fireplace, too."

"Fi' wood v'y low. Outside v'y cold. Fi' wood won't last till spling."

"Well, chop down the carriage house."

"Yes, boss. I get plenty wood quick."

Ridley strode around the big room, booting chairs back into their proper places. Bottles were scattered over the table. He gathered them in the refuse bin by the stove. He turned and saw Al facing him.

Al said: "Letty will never come back to me."

"No one in this country can say *no* to a Ridley. Get that through your head. You're a Ridley!"

"I talked to Dennis before I went south last summer. He said. . . ."

"The hell with Dennis. I've carried the Stinchfield Cattle Company on my shoulders for the last four years. Where do you think Dennis got the money to play the honky-tonks . . . those big, fancy honky-tonks in Helena? From me. From *us!*"

Al raised his voice. "I'm not talking about Dennis. I'm talking about Letty. Letty won't take Dennis's orders or yours, either. Letty will do what she likes."

Jawn growled: "Yes." A heel of liquor from one of the bottles had spilled on his wrist, and he stood wiping it on a handkerchief. "I wouldn't trade Letty for ten of him. And her mother was a quarter-breed Blackfoot, did you know that? Sometimes it makes a man wonder." He rammed the handkerchief back in his pocket and said: "But she'll come! She married you, didn't she? She's your wife."

Al heard the creak of cold boards and realized that his mother was at the head of the stairs, listening. As soon as he got the chance, he stepped into the hall and looked up the stairs. She stood on the topmost step, clutching the balustrade. He tired to get her back in her room. He said: "You shouldn't be out here. Wait till the house gets warm."

She hissed for him to be quiet. Her eyes turned in their deep sockets. "Don't let him know I heard. He'd guess what we were about."

"What do you mean?"

"You can't let him bring that creature here. That shameless . . ."—she hunted for a word and said—"*thing.*"

"Now, Mother."

"Well, she is! Everyone in the country talks about her, first chasing down to see Jack Kansas, and then that *friend* of yours, Warren. I've never told you this before, but she's part Indian."

He tried to reassure her and get her back to her room. "Yes, I know. Her mother was supposed to be part Indian, but that's nothing. Lots of good people are part Indian."

"*My* son will not be mixed up with a bunch of 'breeds."

"Don't worry, Mother."

He got her inside her room and closed the door. It smelled gassy from the little circular wick kerosene burner that she had lighted to heat it.

"You'd better dress and come downstairs."

"No. He thinks I can't get up and down the stairs. I want him to go on thinking that. We have to get away from here. The two of us. You have a team and a cutter, don't you? We'll take that. We'll go west to Fort Wells, and, when it's warmer, we'll go on to Benton or Helena. From there we'll get a coach to Salt Lake City, and we can take the Union Pacific back to Saint Louis. The Whimples are my cousins. Mister Whimple owns a large . . . oh, a very large warehouse there. They're fine people. Georgia stock. That's what you want to marry, a real, nice *Southern* girl."

To quiet her he said: "Sure, Mother. Sure. You lie down now until the house is warm."

X

"Father and Son"

When he went downstairs, his father was gone. He returned about ten minutes later and said: "I sent Curly after her."

"She'll not come."

Big Jawn lighted a cigar and stood straight, grinning with his powerful teeth clamped on it. "She'll come."

Daylight was gray, and the wind had picked up a little. Ridley kept walking to the front window to see from one of the edges that were free of frost. Shortly after noon he said: "What did I tell you? She's coming. Get this through your head, Son . . . nobody says no to a Ridley."

She dismounted at the carriage entrance, turning her horse over to Curly Forbes, and Ridley jerked the door free of the frost to let her in. She saw Al and stopped with a shocked look in her eyes. He knew then that his father had got her there on some pretext, that this was the first she knew of his return.

She spoke to him, and asked: "How's your mother?"

"Why, all right. She's in bed."

Jawn said in a big, jovial voice: "Letty, child, I heard some foolishness about you promising never to come here again. You'll have to forgive me, girl, but I got you here any way I could."

She stood with her shoulders back and her head high.

91

There was defiance in her eyes. She started back toward the door, but Jawn Ridley pushed it shut and stood with his back against it.

"Now, now. Think it over. Al is your husband. You married him. Those weren't empty words. He shouldn't have run out. He did, and now he's sorry. It took some nerve to come back. Think well of those things. Now, let's take off your wraps."

Seeing victory in her hesitation, Jawn Ridley came forward, plucked off her hat, and commenced untying the shawl that was under it. He did it with an almost forgotten gallantry, a gentleman of the old South.

She wore a short sheepskin coat. A rough blanket around her waist served as chaps. Over her boots, pulled high on her legs, was a pair of very large and heavy German socks.

She walked around behind a divan while pulling up her riding skirt to remove the socks.

Ridley, with his back turned, said to Al: "She's your wife. You should go back there and help her."

Al, flushed and sick-looking, started off in another direction. Suddenly furious, his father seized his arm and flung him around. He grabbed him by the front of his woolen shirt. He lifted him so that for a second his feet were entirely off the floor.

"What's wrong with you?" he said through his teeth.

"Let me go!"

Ridley rammed him to arm's length and jerked him back. He did it again and again. Al's hair spilled over his face. His shirt tails were out.

"Go over there to your wife."

Al Ridley wanted to stand up against his father. He wanted to be the man he had learned to be at Medora and the other construction camps along the N.P. Instead, he did as his father said.

Letty had finished taking off the socks. She stared at them from beyond the divan.

When Al stopped about ten feet from her, his father cried: "That's your wife! Take her in your arms!"

Al cried: "Leave me alone!"

Letty started away, looking at Ridley like he was a madman.

"Take her in your arms," he said to Al. "Do you hear me? . . . take her in your arms."

When Al still made no move, Ridley vaulted around the divan and swung his open hand to his son's jaw. The blow drove Al halfway across the room. He hit the floor with a force that raised dust from between its boards. He lay on his back with blood running from the corner of his mouth.

Letty cried: "Leave him alone!"

"I'll leave him alone when he acts like a man. I swore once I would make a man of him or kill him. You stay out of it." Ridley stood over him and bellowed: "Get up!"

Very slowly Al got to his feet. He stumbled and fell. Ridley started to follow, but the girl got between them. Sitting on the floor, she got his head in her lap. Unnoticed, Mrs. Ridley was screeching from the stairs.

Ridley strode through the big door and bellowed up the stairs: "Go back! Go back. You've had your turn with him. You made him the yellow milksop he is. Now it's my turn. I'll make a man of him or kill him." She must have come on for a step because he started with a half lunge, shouting: "Go back to your room!"

After a time, Ridley returned, closing the door. He wiped sweat from his forehead. He looked at Al and Letty. She held his head to her bosom. His mouth left a round circle of blood on her shirt.

Ridley said: "Sit up. Put your arms around her. That's your wife."

"Leave him alone. Get him a drink."

Ridley got a bottle from the sideboard.

"Not that. A drink of water." She said, half weeping: "Oh, leave us alone."

Jawn Ridley went to his office. It was too hot with the fire roaring. He tried to open the window, but it was stuck fast by ice. He sat down behind his desk and stared across the room.

At last he got up and went to the kitchen himself. The Chinaman was not around, but a kettle of water was boiling on the cook stove. He took it with him to his bedroom and shaved. He trimmed around the edge of his hair a little, removing some of the gray. He put on a white linen shirt, decided that was too noticeable, and changed to gray wool, knotting a small, black kerchief at the collar.

He cleaned up a slight razor nick in his chin and went back to the big room. For a startled second he thought she was gone. The room was shadowy, and she was seated in a straight chair beyond the divan.

Al had been laying full-length, a damp towel over his bruised face. He sat up quickly when he saw his father. Ignoring him, Jawn said: "It's dark in here. Why don't you light a lamp? My dear, you must be famished. I have an idea where my cook went, but he has some bread baked, and we can fry some bacon."

"I'm not hungry," she said.

"It's been a long time since breakfast. Food and cup of coffee will help all of us."

She said: "Where is Missus Ridley?"

The question surprised him. "Upstairs. Why?" She didn't answer him. "We'll take her something to eat. As I said, my cook must have gone somewhere. Will you favor us by preparing something, my dear?"

Jawn Ridley sat in the kitchen and watched her. There was smoothness and confidence in everything she did.

When the meal was on the table, she said: "Do you want me to call Missus Ridley?"

"No. She's still . . . semi-invalid. She won't come down. Fix a tray for her. I'll send Al up with it."

She put bacon, bread, stewed dry peaches, and a cup of coffee on a large platter and carried it to the front room. A few seconds later, Ridley could hear the stairs creak at Al's steps. He came down a couple or three minutes later, looking pale beneath the bruises of his face. "Where's Mother?"

Ridley said: "Why, upstairs."

"She isn't. Where was she when you were up there?"

"I didn't do anything to her. Damn it, boy, I hadn't seen her for a week, until that incident a few hours ago."

Al hurried through the big house. They could hear him opening and slamming doors, calling: "Mother! Mother!" He went outside bareheaded and without a coat. He looked through the outbuildings.

Letty, at the window, said: "Look, he's going down to the bunkhouse. Make him put something on. He'll get pneumonia."

Ridley, coming up behind her, took hold of her arms.

She twisted and tried to get away. "Let me go!"

"To follow him with his coat and hat? To pamper him like a child?"

"He's frightened on account of his mother. Where is she? What did you do with her?"

"*I* do with her? Nothing! Do you want to know the truth? She thinks you're a corrupt woman. Ever since last summer she's been trying to scheme a way to get herself and Al both away from here, never to come back. I have an idea she hired the Chinaman to drive her to the Landing, or to Fort Wells. That's it . . . Fort Wells. There's a major there who knew some of her people in Saint Louis, and I suppose she has some half-demented idea of causing my arrest for the discipline I just administered to my son."

"Let me go!"

"Where to? Al? Do you really think it would do you any good to go to *him?*"

She screamed: "Al! Al!" She doubled over with sudden, cat-like strength and almost escaped. She tried to bite his forearm. He laughed.

The door rattled, and Ridley spun to look at his son.

"Leave her alone!" Al cried.

"Go away. Follow your mother."

Al said hoarsely: "Leave her alone!" He started for his father. He hesitated, realizing the futility of attacking him with his hands alone. His eyes darted around. He saw the steel bar that served as a stove poker. He grabbed it, and charged.

Ridley hurled the girl from him with a sweep of his left arm and with his right caught the force of the bar. He grabbed it midway and, with a downward twist, ripped the iron bar from Al's fingers.

Al stumbled forward, off balance. Ridley met him with the heel of his left hand. It stunned Al to a stop. He back-pedaled, hit the table, and was balanced for a second with his heels against the floor. Ridley followed. He smashed him with a right and left. Al's knees buckled, and he fell forward. Ridley grabbed him, stood him on his feet. "I should have done this before!" he said through his teeth. "I should have thrown you out when you came back from Saint Louis two years ago and I saw what they'd made of you."

He hit him with his open hand driving him halfway across the room. He picked him up again and knocked him down again. "I said I'd make a man of you or kill you. And I don't care which it is."

Al was unconscious. Ridley picked him up by the collar. He dragged him, limp and flopping, to the door. He balanced him on his feet like a puppet on one string and let him dump face foremost in the snow.

Already the winter twilight was fading. The moon was out, riding in a thin crescent just over the horizon. He could see the tall, slouched figure of Joe Livingstone in the bunkhouse door with the candlelight behind him. Livingstone was looking that way, wondering what was up.

"Livingstone! Come up here. Come and get him. Hitch the cutter and take him to the Landing. Patch him up. Have somebody haul him out to Fort Wells. Have Curly do it and you stay here."

He turned back, booted the door shut, and looked for Letty.

She had been stunned by her fall. Now she was on her feet, backing around the table. She reached inside the tight waist of her riding skirt. She drew out a tiny Derringer. She cried: "Stand back!"

"Girl, put that thing down." Ridley picked up a chair. He thrust it in front of him, and took a step in the protection of its thick, oaken seat.

She fired. There was a big flash of powder and the roar of the ball going high. She fired the second barrel, and its bullet thudded in the seat of the chair. Ridley laughed, tossed the chair away, and kept walking.

XI

"Showdown"

Mrs. Ridley, in Al's cutter, with Wing, the Chinese cook, did not take the turn toward the Landing and Fort Wells, but instead headed eastward toward Bull Sink. The excitement of escaping sustained her for a while, then the bitter cold made itself felt, driving her beneath the heavy buffalo robes that filled the front of the box. The Chinaman, dressed only in quilted cotton, hovered shivering and chattering beside her. After a while, with a robe over him, he became warm, but she did not. She went into violent spasms of shivering, alternating with periods when she dozed.

"Oh, missy, don't go sleep!" Wing would cry, shaking her until she awakened. "You go sleep in strong cold, you die."

"I won't die!" She was positive on that point. "I don't aim to die. I have to get help. He'll murder my poor boy if I don't get help."

Neither of them had more than a vague idea of Bull Sink's whereabouts. After passing the flanks of the Medicine Ridge, a winter breeze struck them. In summer it would have been only a zephyr, but thirty below gave it the fangs of a wolf. They quartered into it, Wing keeping the team headed toward some purplish, bird-track gullies at one side of the Wolftones where someone had told him Bull Sink lay.

Mrs. Ridley had estimated the trip at two hours. In two hours they were only across Sage Creek. On one side of them lay the crazy-running chasms of the badlands, on the other the level prairie vastness. They crossed a coulée within sight of a shack, drifted over and abandoned. Following the low ground was a steady labor through deep snow. The ridges were blown almost clean, but there the north wind struck them with all its bitterness.

They reached Horn Creek, and crossed it, and mounted the height of prairie that would later drop off toward the Bull. With landmarks no longer visible, Wing was hopelessly lost. Given their heads, Ridley horses would have turned back, but these were Dakota stock, and they kept moving in the general direction of home.

The sun, circling the southern horizon, was almost lost in the winter haze. With a sudden lurch the sled dropped over the edge of a steep coulée. It almost overran the horses. It frightened them to a lunging, slip-sliding run, and they ended breast deep in the snow at the bottom.

Wing crawled out from among the robes and tried to maneuver the team. They were tangled and kept lunging at cross-purposes. He went up front, thigh-deep in snow, shivering and teeth chattering, and tried to lead them. He couldn't do it. Almost frozen, he crawled back beneath the robes. For a long time the woman beside him had not moved. He shook her and tried to awaken her. She was cold to his hand. He decided she was dead. He knew that he would die, too. In the darkness beneath the buffalo robes he resigned himself to death. He gave thought to his tong, the Suey Sings, and wondered how his body would ever be found for its return to China.

After a timeless period beneath the robe, he heard voices. At first he gave them no credence, but they became louder. A man shouted—"Hey, down there!"—and Wing crawled out to look.

Two men, driving a heavily blanketed team hitched to a bobsled, had come along the eastern coulée rim and stopped. The men were Sophus Briggs and Harry Layne, and they were just returning from a trip to Briggs's place where they had picked up some salt and turnips that had been left behind the autumn before.

An hour later, at Bull Sink, they carried Mrs. Ridley inside Dehon's cabin, covered her with warm blankets, massaged her arms and legs. Mrs. Dehon produced wine, heated it on the stove, and, forcing Mrs. Ridley's teeth open, they poured it down her throat. The hot wine produced the first real sign of life, and she commenced to whisper.

"She wants the Pecos Kid," Layne said. "I'll fetch him."

The Kid was already approaching the front door. On one knee he listened to her. The things she said meant nothing to him. However, by that time Wing had remembered enough English to tell him of things at The Citadel.

Pecos hurried to the school that was just letting out and got Hernandez. Big Jim was at the stable, fixing ice lugs to the shoes of his favorite appaloosa saddle horse. Telling them only what he knew, and that briefly, Pecos hurriedly got ready to ride.

"Letty?" Big Jim said. "What's *she* doing there? Is she living with Al now?"

"I don't know. It was all garbled, something about Curly Forbes. It's hard figuring out a Chinaman in English, and this one was speaking Chinese. Dennis told me he was hitting the bottle. Afraid Ridley would kill the girl while he was left alone with her. I wouldn't doubt that he'd kill Al. And Letty. . . ."

Hernandez grinned with a shine of his teeth against mahogany skin. "Thees the showdown, Keed?"

"I don't know. This might be it."

They left with the sun skirting the horizon. By the road, it was a long journey to The Citadel, but many miles could be sliced off by cutting directly through the badlands, and that was the course they took up the trail to Trapper's Springs, thence along Trapper Coulée, around a lower spur of the Wolftones, across the Horn and Sage which there came down within two miles of each other.

They reached the prairie rim. The moon was up, riding in a thin crescent just above the horizon. At that season there was little difference between late afternoon, twilight, and night—always the gray sky, the perfect whiteness of the earth.

After long effort, the Pecos Kid's horse faltered.

"Swap with you, Jim," he said.

"By the gods, no. I wouldn't lend old Walla Walla to anybody, I. . . ."

The Kid seized the horse's bridle and said: "Get off!"

"All right, Kid, if you want to act that way about it. But how'm I going to keep up on that broncho of yours, me weighing what I do . . . ?"

"You don't need to keep up. You get there when you can. It could be you'll come in handy even if you're an hour late."

The big gray was a fine traveler, and moved better under Pecos's lighter burden. When Hernandez dropped behind, Pecos rode on alone. He crossed some big sinks and took the climb toward the Medicine Ridge. He found the tracks left by the cutter that morning. They were just beginning to fill with wind-carried snow. He followed the road around the broken face of the ridge and saw The Citadel, rising white against white, visible because of the shadow around it. Lights burned dimly in the big house, and in one of the bunkhouses. Then, distant and muffled, he heard a gunshot, then another. The sounds came from the big house.

He reached the lower corral, crossed the creek ice, came up a steep pitch with the burned-out sheds on one side and more corrals on the other. The lighted bunkhouse lay in front of him, its low eaves almost touching the drifted snow. He was wary now. His right hand glove was off, his fingers on the icy butt of his gun.

A voice he recognized to be Al Ridley's shouted: "Pecos! Pecos, look out!"

He swung over, using the side of his horse for protection. He did it by reflex without knowing where the danger lay. A gun exploded with a streak of powder. The bullet roared over his head, the sound mixing with the splitting crash of explosion. He drew and turned and saw two men struggling in the box of a bobsled. One of them—he thought it was Al Ridley— was flung over the side. He wheeled that way, around the end of a shed, and realized the next instant that somebody was in the bunkhouse door behind him.

A shadow impression against candlelight stamped the man's identity. It was gangling, loose-jointed Joe Livingstone. Pecos turned with his seat far back in the saddle, one boot thrust out hard against the stirrup, and fired. He missed, and kept firing. Joe Livingstone, in his limber manner, was dodging around the end logs of the cabin, shooting back at him.

Pecos hit him with his third bullet. The force smashed Livingstone back against the logs. A muscular reflex brought him lunging to his feet. He tripped over his toes and fell face foremost in the snow. He was loose and limp with his arms outspread. It was the end of his long trail from Utah.

There was shooting from the sled box and behind the sled. Al Ridley shouted: "Kid, I'll take care of this one. Go to the house. She's up there with him."

Pecos went on, urging the appaloosa to a gallop, reloading his gun as he went. He followed the horse trail that marked the carriage path. He could see Ridley's massive silhouette against the front window. He rode toward the carriage entrance, expecting a blast of gunfire from the shadows, but none came.

He got down, reached the door with three long strides, worked the catch. The door didn't open. For a desperate moment he thought it was barred. He drove one foot against it. It broke free of the frost holding it and spilled him inside.

He got up and ran through the arch into the big room. A lamp on the table was upset. A candle burned. He saw Ridley pivot from the window. Ridley, alarmed by the shooting, had just buckled on his pearl-handled revolver. He was on the point of drawing, but he saw it was the Pecos Kid and checked himself.

"Get out of here!" Ridley thundered.

"No, seh." Pecos looked around. Letty Stinchfield stood with her back against the far wall.

She spoke his name and started forward. He motioned her back without taking his eyes off Ridley. "No, seh," he said. "This time I'm not getting out. Not even with Letty. Letty, you go yonder. I wouldn't want you to get hit by careless bullets. I came here to settle up with Jawn. This is what we've been headed for all the time. This is the finish."

Ridley took a deep breath. He pulled his lips tight, revealing his teeth. "Gunman!" he said. "Quick hand and a limber wrist. Five minutes a day shooting at a tomato can. I've never had time for that. You didn't come here to fight with me. You came to kill me."

"Take off your gun."

"And then . . . ?"

"I said to take it off. Unbuckle yours and I'll unbuckle mine. I'll fight you any way you choose."

Ridley laughed. Hs hands closed on the buckle of his gun belt. He opened it, letting the heavily weighted holster swing around his waist. He let it drop with a thud to the floor. Pecos's belt was already loosened. He wrapped the cartridge-heavy belt around the gun and holster and tossed them to the divan.

Ridley, still showing his teeth in a savage smile, said: "Any weapons I choose? Why, that's a duel, Major."

He turned his back and strode to the fireplace. Hanging above the mantel, dusty and cobwebby, were Sioux, Cree, and Blackfoot weapons. The display was centered around a shield and crossed lances. He flung the shield away, got down the lances, and hefted one in each hand.

"Your lance, Major!"

Pecos had started forward. It was the girl's scream that warned him. Pecos wheeled on a one-boot pivot. The spearhead of heavy H.B.C. iron flipped past and buried itself in the paneling. Ridley did not hesitate. With the momentum already started he came straight on, the second lance in both hands.

Pecos let his pivot foot go from under him. He hit the floor, twisting over. He was on his back with Ridley over him, desperately trying to change directions, and swing the lance downward. Pecos doubled his legs, knees under his chin. His body uncoiled with shoulders braced on the floor. His boots struck Ridley in the abdomen. The big man was bent double. His charge had been brought to a stop. He reeled backward, lance rattling onto the floor. His mouth was open, his eyes staring. He hit the table and rebounded. His knees bent. He might have gone on his face, but Pecos, coming to his feet, straightened him with a right and left to the jaw.

Ridley's head bobbed crazily. It rolled as though on a boneless neck. He was still on his feet. He retreated, and Pecos, following, smashed him to the floor. Ridley rolled over. He still wasn't out. He had the sort of brute brain that clung to consciousness. He retreated with both hands out for protection.

"No." He wiped his mouth. It was bleeding. With the back of his hand he smeared blood all over his face. "No, Warren. Old . . . Army men. Stars and Bars. Thicker'n water, Warren. Word of honor, Warren. I'll get out . . . out of the country. What's here . . . he can have. Al. Al and his mother. I'm licked. Texans never kick a man when he's down."

"Get out!" Pecos said. *"Get out!"*

Ridley turned. He seemed to stumble. But he stumbled directly to the spot he had dropped his revolver. He pulled the gun and twisted over with a quickness one would not think possible from one of his size. Pecos, with a backhanded sweep, knocked the candle off the table, and dived headlong for his own weapon.

The cartridge-filled belt, wrapped tightly around the holster, gave it weight, so the gun drew to his one-handed grab. On one knee by the divan, he fired. The room was laced and cross-laced by gunfire.

He heard the thud of lead finding its target. He had an impression of Ridley's stumbling shadow against the window. There was a sharp crash. Cold air whipped across the room.

Pecos stood. He groped his way around upset furniture. He saw Jawn Ridley, lying across the window sill, his head and shoulders outside, his arms dangling.

"He's dead," Pecos said in an empty voice. He turned away. "Letty." Then with sudden fear he cried: "Letty!"

She ran to him. She almost fell. She saved herself by clutching him around the neck. She was crying with her cheek pressed against his breast.

Suddenly she pulled away and said: "Al! What happened to Al?"

"I don't know."

She ran to the door.

"Where's your coat?" Pecos said, and they wasted time finding it.

The shooting by the lower corrals had stopped. He remembered hearing none when he came to the house. He said: "Ride my horse. I'll go afoot."

Pecos ran beside her, holding to the latigo. A man was walking that way.

"Al?" she asked. "Is that you, Al?"

The voice of Hernandez Pedro Gonzales y Fuente Jesús María Flanagan answered: "I weesh you would come here and settle a dispute between me and thees husband of yours, *señora,* for both of us claim one notch for thees gunman, thees shoots-in-the-back, Curly Forbes."

Al was by the sled box, a Winchester in one hand, staring across at her.

She dismounted and ran to him, her boots sinking with each step deeply in snow. "Oh, Al! I thought he'd killed you, Al."

She meant that Jawn Ridley had killed him, but Al thought she was talking about Curly Forbes.

"He's dead. I killed him." He saw Pecos. "My mother. She went somewhere. We have. . . ."

"She's all right, kid. They're taking care of her at Bull Sink."

It took Al a second to realize that Letty was there with her arms around his neck. It was the same way she had hung to Pecos a while before—only it wasn't the same, either. It meant more. It meant that Al needed her, and she knew it.

"Al," she kept whispering.

He put his arms around her. He drew her hard against him and kissed her. Their lips were pressed together for a long time.

"That's how it is," Pecos said to Hernandez, turning away. "We're flashy, but women get away from us. We lack stability. You'll not find many women that'll tie themselves to the saddle strings of a drifter."

"Women, women, women." Hernandez snapped his gloved fingers. "Do not attempt to inform your Hernandez on the subject of women. Twice as much trouble have I had escaping from women than from deputy sheriffs, even. I tell you, when the chinook blows warm, your Hernandez will say good bye to thees range and return to Fort Benton to gladden the hearts of *five hundred* women."

"Oh, hell, Butch. There aren't five hundred women in the whole town." The Pecos Kid grinned.

"There will be when the word is about that their Hernandez has arrived." Ignoring the intense cold, he slid his bullet-riddled fifty-dollar hat to the back of his head, and, plucking an imaginary guitar, sang . . .

¡Ay, ay, ay, ay!
¡Canta y no llores!

The Conestoga Pirate

Eight years before the advent of the Pecos Kid, Dan Cushman created the character of Comanche John, a Montana road agent. His first appearance was in the story that follows, published in *Frontier Stories* (Winter, 44). In this adventure, as well as in the next to appear, "No Gold on Boothill" in *Action Stories* (Summer, 45), he was called Dutch John. It wasn't until publication of "Comanche John—Dead or Alive!" in *Frontier Stories* (Winter, 46) that the character's name was changed to what it would remain in the numerous adventures that followed in various magazines and in three novels: MONTANA, HERE I BE (Macmillan, 1950), THE RIPPER FROM RAWHIDE (Macmillan, 1952), and THE FASTEST GUN (Dell First Edition, 1955). For the sake of continuity within this saga, the character's name has been changed to Comanche John in this story and in "No Gold on Boothill."

I

The pack horse grazing near the campfire snorted, stood with lifted head, peering into the twilight.

"Bear likely," said the grizzled man, jiggling the venison in the long-armed skillet. "Saw a trail over yonder in the cottonwoods when I fetched kindling."

But his younger companion was unconvinced. His eyes tried to pierce the gloom that deeply hung in the underbrush. Then, distantly, came the *clack* of hoofs on rocks.

The grizzled one, hearing the sound, pushed the skillet to a cool edge of the fire, stepped away from the direct light while his hand went to the long-barreled Navy six at his belt. For many seconds the two listened.

The elder man was under medium stature. His hair, once dark but now silvered, fell to his collar. He was dressed from hand to foot in buckskin. His companion was far younger—in his early twenties, although his beard tended to deny his youth. He was slim, supple as a young birch, stood with the confidence of one long used to the wilderness.

"Sounds like two horses to me, Bogey," the young man said. "Some trapper, I suppose."

Nearby a horse snorted and whinnied. An answering whinny came from the direction of the trail. The *thlot-thlot* of hoofs hesitated, and grew louder. In a moment, a lone rider, leading a pack horse, appeared in the fringe of firelight.

He paused there, partially hidden in shadow. A black slouch hat was pulled low over his eyes. His face was covered with matted beard that was no less black or disreputable than his headgear. When his eyes fell on old Bogey, he gave a shout of pleasure.

"Well shoot me for a Blackfoot, if it ain't old Bogey!" He leaped from his mount, strode over, extending his hand.

"Comanche John!" Bogey pumped the traveler's hand vigorously. "I heard tell you up and went to Mexico."

"No Mexico for me. I been in Californy."

"Gold huntin'?"

"Yep. Come over from Placerville this summer. Camp there got too full of law and order." Comanche John circled his neck with a grimy forefinger ending with a circular motion by his left ear indicative of a hangman's noose. He winked, shot a spurt of tobacco juice at the fire where it spluttered on a hot coal. "There was some lonely wayfarers relieved of excess weight which they carried, and a pack of folks suspected me. Of course, I was innocent as a babe unborn. . . ." His matted whiskers parted to reveal a set of tobacco-stained teeth when he smiled.

"This here is Wils Fleming, my pardner," Bogey said, motioning to the tall young man. "Wils, shake hands with Comanche John."

Comanche John was medium in stature, perhaps thirty-five years old, although there was about him that peculiar ageless quality that years in the open so often give a man. Wils could tell he hailed from "civilization" because he wore gray homespun trousers and horsehide boots rather than the fringed buckskin of Indian country. His eyes were hard, calculating, and perhaps cruel; his manner of wearing his Navy pistols—slung low and far forward—testified to his expectation of trouble.

"Which way you headed?" John asked.

"The Deer Lodge Valley," answered Wils.

"Deer Lodge! No Deer Lodge for mine."

"No?"

"No, sir! Me, I'm trailin' for the real diggin's . . . the Grasshopper . . . Bannack!"

"Bannack?"

Comanche John snorted. "Don't tell me you ain't heard tell of Bannack yet. It happened nigh three months ago."

Wils and Bogey registered in the negative, drew closer, listened.

"It was thisaway. I was headed up to Orofino from Salt Lake, but I met a fellow named Joe Graves t'other side of Fort Hall. He and two half-breeds was headed down for provisions. He'd come from Bannack . . . said the gravel of the Grasshopper was yellow with the stuff. Greatest strike ever in the Northwest. There'll be a rush for it when the news gets to the Salmon River diggin's. But I'll be there ahead of 'em."

Bogey, listening, commenced rubbing his palms. Wils looked thoughtfully in the fire.

"Better come along," Comanche John urged.

"How about it, Wils?"

"Sure, I'm for it."

"Got provisions?" John asked hopefully.

"Little. Managed to pick up some flour at Fort Hall."

"Good. I ain't got any myself. Been livin' on jerky straight for the last two or three days. But share and share alike is my motto. . . ." John glanced first at Bogey and then at Wils while his thumb ran back and forth in the strap that held a pistol—but the implied threat in this action was not necessary. The two gladly invited him to share their meager supplies.

"Flour will be worth more'n gold dust over in Bannack before spring comes, I reckon," John said. "Joe Graves and his 'breeds won't get back with a wagon train before then, and a man can get mighty sick of deer meat in that time."

This meeting was at the mouth of Horse Creek on the Snake River, in the wild Northwest, a Northwest of two or three roads, a couple dozen beaten trails; a country dominated by the Hudson's Bay Company, the American Fur Company, and the Blackfeet. Ten years before a half-breed named Benetsee unearthed a fragment of gold worth about ten cents from a prospect hole he had scratched out with the branch of an elkhorn at Deer Lodge. But the great strike waited on John White who, on July 26, 1862, sunk his pick into the gilded sands of the Grasshopper, at a spot that was later known throughout the world as White Bar, a symbol of riches. It became Bannack, and it was toward this Eldorado the trio traveled up the Snake, crossed the barren lava expanse to where Lost River and Birch Creek sank away in the thirsty formations, and on the second morning they turned up a sage-dotted plain that separated two northerly running mountain ranges, following a trail that would lead them through the rugged Bitterroots by way of Lemhi Pass, and on to Bannack.

At late morning, Wils reined in, pointed out a string of white dots several miles ahead, dots that wound serpent-like, kicked up a haze of dust that hung blue in the fall atmosphere. "Wagon train," he said. "Suppose they're headed for Bannack?"

By noon they overtook it. Evidently the train was on the point of leaving the trail, for it had turned eastward, and then paused for the noon meal.

In all, there were about thirty wagons. Many were pulled in tandem by six or eight horse teams. In these arrangements, the canvas-topped schooners would be in front with one or more loaded supply wagons in the rear. As the trio rode by, the faces of women and children peered from the rear puckers of several schooners.

"Settlers," Bogey growled as if the word had an unpleasant flavor. "Saw a train of 'em on the south Snake two years ago. Country's gettin' right crowded."

At one wagon they noticed several men gathered, watching their approach.

"Be you headed for Bannack?" Comanche John asked as soon as they were within speaking distance.

"Bannack?" asked one. They glanced at one another. Obviously the word was new to them.

"Sure . . . the Grasshopper diggin's. Biggest gold strike the Northwest ever seen. Bigger'n Fraser or the Salmon."

"Did you say gold strike?" A tall, finely built man had ridden up just in time to hear the end of John's remark. He rode unusually erect. He was perhaps thirty. Unlike the bearded men who were grouped by the wagon, he was clean-shaven except for carefully groomed sideburns that extended lower than the base of his ears. There was about him that which stamped him a man of the world—but for all that, it was plain the others did not look on him as their leader.

"Bet your life it's a gold strike," answered Comanche John. "At Bannack, over the Bitterroots. Up two hundred miles to the north."

"When did the strike take place?"

"July. We heard from the first man out."

"Plenty for us all, so I hear tell," Bogey put in.

There are few who can resist the lure of gold. Already the words had wrought a noticeable change on the ever-growing group at the wagon. But there was one ancient man, bearded, lean as a scarecrow, who stroked his ragged gray beard and shook his head. "We came to make homes," he said. "We're headed for them mountains yonder . . . for Paradise Valley."

Comanche John was unimpressed. "Paradise Valley? I never heard of them diggin's."

"They're not diggin's. Not gold diggin's, anyhow." The gray one fixed John with his Old Testament eyes. "Paradise Valley is broad and grassy. There's good pure spring water and black soil. We didn't come to dig gold . . . we came to farm."

"Farm!" John aimed a spurt of tobacco juice at a wagon wheel. "Farmin's for squaws and Chinee."

"Farming is the most noble of callings! Farming is God's work!"

"A sky pilot!" John evidently considered a person of such ilk beneath his contempt for he turned his attention in another direction. His eyes sought out a man who seemed to be their leader. "Got plenty of beans and flour for the winter?"

"More than enough. We planned to have enough to carry us until our first harvest."

"Fine." John rubbed his hands. "Share and share alike's my motto. Long as we tell you how to get to the diggin's, I reckon you folks won't object to us takin' our share of the provisions."

The leader—his name was Matthew Ebbert—did not immediately comment on this. His eyes were thoughtful. A good portion of the group appeared to be awaiting his decision, but one of the wagoners struck fist against palm with resolution.

"I'm headed for Bannack," he announced.

A woman whose face looked out from beneath the tunnel of a long sunbonnet clutched him by the arm. "Jason, I don't want to go to a mining camp," she half whispered. "I want a home . . . our own land. . . ."

But her husband was determined. He jerked his arm away. "To hell with farmin'. This is our chance to get a stake. It's Bannack for me!"

His words seemed to stampede a good portion of his fellows. "Bannack for me, too!" shouted one, and another: "Farmin' can wait, gold won't."

"What say you, Ebbert?" one asked of the leader.

Ebbert still hesitated. He glanced at the faces around him. The temper of the majority was apparent. Then he spoke reluctantly: "I say, those who want to go to Bannack, go. And those who want to go to Paradise, go."

"But that will mean splitting the train!" cried the parson.

Ebbert nodded grimly.

"Who's talking about splitting the train?" The question came from a girl who had ridden up just in time to hear the parson's remark. She sat her horse like a veteran. She wore a split buckskin skirt and beaded jacket. Her hair was tucked beneath a broad sombrero.

The parson turned to her. "These fellows have brought news of a gold strike up north somewhere, and now your paw says, split the wagon train."

"No. We can't do it. We all started together . . . for Paradise Valley, and that's where we're going." She glanced around, her eyes troubled at finding that her words had won so little support.

"No, Nora," Ebbert answered. "I'm afraid it's not that easy. Some of the boys want to go to the valley, but most lean toward Bannack. The wagon train will be split whether we want it or not."

"You, Boone." She now turned to the tall, shaven man who had ridden up a while before. "You can stop them, can't you?"

"Sorry, Nora. Afraid I can't. Your father's right. We'll have to split. There's no other way."

She looked searchingly at Boone for a moment, then back to her father. An expression of doubt appeared in her face.

"But we're going to Paradise . . . ?"

"Well. . . ." The word drifted off uncertainly. Matthew Ebbert was plainly uncomfortable. He ran fingers through his whiskers, gazed off at the white clouds that flecked the deep autumn sky over Saddle Mountain.

"You don't intend to go to this . . . this . . . Bannack?"

"Yes, Daughter," he answered with decision. "We're going to Bannack. Paradise Valley will have to wait."

Hearing this, the parson snorted with disgust. Nora turned to the tall man—he was evidently more than just a friend. "Boone, how about you?" she asked.

"It will have to be Bannack," he answered, a note of softness creeping into his cold voice. "It's our chance for a fortune, Nora."

Thus rebuffed on all sides, the girl seemed to resign herself. "Then, of course, I'll have to go, too." Her even tones masked the turbulent emotions that were sweeping her.

The parson had stalked off toward his wagon. But now he turned, and his spindly legs carried him back. "Then by jimmys, I'll go to Bannack, too," he announced, his high voice quavering with emotion. "I dreamed of a farm in Paradise Valley . . . a place where I could live out my last few years in peace. But I'll give that up."

"But there'll be plenty going on to the valley, Parson. You can go along with them," Ebbert said.

"No. If Boone and Nora go to Bannack, I go, too." He sighed. "I've dreamed and dreamed of marryin' them in their own little home in Paradise Valley. But if it's to be Bannack. . . ." He tossed his hands in a gesture of resignation.

"But Parson. . . ." Nora was on the point of objecting to his sacrifice, perhaps say another minister could be found, but she paused, afraid of hurting the old man's feelings. Then, for the first time, she took notice of the three whose story of Bannack gold had disrupted the unified purpose of the group.

Her glance swept over Comanche John, whose lips curled in amusement at the scene, and over Bogey who seemed taken aback by the vigor of her objections, to fasten themselves on Wils. He sat his horse, tall and impassive. Although he was the youngest of the trio, there was something in his manner that stamped him as their leader.

"Why couldn't you let us go our way in peace?" she demanded. "Why did you have to come with your story of gold? If you'd waited another day . . . yes, another hour or two, we'd never have met." Her eyes darted fire. "See what your news has done? It's split our group. Before you came, all they wanted were homes. Now they're mad with lust for gold. . . ."

Without giving him time for an answer, she swung her horse around, cracked her quirt, went galloping to the far end of the train. But the last glimpse Wils caught was not of eyes that darted fire: it was the face of a girl whose lip trembled in disappointment.

Comanche John whistled admiringly. "Ain't she the scorpion?" he asked.

II

Fewer than a third of the party held to the original purpose. Grimly, perhaps a little regretfully, these drew their wagons from the line and headed northeastward in the direction of a low flank of the Bitterroots, around which lay their valley. After they were gone, Matthew Ebbert strode over to where Wils, Bogey, and Comanche John had dismounted and now sat in the sagebrush, eating jerky.

"Any of you men ever been to Bannack?" he asked.

Wils shook his head. "There wasn't any such place as Bannack when I came over the Lemhi Pass last fall."

"But do you know how to get there?"

"Sure. Just go up Birch Creek here. You drop over the divide and follow the Lemhi River until you see the pass toward the east. Bannack is on the other side . . . maybe forty miles."

"How do you recognize the pass when you reach it?"

Wils shrugged. "Just have to know, that's all. Maybe I could draw out sort of a map."

"No. I'd rather have you guide us."

Wils looked questioningly at his companions.

"We haven't much money," Ebbert went on. "But we have plenty of supplies. There are many supply wagons loaded with flour and with grains we intended to use for seed. We'll give you an equal share."

Comanche John rubbed his hands. He knew the supplies would be worth a fortune in the new-born settlement that winter. "An equal share, hey?"

"It would be more than you'd need for an entire year . . . even if you had a family."

"Go ahead, Wils," John urged.

"All right, we'll guide you," Wils answered.

Gleeful at this, Comanche John sawed off a large chunk of jerky with his Bowie knife, poked it in his cheek with his thumb to let it soak like a dried-out chew of tobacco. "Share and share alike is my motto. Once we get to Bannack, we'll divide the stores up equal!"

A horse kicked dirt as it was pulled to a stop. "What's that about dividing the supplies?" a man asked.

Wils looked up and recognized Boone Logan. A second later, six others came to a stop behind him. There was something about these men that set them apart from the honest homeseekers who made up the bulk of the party.

Ebbert answered: "I've offered these men equal shares in the supplies provided they guide us to Bannack."

Even though he maintained a poker face, there was no doubting Boone Logan's opinion. "We can get along quite well without them," he said coldly. "If they're short on provisions, load their pack horses with flour, beans, whatever they want. But no more of this about guides."

"Have you ever been there?" Ebbert demanded.

"Where?"

"To Bannack . . . or over Lemhi Pass?"

Logan hesitated. "No. But two of the men here have been to Fort Benton . . . Mex and Jodel."

Ebbert turned to them. "Have you ever been over Lemhi?"

Mex and Jodel exchanged glances. Then one of them spoke up—it was Jodel, a greasy-looking man with a heavy, truculent face. "No. We went east of the mountains, from Fort Laramie."

"We need someone who has traveled the pass." Ebbert's manner of saying this indicated his mind had been made up.

Boone Logan turned pale around the lips, and his hand clutched the reins until his knuckles turned white. But he said no more. After meeting the elder man's steady glance for a moment, he cracked his quirt sharply across his horse's belly, started off at a lope, his followers at his heels.

Comanche John, thoughtfully masticating his jerky, watched him go. "That fellow's right nasty," he commented.

"Boone Logan is my future son-in-law," Ebbert said with a note of disapproval of John's opinion.

But John was undismayed; he picked a string of jerky from between his teeth with the point of his Bowie, and then answered: "I don't give a damn if he's your blood brother. I'll call a snake by his true name whenever I run onto him."

Ebbert turned away, his face troubled.

The wagons, Bannack-bound, soon started. All afternoon they creaked up the valley of the Birch, pausing only after the sun dropped from sight beyond the Lemhis. Wils, Bogey, and Comanche John were just cleaning up after the evening meal when a girl appeared in the firelight. It was Nora Ebbert.

"I'm sorry I lost my temper this afternoon," she said simply.

Wils was a little ill at ease, not used to having women—and especially ones as beautiful as this—insert themselves into the light of his campfire. He studied her for a moment as she stood there, her eyes mysterious in night shadow, the firelight golden in her hair. "That's all right," he said with one of his best smiles.

She went on: "It wasn't your fault the wagon train split. It was the fault of those who would rather seek gold than something more worthwhile." Then she dropped the subject. "How far is it to Bannack?"

"About three days on horseback, but much longer for the wagon train. We'll be lucky to get there in ten days. You can never tell about October."

"You mean it might storm. What then?"

"Then we'll probably be on this side until spring."

"Are you through with your supper?"

"Yes."

"Will you come to our wagon? Father sent for you."

The two walked across the piece of ground that the wagons circled. It was dark now, and the wagon tops shone ghostly white in the flickering light of a dozen campfires. There was talking and laughter, and someone played a banjo. It seemed strange and unreal to Wils—this center of light and sound in the midst of the vast wilderness, a wilderness that seemed to crowd in with the night. As if in recognition of his thoughts, the wilderness intruded even more closely when a coyote howled on the hillside.

"Is there just you and your father?" Wils asked.

"Yes. Mother died four years ago, in Missouri. I have a brother in California. Father and I left this spring for Paradise Valley. Boone . . . Mister Logan . . . had been there. He told us about it."

"It's too bad we had to spoil your plans."

Nora smiled. "One never knows what is for the best. . . ."

Matthew Ebbert had questions concerning the route. They talked for half an hour. When Wils started back to camp, he was accosted by Boone Logan.

"Come in, Fleming," Boone said cordially, motioning toward his wagon.

Wils followed the big man up the stairs that were dropped down from the high wagon box. Inside, Logan dug a live ember from the stove, held it to the wick of a tallow lamp that he blew to flame. He motioned his visitor to a chair, eased himself to the edge of the bunk.

"I'm surprised you'd want to be slowed up on your trip to Bannack, Fleming. Why don't you go on and leave us? Get there before the good placer ground is all gone. We'll find the way, provided you leave us instructions."

Wils had expected something like this. But why was the man so determined they should not go along? Surely it was not the share in the provisions—Logan himself had offered to load their pack horses with food. Perhaps it was something more personal, but Wils dismissed the idea.

"I don't mind being held up a few days," he said. "I'd hate to see this outfit start the wrong trail through the Bitterroots. If it blizzards, which is likely, there'll be no track to follow. And there are plenty of false breaks which lead only to blank walls three thousand feet high."

"Don't be swayed too far by your charity." A sarcastic note had found its way into Logan's voice. "I've had no trouble guiding this train up till now."

Wils fastened Logan with his cool, gray eyes. "Why are you so damned set on getting rid of me?" he asked in an even tone.

"Maybe it's because, as guide, I don't care to have my position undermined."

But his words did not ring true. Suspicious of Logan from the start, Wils now became convinced that there was something underhanded, perhaps sinister, afoot. For some reason, a vision of Nora flashed in his mind. It was distasteful to associate her with this man—her future husband. What, he wondered, had prompted her to accept Logan's offer of marriage—but true, he was handsome, and a man of the world.

"I've accepted Ebbert's offer, and I'll stick to it," Wils said.

"Maybe this will help you alter your decision." Logan pulled a weighty buckskin bag from his jacket pocket. It jingled when he tossed it in Wils's lap. "Couple hundred there," he commented.

The action was unexpected. Wils allowed the money to lie for a moment, then the full import of it appeared to him. So Logan expected him to sell out for this poke of gold coin! He threw it to the floor at Logan's feet, stood up.

"I'll get my gold in Bannack," he said coldly.

Logan's eyes narrowed until they became slits, cutting his deeply tanned face. The veins stood out on his temples. He crouched forward, buckskin tightening around the tensed muscles at his shoulders. Wils watched the hand that hovered for a moment over the pistol butt. Then Logan relaxed a little and spoke. "I advise you and your friends to be gone when morning comes, Fleming. And if you mention this little episode to Ebbert, or to Miss Ebbert. . . ." He did not complete the threat, at least with words, but his fingers significantly tapped his gun butt.

Wils answered: "I intend to guide this train to Bannack. As for the Ebberts, I'll tell them what I choose."

Their eyes met for a few seconds, then Wils turned, leaped down from the wagon, and hunted out the low-flickering campfire where Comanche John, having become mellow in the early autumn starlight, played low and dolefully on a mouth organ while Bogey sang:

Oh, I'm goin' to Orofino
That's the place for me,
I'm goin' to Fraser River
With the washbowl on my knee.

★ ★ ★ ★ ★

The train started with the dawn. Soon left behind were the barren, sage-dotted lava plains. Here the country was greener and more rugged.

Boone Logan kept to himself during the morning. At noon he spoke briefly with Matthew Ebbert, and after that he and his six companions—Mex, Jodel, and the rest—disappeared until nightfall. "Scouting for Blackfeet," someone said, although this was not hostile country.

The next day also passed uneventfully, but Wils did not relax his caution. He knew Logan would sooner or later attempt to carry out his threat.

On both afternoons Wils and his two companions rode ahead to choose the train's campsite. On the third afternoon Wils was ready to start, but neither Bogey nor Comanche John were to be found—they were behind somewhere catching trout for supper. So Wils set out alone.

After traveling several miles, he caught sight of a rider out ahead. He urged his horse to a gallop. It was Nora Ebbert.

"Hello, Wils." She smiled. "Looking for a campsite?"

He nodded, was about to say something when a herd of deer caught Nora's eye. They grazed on a hillside a short distance from the trail.

"Look!" she exclaimed. "A white deer."

They reined in. "Looks like an albino," Wils said.

They headed up the hillside, but the deer, alarmed at their approach, started off on little stiff jumps and were soon hidden from view by a rise of ground. When the riders gained this point, the animals had found shelter in a patch of evergreen.

It had been a greater climb than Wils or Nora had imagined. They paused to rest their mounts after the steep ascent. From this vantage point could be surveyed a great, undulating expanse of hilly country. The wagon train was not yet in sight, but from that direction came a group of swiftly riding horsemen.

"Wonder who they could be?" Wils pondered as he watched their approach.

The girl shook her head. "Maybe they're strangers."

"No. They're from our outfit. They're in too big a hurry to be going far, and, besides, they have no pack animals."

A troubled expression knit Nora's brow when they started down the hillside.

When they came to the trail, Wils asked: "Who are those men of Boone Logan's?"

"Men of Boone's . . . ?" Nora seemed upset by the question. She glanced sharply at Wils, then away.

"Yes. Jodel and that bunch. They aren't like the rest of the party."

After a moment's silence she answered: "We met them at Fort Laramie. Some of them Boone knew . . . he had been out here before, you know, along the Overland Trail to California."

"Were they planning to live in the valley?"

"I don't suppose so. Boone said we would go through Blackfoot country, so we would need them to scout for war parties."

Wils dropped the subject. For the next couple of miles the girl seemed preoccupied with some problem of her own.

The trail now led through a flat that was spongy with water. Wils examined it doubtfully. "Wagons can't get through there. Too heavily loaded." He looked for a route on higher ground. A hillside invited his inspection. As he pointed his horse up the climb, he did not notice how near the riders had approached from down the valley.

A shot cracked. The wind from a bullet fanned his cheek,

flung up a shower of rock fragments where it plowed the dirt.

Wils turned his horse. More guns spat out. Bullets kicked up dirt on every side. Down the hill his horse plunged. A jutting flank of the hill gave temporary protection. He looked around for Nora. She was still in the swampy depression and hidden from the horsemen.

"What is it?" she cried.

But he had no time to explain. He lashed his horse to a run, motioned for the girl to follow. In a few seconds she was abreast of him.

The protecting flank of hill was soon left behind. Before them was a broad spread of land destitute of protection. Two wind-sculptured fingers of sandstone stood out from the rimrock eight hundred yards to the right. Toward these they spurred their horses.

The spat of gunfire from behind rose over the clatter and thud of hoofs. A bullet cuffed the ground ahead. Another, striking a rock, droned hornet-like as it glanced away.

Wils unholstered his pistol. It was a new type, throwing a slug no more than half the size of the conventional Navy Colt, but it carried like a rifle. He was tempted to risk a shot. The riders were grouped, making a good target. He fired. One of the horses faltered, drove nose downward to earth, its four feet pointed skyward for a moment, and the rest was obscured in dust.

Suddenly the shots and the pursuit stopped. Once gaining the security of the rocks, Wils and Nora looked back. The riders had formed a group and sat looking in their direction. A hundred yards in their rear the fallen horse was a still, dark spot in the crisp autumn-hued grass, and from it a man came limping.

"Too bad I got the horse," Wils muttered. He looked across at the girl. Her breast rose and fell excitedly beneath her buckskin blouse. Her hair had escaped from beneath the sombrero; wind-blown, it hung down her back in loose, brown masses that reached the saddle cantle. Her eyes danced with excitement and anger.

"Those . . . highwaymen!"

"I doubt that they're highwaymen," Wils answered. He had an idea of their identity.

"I wonder why they quit following so suddenly?"

Wils shook his head, watched the riders who picked up their unmounted comrade and started back in the direction from whence they came.

"My hair," Nora laughed. She started tucking it back beneath her sombrero. "It got lose down there. Strange thing, as soon as it did, they stopped shooting. It must be a charm."

"Yes," Wils smiled. "It may have been more of a charm than you think."

From a distance, he estimated, they would mistake her for a man. They probably thought her to be old Bogey who wore buckskin and rode a bay horse, too. But Bogey's hair was cropped off at the collar. Nora's long tresses flying behind would be instantly recognized.

The two circled the rimrock until they sighted the train. It was then near sundown, so they signaled the lead team, and the wagons creaked into a circle. Soon a dozen campfires sent pillars of smoke into the chill autumn air.

III

The trout that Bogey and Comanche John had snared from the creek tasted excellent after their dreary deer meat diet. While Wils ate, he told of his experiences of the afternoon.

"It's that blasted Logan and his gang!" Bogey's voice shook with anger.

"Yep!" Comanche John, who took man's perfidy as a matter of course, was inclined to a practical view. "It would be a pretty rough job cleanin' 'em out. I reckon I'll have to treat this Logan to a pistol ball. You know what the fee-losopher said . . . 'when the head is gone . . . ?' "

"That will be our last resort," said Wils.

"Last resort!" John paused in the course of taking a great bite from the boiled trout he held in his fingers. "Down in Californy, where I hail from, killin' was the first resort."

Their conversation was interrupted by the appearance of Matthew Ebbert. "Can I speak to you a minute?" he asked of Wils.

Ebbert led the way to his wagon. "Nora told me what happened," he said. "Who were those men, Wils?"

"Couldn't see their faces."

"But you have an opinion."

"Sure. I think they were those men of Logan's."

Ebbert walked for a while in worried silence. There was no

doubt he, too, suspected them. "Boone was with the train all afternoon."

"But his men . . . Jodel and the rest?"

"We aren't sure. We mustn't condemn anyone without proof. You're likely to meet highwaymen along the trail any time." But Ebbert's attempt to palliate the circumstance was weak.

"By the way, why was Logan so set against me joining the train in the first place?"

"He's a strange man in some ways. It might be . . . well, he has a jealous disposition."

"Jealous?"

"Don't misunderstand me. I'm not doubting my daughter. But it might seem to him that Nora is paying you too many favors."

"Then you believe he was at the bottom of this thing?"

"I don't say that. I don't even believe it. He's a man of importance in Missouri. Comes from one of the best families. He was educated for the bar. He wouldn't stoop to . . . murder."

They were now at Ebbert's wagon. The stovepipe, thrust through the canvas roof, belched smoke, and from the doorway wafted the odor of baking bread.

"Have a bite with us?" Ebbert asked.

Wils accepted with alacrity. Inside, Nora was just placing the loaves to cool. She smiled when he entered.

There were two others in the wagon. One was a heavy-handed teamster named Ceiver; he had belligerent black whiskers. The other was his wife, Prudence. She was also muscular and belligerent.

"Heard about the trouble you had this afternoon," Ceiver growled, "and, if you want my opinion, we made a poor choice in a man to guide us. We should have found one without so many enemies."

"Now, Tom," Ebbert temporized. "There's just a possibility we're harboring the enemies right here in our own group."

But Ceiver scorned the suggestion. "I know what you mean by that. But you have no cause to suspect them. Why would those boys start out to kill Fleming? Or Nora? No. It's some personal feud of his own."

Wils had taken this much in silence, but with mounting anger. He started to address Ceiver, when Prudence cut him off.

"Don't pay no heed to my man there. He's bull-headed as a porkey-pine in August." She turned on her husband who obviously quailed beneath her glance. "Ceiver!" she boomed. "Keep your birdcage shut. This young man's here as a guest." Then to Wils: "Prudence Ceiver's the name. Glad to meet wi' ye."

They shook hands. Her palm was hard and big-boned like a man's.

When Wils returned to camp, neither Comanche John nor Bogey was in sight. But shouting voices attracted his attention to the right, beyond a small knoll where a wagon had been pulled some distance from the circle. He imagined hearing Bogey's voice.

Gripped by an unexplainable foreboding, he started over to investigate. His walk soon quickened to a run. He made the top of the knoll, burst around the wagon. And there was old Bogey with blood streaming from the corners of his mouth. It had run down his chin and saturated the front of his buckskin shirt. He was on hands and knees, and standing over him was Boone Logan.

"Bogey!" Wils shouted, flinging aside the men who stood watching.

Logan turned on him. Wils pulled up, dropped his hand to his pistol, but something rammed him in the back. "Stick 'em up," a harsh voice sounded in his ear.

Wils turned his head, glimpsed the leering, greasy face of Jodel.

"Ever see a man shot through the spine?" Jodel growled with a lopsided smile that exposed a row of snaggled, yellow teeth. "They just lay and kick, like a chicken with his head cut off."

Wils could do nothing but obey. He lifted his hands. Boone Logan, who had watched this, smiled coldly and turned his attention once again to the old man who was just struggling to his feet.

Bogey made an effort to put up his fists and fight back, but his guard was flecked away. Logan swung a terrific right-hand smash. It caught Bogey high on the cheek. He staggered as if hit by a sledge, would have gone down had not his assailant stepped in and seized him by the hair. Logan thrust him back on his wobbly legs, then drove another blow. It made a sickening thump when it landed—like a hammer striking a pumpkin. When Bogey went to the ground, he struck across the extending wagon tongue. He lay there as if his back were broken.

"Logan, I'll kill you for this," Wils said.

"You aren't in a very good position to talk of killing." Logan smiled.

With a brutal laugh at this, Jodel thrust the barrel of his pistol against Wils's spine with a force that, coming unexpectedly, all but knocked him from his feet.

Logan nudged Bogey with the toe of his expensive boot. "That's what happens to those who come around and make threats. Take him back to your camp." Then he turned and started toward the circle of wagons.

Wils, still covered by Jodel's revolver, gathered the old man in his arms and carried him away. At camp he found Comanche John who had returned after picketing horses. Wils told briefly what had happened. By that time, Bogey had started to come around. When Wils looked up, John was gone.

On glimpsing signs of approaching consciousness from Bogey, John had strolled leisurely in the direction of Logan's camp. The twilight was deepening, but he could still see well enough. Over there, six men had gathered around a newly kindled campfire. John approached quietly, sat on the wagon tongue watching for several seconds before anyone noticed his arrival.

"Hello, boys," he said cordially. "See you beat up old Bogey. That's somethin' I been longin' to see done for quite some spell."

They scrutinized him doubtfully. "You mean you're glad to see him beat up?" Jodel croaked.

"That's right. We ain't travelin' together any more." Comanche John's disreputable beard parted to expose his teeth in a lop-sided smile. "Surprised, ain't you?"

"What do you want?" one asked suspiciously.

"Reckoned maybe I'd jine up with you."

They looked at one another questioningly.

"I'd be right handy," John hastened to assure them. "For instance, I might give you a few tips on pumpin' lead. You was right awkward in that little affair this afternoon. . . ."

"Hush up!" Mex, the dark one, said, looking off toward the other wagons.

From that direction someone was approaching. It proved to be Tom Ceiver, the man Wils had met in Ebbert's wagon a few minutes before. Ceiver nodded shortly to the six near the fire, looked suspiciously at Comanche John who still roosted on the wagon tongue.

"Why hush up?" John asked. He gave the impression of carelessness, but his eyes watched narrowly every move the others made. Then he explained to Ceiver. "I was just ruminatin' with the boys on what a botchy job they made of that shootin' this afternoon. Now for instance . . ."—he nodded to Jodel—"you, Jodel! Step over there away from the rest. About a step or two more. There. That's fine. Now I'll show you a little gun trick I learned in Californy." Jodel was nervous, but John spoke soothingly. "Don't hop around so much. Stand real still, it works better thataway."

Then, with scarcely a perceptible movement, with a hitch of his shoulder only, it seemed, the Navy pistol flicked from its holster. A report split the twilight air. Jodel sagged. Without a word, or a movement of his hands, he pitched head foremost in the dust. The bullet had found his heart.

Such was their consternation at this act, none of the others spoke a word. They drew back instinctively.

Comanche John held the gun muzzle up, blew the smoke from the barrel. "You see, it was right easy. Nice, clean job. Californy-style. If any of you boys want more lessons, just say the word."

John spat distantly at the campfire. Gun in hand, he stepped sidewise around the wagon. There he leaned almost double and watched the group from underneath, but none seemed to have stomach for a fight.

"That was murder! Plain out-and-out murder!" It was Ceiver's outraged voice. "He won't get away with this, I'm telling you . . . !"

"What was that shot?" Wils asked when Comanche John returned to camp.

"That? It was me givin' our friend Jodel a lesson in the

135

fine art of pistol shootin'.'"

"What do you mean?"

"I just killed Jodel."

"By crackies, I was aimin' on gettin' him myself," Bogey said through swollen lips. He was propped against a bedroll, unable to move about.

"Yes, sir, nice and clean a job as I ever turned in . . . 'less maybe it was that guard I picked off the Yuba coach that time. A-course the guard was tougher because he had me dodgin' buckshot." John set to loading powder, ball, and cap in his pistol's empty chamber. He took considerable time about it, then minutely inspected each load in his other gun. One cap failed to please him, so he inserted another one. "Can't be too careful about these things," he muttered.

"I suppose all hell will break loose now," Wils said. "But I guess it doesn't make much difference. I made a promise to Logan when I was over there with a gun in my back, and it's a promise I aim to keep."

"Now don't go off half-cocked with your powder wet," John cautioned. "I'll get him when the time comes."

Wils shook his head.

John fished a gold piece from his jeans pocket. "Tell you what, I'll flip you for him."

But Wils wasn't listening. His attention was drawn to the people who were running to the place where Jodel lay dead. "There's likely to be trouble," he said. "Maybe a lot more trouble than we cut out for ourselves."

"Hmm-hmm." Comanche John pocketed the gold piece. His eyes grew shifty. Evidently he had not forgotten a similar group that became the law over in Placerville. "That's somethin' else they have over in Californy," he muttered, "them pesky Californy collars."

John went quickly over to where his horse was staked, ran

hand over hand up the picket rope until he grasped the halter. He led the animal to where his saddle lay, threw it on, pulled tight the cinch. Almost before Wils or Bogey realized what he was about, he was mounted and signaling farewell.

"I'll be seein' you in Bannack," he grinned.

"Wait! If you're goin', we're goin', too." Bogey attempted to get up.

But Wils restrained him. "It's no use, Bogey. You can't travel tonight."

John snapped his quirt, and the horse started off toward the trail.

"There he goes now!" someone shouted. A dozen men came running. A rifle cracked. The horse stumbled, went to his knees, sent John pitching over his head to the ground. He lay stunned for a fatal moment, attempted to regain his feet, but they had borne down on him.

"Stick 'em up. We got you covered," Ceiver shouted.

Wils ran to the scene. He elbowed his way through the men who obstructed him, tried to speak, but no one would listen.

"Here's his pal, let's string him up, too." It was one of Boone Logan's five remaining henchmen.

"String 'em both up," a wagoner cried.

"Get a rope!"

A rough hand was laid on Wils's shoulder, spun him around. He jerked away. With a continuing movement, he whipped his pistol from the holster, backed away. The mob fell silent—hesitated.

"Release him!" Wils said, motioning toward Comanche John with the muzzle. But he noticed the eyes that had been on him now shifted to something in his rear. He dared not glance around. A footstep cracked the dry grass behind him.

"Drop the gun, Fleming." It was Logan's cool voice. "It

wouldn't hurt my feelings to have to pull this trigger."

Wils dropped the gun, slowly raised his arms, turned. He noticed Ebbert a few steps at Logan's rear, and running to catch up came Nora and Prudence Ceiver.

"What's going on here?" Ebbert demanded.

"This man killed Jodel," one of the wagoners answered, pointing to Comanche John. "We're going to hang him."

Ebbert raised his hand in a gesture that asked for coolness and deliberation.

Tom Ceiver spoke up: "A murderer deserves to get hung. And this murder was in cold blood. I saw it." He advanced on Ebbert, his black whiskers bristling.

"I'm still running this wagon train," Ebbert said coolly. "And there'll be no lynching. If there's anyone hanged, it will be after a fair trial."

"All right, let's hang him after a fair trial," Ceiver answered.

The word trial seemed to make Logan coldly furious. He whirled on Ebbert, glowered down on him. "What damned women's talk is that? String these two fellows up!" Then he caught sight of Nora and said no more.

"I don't know what's in the back of your mind, Logan." Ebbert's use of the name Logan instead of Boone called attention to the rift that was growing between them. "You may think it's time to take command. But I don't. I'll do the ordering here just as long as these men here want me instead of you." He turned, faced the group. Not one pair of eyes challenged him. He nodded toward Comanche John. "Bring him to the wagon." Then to Wils: "Take your gun, but don't cause us any more trouble."

IV

A great bonfire crackled beside Ebbert's wagon. He presided from a chair that had been moved down for him. At one side ranged six wagoners who were chosen as a jury. Comanche John, apparently but little perturbed, sat in the center of things, chewing tobacco and spitting at the fire.

The trial had not yet begun, but Parson Joe had seized the opportunity to speak his mind. "See what happened when you chose gold instead of Paradise Valley? A killin' already, and now probably a hangin'. The next thing we'll be fightin' amongst ourselves . . . you mark my words. It ain't followin' the Lord, that's what it ain't. Sometimes I think it must have been the old boy with the horns hisself which sent these three fellows into our midst to lead us from the true course . . . to send us off to this Gomorrah of a city called Bannack. . . ."

"Why'd you come, Parson?" one of the wagoners asked with a laugh.

"It wasn't for the gold. I'd ten times rather have gone to the valley. I come because here was where I was needed the most."

"Court will come to order," Ebbert said. "We're here to try a man for murder."

The trial took about ten minutes. The jury seemed not swayed by the testimony of Logan's henchmen; what influenced them most heavily was the word of Tom Ceiver, for he was one of their own number. He damned the crime as a black one.

"It was trickery, that's what it was. He shot Jodel down without giving him a chance. If it had been a fair and square gun duel, it would be different. But this wasn't. I say, hang him."

Then Wils told his story, and Bogey recounted the beating he had received at Logan's hand.

But Logan stood up and denied everything. "I never struck this man. He got bruised up in a fight over at his own camp. Now they've thought it over and are trying to pin it on me in hopes it will win sympathy for that murderer there. A fine story!" He laughed and most of the jury laughed, too. But one person who did not smile was Nora Ebbert. She looked grimly into the crackling fire, and her jaw was set.

"Well boys, what's your decision?"

The jury did not hesitate. "Hang him," they chorused.

Parson Joe, who had anticipated the verdict and perhaps inwardly applauded it, stepped forward as nimbly as his shaky old legs would carry him. It was a great moment in his ministerial career, and he intended to make the most of it. He addressed Comanche John in sepulchral tone: "You are about to meet your Maker, and I'm willin' to give spiritual assistance and succor in your hour of need."

Comanche John grinned at the parson, aimed a spurt of tobacco juice at the fire. "Reckon it's a little late for me to be doin' much prayin', Parson."

"It's never too late to come into the fold, brother. It says right in the Good Book . . . the Lord is a skillion times happier over gettin' back one single lost sheep which has strayed than in keepin' all the rest of his flock. 'For the last shall be first and. . . .' "

"I ain't strayed from the fold. I ain't ever been thar." John guffawed. "Besides, Parson, I ain't a sheep, I'm a wolf."

"Is there a tree hereabouts?" someone asked.

John turned from the parson, directing his attention to the speaker. "Do you know how to tie the knot? I reckon I'll have to teach you Missouri farmers how it's done. Them Californy collars is tricky affairs."

"We'll tie it to fit your neck. We may not know much about a Californy collar, but we're right handy with Pike County cravats guaranteed to wear a lifetime."

"By the way, where is a tree?" Ceiver asked.

The question struck everyone silent. Indeed, where was a tree? Along the creek were willows, and here and there a few spindly quaking asps. These wouldn't do for a hanging. Besides, it was now dark. Stringing a man up would not be as easy as it first sounded. They pondered, spoke together in low tones. "How about it, Ebbert?" one asked.

"We'll wait till morning." Then to Ceiver: "You've taken lots of interest in this thing. I'll make it your responsibility to watch the prisoner until sunup."

They decided to keep John in Ceiver's wagon. Prudence left to stay with Nora for the night. Over a bench that sat by one wall they tossed a quilt; there Comanche John, tied hand and foot, was told he could sit or lie as pleased him. There seemed little chance for him to escape from his bonds, but to make doubly sure two guards were posted at the door of the wagon, while Ceiver himself flopped down on the bed inside. Thus Comanche John was between them.

The bonfire slowly died to a bed of ghostly blue flicker. A cold wind, reminder of approaching winter, sprang from the north. It bent down the dry grasses, moaned complainingly around the sides of the wagon. The two guards outside pulled their jackets more closely about them, and finally they

141

crawled inside. Ceiver snored.

At his own camp, Wils lay watching the moon climb high from the jagged horizon. Two hours passed before he crawled quietly from his bed. Bogey made a movement to follow, but Wils restrained him. "I'll get along better alone," he said.

He made a wide circle, then slowly crept toward the wagon where John was held prisoner. Up above, the moon shone intermittently. He advanced only when it was hidden. Whenever its edge broke from behind a cloud, he would lie flat in the grass. Thus he advanced until a bare forty yards separated him from the wagon. The moon brightened; he watched, but there was no movement near the wagon, no sign of the guards.

A cloud sailed over. In the moment of darkness he rose on hands and knees preparatory to going closer. He would chance it all the way to the wagon this time. But he stopped. Quickly he dropped flat again. Someone was there. He could make out a vague shape—a head and shoulders that, like a shadow, moved along the canvas wagon top. For many minutes he lay still, watching. But no sound came to his ears, and the shadow was not again visible. He began to think his eyes had played him false.

Someone shouted. There followed the thud of running feet. Off in the darkness a horse snorted. It was followed by the sound of galloping hoofs. From beside Ceiver's wagon, several guns cut loose, sending red streaks of flame toward the retreating hoof beats.

Many voices sounded. "He got away!" were the words on many lips. The question came—"How?"—but apparently none could answer.

Wils dared not wait to learn more. What if they should discover him gone from his bed? He ran swiftly back to his camp, pulled off his boots. Even while doing this, someone was approaching from out of the gloom.

Wils asked with feigned drowsiness: "What's the shooting?"

Two men drew near. One recognized him. "The tall one's here," he said.

"How about the other?"

"He's here, too."

Wils began pulling on his boots. "You still haven't told me what the shooting was," he complained.

"Yes, what the thunder's going on?" Bogey put in.

"Your pardner got away. Somebody slit the canvas behind him and cut his ropes in two."

Darkness hid the surprise on Wils's face. This had been his own plan. Bogey, of course, still thought Wils had done it.

Someone else approached. "Find them?" By his voice, it was Boone Logan.

"They were here, in bed."

Logan grumbled something and turned away.

The fire was again burning brightly when Wils and Bogey reached the scene. Cursing and pacing back and forth was big Tom Ceiver. "Took my guns, the dirty thief!" Then he spied Wils. "He's the fellow that cut 'em loose. He had plenty of time to get back and play 'possum."

There followed ugly mutterings among the men. "Ought to string 'em up and not wait for morning this time," someone said.

"Hold on!" It was Matthew Ebbert. He was emerging from Ceiver's wagon. "We have no reason to believe that Fleming here had anything to do with it."

Ceiver paused, looked incredulous. "What? No reason? Why, it's as plain as light. Who else would want to cut him loose?"

"Maybe you, Ceiver."

This knocked the breath from the black-whiskered man for a moment "No time to joke," he finally answered.

"I'm not joking."

"Not joking! I never heard anything so ridiculous in my life."

"Then maybe you could explain why your Bowie knife was laying on the wagon floor right where Comanche John's ropes were cut?"

In proof of this, Ebbert held the Bowie out in the light of the fire. Unusual in design, it had a handle mounted with a young deer's hoof. Many recognized it instantly. Ceiver's jaw sagged. He was too astounded for the moment to deny anything.

His wife's voice cut in: "You sure been a hero tonight, Paw. Not only do you cut him loose, but you furnish him a brace of pistols."

Ignoring Prudence, Ceiver turned on Ebbert: "It's a damned lie. I never cut him loose, and you know it. You're trying to shield somebody. The last time I saw that knife it was sticking in the table top at the back of the wagon."

But few were listening to him now. They still snickered at his wife's words. Off in the shadow, Logan glowered.

Ebbert said: "We'll never settle it tonight, and we'll never catch Comanche John, either . . . not that it makes much difference. I don't imagine he'll bother us any more. Let's roll in and get some sleep."

As Wils turned toward his camp, he noticed Nora for the first time. She stood at the door of the wagon. Her lips were drawn in a firm line. But when she caught Wils's glance, the line softened, and she smiled.

Bogey spent a poor night. His back pained where it had struck across the wagon tongue. Next morning, when he attempted to ride, his face grew white, and he nearly fell to the ground. Nora, who saw him, insisted that he ride in her father's wagon. Reluctantly he accepted. "Shunted off with the women," he sighed as he lay down in Matthew Ebbert's bunk.

Wils discovered that the knife incident had not convinced the wagoners of his innocence. They were cold toward him. He kept to himself at the head end of the train.

At mid-morning they passed over a low divide from where the waters flowed north—north, but not to Bannack. This stream, the headwaters of the Lemhi, was turned away by the snow-burdened Bitterroots, divide of the continent which reared mightily to the east. It flowed westward to join the Salmon—treacherous River of No Return—and roar down unconquerable cañons, at last to falter and join placidly with the Snake flowing to the Pacific. Beyond the Bitterroots sprang headwaters of the Gulf-bound Missouri.

In the afternoon Nora joined him. They rode together for several miles without either mentioning the happenings of the previous night.

She asked: "How long before we reach Lemhi Pass?"

"About four days if everything goes right."

"And how long to Bannack?"

He calculated. "Two days more, barring storms."

Storms! Nora looked off at the forbidding mountains with a shudder.

Wils pointed north. "The pass is over there, around that peak . . . though you can't tell it's a pass from here."

"You mean a wagon can get through the mountains there?"

"It can if it hurries." When Wils spoke these ominous words, his eyes were on the black bank of clouds building over the northern horizon.

145

"Do you suppose Comanche John is beyond the pass already?"

"Perhaps . . ."—and after a pause—"I suppose you believe I cut him loose."

Nora shook her head. "No, I don't believe you did it. I thought the question was settled last night."

"You mean Ceiver actually did free him?"

"I prefer to believe that." Nora smiled. "It's handy to believe it."

Wils studied the girl's face, but it told him nothing.

She went on in a musing tone: "Some of the men are a little worried over the prospect of meeting Comanche John when they get to Bannack."

"I suppose you'll marry Boone Logan when you get there . . . ?" Wils didn't realize he was saying these words until they had already passed his lips. It was as though his most intimate thoughts had found the power of speech. Nora looked at him with a startled, searching expression, then turned her eyes away. A minute passed. The *clack* of hoofs on stones and the soft creak of saddle leather were the only sounds that filled the void these words seemed to have pointed out between them.

Her voice, when she answered, was scarcely audible: "Yes, we are to be married at the end of the trip."

"I gathered as much from things the parson said." Wils tried for a pleasant, perhaps casual, tone, but a tremor in his voice informed against him.

Suddenly, impulsively, the girl pulled her horse to a stop, faced about. Her eyes were intense to the point of tears. "Wils! Does it make any difference to you . . . that is . . . oh, I don't know what I'm trying to say!"

She made a move as if to turn her pony toward the train, but Wils grasped the bridle. For a moment he was so near he sensed the warmth of her body—could inhale the fresh redolence of her hair. Their eyes met.

He spoke huskily: "Yes, it makes a lot of difference to me."

His arm reached out as if to grasp her about the waist, but her horse jerked, twisting the bridle free of Wils's fingers. Nora drove her heels to the animal's side, sent it galloping toward the train. Her eyes were turned away when she passed him and her lips were drawn in a thin line. The hint of a sob was catching at her throat.

The coolness that had grown between Matthew Ebbert and Boone Logan had become obvious to all. Preoccupied and serious, Ebbert would joggle along in the high wagon seat, or walk silently beside his mules, while Logan who, until now, had been his frequent companion, spent his time in conference with first one and then another wagoner. He seemed to have plenty to talk about.

For Wils's part, he took no chance on ambush these days. Never did he ride beyond sight of the train, and after dark he took the precaution to carry his robes away to a secluded spot where Logan's men could not find him while he slept. He had no hankering for a knife between the ribs.

The evening after Wils's conversation with Nora, Matthew Ebbert hunted out his lonely campfire.

"I don't like the feel of this wind," Ebbert said by way of introduction. He wore a homespun shawl as protection against the breeze that, judging from its piercing bite, had been born on snowfields.

"It doesn't feel good," Wils answered laconically—he had faced the uncertainties of Northwestern winters long enough to expect the worst.

"What if the pass gets snowed full?"

Wils shrugged. "Then we'll have to winter at Fort Lemhi."

"And wait until spring?"

"We have plenty of provisions. If some are in a bigger hurry, they might be able to make the pass on horseback."

The lines on Ebbert's face seemed deep tonight, its bold relief accentuated by the fire that flickered alternately light and dim in the cutting wind. Wils guessed there was something in addition to the possibility of blizzard that worried him—and this supposition was strengthened by his next words.

"I'd like to talk to you, Wils . . . something important. But it's too cold here for an old man. We can go to Ceiver's wagon. Prudence and Nora are keeping Bogey company. And Ceiver . . . well, he's not there."

Wils poured water on the fire, then dug it under. It was evergreen country here, and the wind might carry lingering embers to the inflammable needles. After the fire had become a steaming heap, he started with Ebbert for the wagon. It was so dark that neither of them noticed the shadow that lurked a few rods at their rear. They entered Ceiver's wagon and closed the flap. It was draughty cold, darker even than outside. Ebbert felt around for the little iron stove, but the fire had long been dead.

Wils asked: "Want me to run over to your wagon for a light?"

"No. I'd rather you wouldn't. No use advertising our being here. It would only worry them more than they are already."

Ebbert struck flint on steel. After several unsuccessful attempts a spark took hold, and the tinder flared. He applied it to the wick of the tallow lamp. The interior of the wagon became visible in the smoky, yellow light—flickering light, for the flame bellied as if each flare would be its last as the wind sought out a hundred crannies for entrance.

Ebbert started in his tired voice: "Things haven't been going too well. You have probably noticed Logan's confidential talks with the men. He's been spreading it around that you released Comanche John and the two of you . . . are planning an ambush."

"So that's what he's been saying."

"It was only tonight I learned from Ceiver what it was. Many believe him . . . even Ceiver."

"Ceiver's always been suspicious of me."

"You see the position in which it places me."

Wils pondered a moment. "Just one question. Do *you* believe it?"

"No. I've always trusted you."

"How does Logan say this ambush of mine is to be carried out?"

"He says you won't lead us to Lemhi Pass at all. Instead, you will lead us along some blind trail . . . one which allows no retreat . . . and there Comanche John and his gang will kill us all. After that, the train and supplies will be taken on to Bannack and sold for a fortune."

"Apparently I have it well planned. Well, what do you suggest?"

Ebbert shook his head. "It's not easy. I can't see Logan's purpose in spreading such a story. He admits he's never been through the country, and yet he wants to guide us. I hate to say this, Wils, but the men won't follow you much farther."

"What does Logan suggest for me, the rope?"

"Yes. And he's found support . . . with Ceiver, for instance. They say . . . 'if we let him go, won't he ride ahead and lead the gang back on us?' "

"Nice fellow, Logan. He has ideas. I wonder. . . ." Wils pondered the uncertain flame of the tallow lamp. In the interim the wind moaned drearily, set to flapping the loose ends of canvas, made the wagon shake with interrupted rhythm on its leather springs. Wils shook his head, evidently in dismissal of some thought he had not put in words.

Ebbert said: "It's unsafe for you to be here another day. Tonight there's a meeting in Donovan's wagon. In fact, it's going on now."

"Weren't you invited?"

"No. They didn't ask me because they know how I stand."

"It appears Logan is taking over the command."

"Yes."

"So I'd better leave tonight?"

"It's the only safe way."

"I'm not looking for a safe way."

"Perhaps not, but you can't guide us if you're dead."

Wils smiled. "No, only in spirit."

"I'd prefer you in the flesh. Now, here's my plan . . . but first, how far is it to Lemhi Pass?"

"Maybe two days for the train."

"No, by horseback."

"Six, maybe seven hours."

"Good. I'll ride there with you tonight. We'll start now. Then I'll have time to return and guide the trail. You can go on to Bannack."

"But how about Bogey? He still can't ride."

"He'll be safe, I believe. None of the men is suspicious of him."

"Very well, I'll take you to the pass. Once there, you can't get off the trail except in this direction." Wils pointed straight down. "One thing more . . . the provisions. . . ."

Ebbert paused. Some sound outside the wagon attracted his attention. Wils, too, heard it. They both listened. It was an indescribable sound, more motion, it seemed, than anything else—as if some weight had been placed at one side of the wagon, interrupting, for a second, its rhythmical shaking. For a moment only the moaning wind, the fluttering canvas, and the soft creak of the leather springs filled the void of silence. The elder man smiled, relaxed. "Thought I heard something. Guess this business is getting me a bit jumpy. But what I was. . . ."

The sentence was never completed. Close, almost inside the wagon, a gun crashed. Ebbert, struck, spun on the balls of his feet. His hands clutched the table edge. Then he slumped to the floor.

By reflex, Wils whipped out his gun, spun toward the opening at the front of the wagon from whence the shot had come. But the killer was gone. Wils had no opportunity to fire a shot in return.

A second later Prudence Ceiver rushed in. "What was . . . ?" she started, and her eyes fell on Ebbert's still form. She pulled back in shocked horror. Then she stared at the gun in Wils's hand. He guessed the thought in her mind.

"It wasn't me. Somebody shot through the front."

Nora Ebbert followed Prudence through the door. She looked, for a moment, at her father. Then, without uttering a word, she dropped to her knees at his side. After several seconds she whispered his name.

Outside someone shouted: "It's in Ceiver's wagon." A moment later the wagon seemed full of men. They pushed to glimpse the dead man on the floor. Nora, oblivious to them, stared at his still form and kept repeating his name.

Someone forced his way through the crowd. It was Boone Logan. He lifted the girl to her feet. "Nora, you'd better go," he said softly. Then to Prudence: "Take her to the wagon." The men made way for the two women as they left. Logan turned, pointed an accusing finger at Wils. "Grab that man. He's the murderer."

"I never killed Ebbert," Wils answered evenly. "He was shot from outside . . . through that opening."

Ceiver came forward. "Let me examine your gun. If there's an empty chamber, we'll know you're the man."

Wils's mind raced over past events. He had fired one shot during the trip—the day he and Nora were pursued by the six riders. With a shock it came to him that he had never reloaded the empty chamber.

But Logan was unaware of this. He cut in: "No use looking at his gun. He's had time to reload it."

Wils's hopes rose. Would Boone Logan unintentionally be his salvation? But no. The others were all looking expectantly at the gun. He must act, and act quickly.

He made a bluff at it. "All right, Ceiver, I'd be glad to have you examine my gun." He stepped forward as if to offer it butt first, for examination. In doing this, his step carried him opposite the slit in the canvas through which Comanche John had gained freedom, a slit now loosely sewed together. He hurled himself shoulder first at the spot. There was a rending of cloth, and within a second he was on the ground outside. He leaped to his feet, slipped away in the darkness. Men fell over one another rushing from the wagon. Someone fired at random off into the darkness.

Swiftly, but silently, Wils circled the camp. A deeper shadow ahead marked a grove of evergreens by the creek where he had moved his bed, intending to spend the night safe from Logan's treachery. It was so dark he could see scarcely a yard ahead. His feet groped down a rock-strewn incline. Nearby he could hear the creek rolling over boulders. Something seized his feet, tripped him. A picket rope. Here was a piece of fortune! Hand over hand he ran down the rope until his hand reached a horse's halter. He led the animal away.

The general form of the country was now emerging as his eyes grew more accustomed to the darkness. Off there were the rough outlines of the hills, and just ahead the deep blackness of the evergreen grove near the creek. He led the horse into the grove, saddled it, quickly rolled together a robe and a piece of jerky and tied these behind the saddle. Then, mounting, he gave the horse rein to pick his way up the creek. From the camp came a medley of excited voices. The voices were angry, but any attempt at pursuit was frustrated by the darkness.

That night he did not pause. Morning dawned gray, a subdued light filtered through low-hanging mists. The mountains were close now. Evergreen branches frequently slapped at him as he rode along. Toward noon he shot a blue grouse that roosted in the low branches of a lodgepole. He paused an hour to roast it, then rode on. By mid-afternoon he was at the gulch through which the trail climbed up toward Lemhi Pass. Here, at last, he paused to make a decision: should he continue to Bannack, or should he keep watch on the wagon train?

V

The next morning Matthew Ebbert was laid away in a lonely grave beside the trail. Parson Joe stood by the rocky grave and preached a sermon—fervent but with a brevity demanded by the exigencies of October. Then, leaving a pine slab hopefully reared against the timeless seasons, the train creaked north.

In the excitement, none seemed to have remembered the existence of old Bogey. After the funeral he found himself alone with Nora and Prudence.

"Don't you believe a word about Wils shootin' your paw," he said to the girl. "That boy ain't got a deed like that in his hide."

Nora didn't answer. She did not wish to believe in Wils's guilt, either. But what else could she believe?

Bogey could read this thought in her eyes, so he went on: "Of course, I've got no way of provin' just who did commit the murder . . . though I got a pretty close idea. But it couldn't have been Wils."

"Why?" growled Prudence, not unsympathetically.

"Why? Because, first off, Ebbert was the best friend Wils had in the train. If Wils had wanted to shoot somebody, he'd have chose Logan . . . there'd be some sense in that. Second, if he'd fired that shot . . . mind I say *if* he had . . . why, he'd have lit out *pronto*. He had the time. He

154

wouldn't have waited with a pistol in his hand."

All this seemed plausible, and for a moment Nora found herself believing it. But there was the fact of Wils's flight, a tacit admission of guilt that cast doubt on anything Bogey could say.

She asked: "But why did he run away?"

The old man was silent for a moment. "It's got me stumped," he admitted.

"All he needed to do was show his revolver for examination. You said so yourself, Prudence. . . ." Nora, almost in tears, pressed her hand to the elder woman's breast.

Prudence patted her soothingly. "There, there honey. If it's true, it's best to face it."

"It ain't true!" cried Bogey.

"Hush up, you old varmint. Can't you see what you're doin' to this here pore child?"

With a sigh, Bogey lay back in the joggling wagon, gazed thoughtfully at the half-translucent canvas ceiling. Slowly an expression of determination became fixed in his eyes. Later, when Nora had moved up to the driver's seat, he asked: "You had a good look at Ebbert after he was dead, didn't you, Prudence?"

"Sure. Helped lay him out in his last bib and tucker."

"Where did the bullet hit him?"

"Right above the heart."

"Go clean through?"

"Yes."

"Come out lower than where it went in?"

"A bit lower."

"Must have been fired from somewhere up above."

"I see what you're getting at, but it don't prove a thing. It might be that Ebbert was leaning forward when the bullet hit him. Or it might have glanced from a rib. Besides, Wils was considerable taller."

Bogey grunted, pondered for a moment. He thought: *if the bullet was aimed down, and if it passed through Ebbert's body, then it is to be found somewhere in Ceiver's wagon.* He asked: "By the way, did you see where the bullet lodged?"

"No!"

"Did you look?"

"A little."

"Hmm. I'd like powerful well to find that bullet." Bogey sat up with a movement that indicated his invalid days were over, sprained back or not. "Yes, sir, I have to find that bullet."

"What can that prove?"

"Plenty. I can prove it didn't come from Wils's gun."

"But his gun ain't even here."

"Maybe not. But I'll lay gold coin against Jeff Davis paper money that Nora remembers it. You see, it wasn't an ordinary Navy Colt like most of the boys carry. It was a new sort of gun, used a one-hundred-fifty grain slug instead of a two-fifty. Had a longer range and a heap smaller bore . . . more powder and less ball. He bought it off a drummer in Salt Lake this spring."

Prudence's eyes lit up. "Say, maybe you fetched yourself an idea." She stepped to the front of the wagon and spoke to Nora through the aperture: "Did you ever notice anything special about Wils's gun?"

"Yes, it had pearl stocks, and an octagon barrel. . . ."

"But anything about the kind of a load it shot?"

"I remember thinking the bore looked like a toy pistol, it was so small. But it carried out a long way. Why?"

"Nothing, honey, nothing at all." She turned back to Bogey with ill-repressed excitement. "Get your shoes on, you old Rebel. We're going to have a look for that bullet."

But they searched the wagon without finding a trace of it. After an hour, they gave up. Bogey returned to his bunk, heaved a profound sigh. "It couldn't just evaporate," he said.

Prudence shook her head in doleful agreement.

That night the train camped on a park overlooking the creek. Next evening, with good fortune, it might reach the pass.

Dawn came through a haze of sifting snowflakes. Boone Logan looked apprehensively at the mountains and cursed, then he ordered the train on. At noon the snow was soggy underfoot. It balled with earth and clung to the wagon wheels in sticky masses; it obstructed and rendered insecure the hoofs of the horses.

Logan held a conference with his henchmen; afterward he prophesied clearing weather and ordered a halt. But his five henchmen rode on—to ascertain, he said, whether it was still possible to travel the pass.

A few minutes after the train halted, the boy who drove for Parson Joe—Tod Warner—appeared at the door to Nora's wagon. He stamped wet snow from his boots, panted from exertion and excitement. "Parson Joe is mighty sick this morning," he said. "He's had the misery all night."

Nora was little perturbed. "It's his lumbago again."

"No, miss. Not lumbago this time. It's in here." Tod indicated his chest.

"A cold?"

"More'n a cold. Chills and fever all night long. Reckon he drank a bucket of water. Thought sure enough he'd die, but he wouldn't let me send for help. But now he's asking for you, Miss Nora."

Nora tossed a shawl about her head and shoulders, followed Tod down the steps. The parson's wagon was a hundred yards distant beyond a clump of quaking asp. She ran most of the way.

Inside, Tod had left a good fire. The parson, with closed eyes, lay beneath a buffalo robe, trembling with ague. He opened his intense blue eyes when Nora leaned over him.

"Not too close, child," he warned in a wheezy, scarcely audible voice. "Not too close, it might be ketchin'."

"Parson, why didn't you send for me sooner?"

"Never mind, child. It don't make no never mind. Nobody can help me now. My sands has just about run out, and the good Lord is makin' ready to fetch me home."

"No. You'll be all right. Tod, put a stone on the fire. We'll wrap it and put it on the parson's chest."

"No, child. No hot stone for me. Nothin' but prayer, and one other thing. . . ." He reached up and took Nora's hand. His palm was hot; the skin was like old paper.

"What other thing, Parson?"

"It's about you. My fondest hope has been to unite Boone and you in bonds of holy wedlock. That's the chief reason I chose Bannack instead of goin' on to Paradise Valley. But now it don't look like I'll ever get to Bannack."

"Parson, don't say that!"

"It's true. By tomorrow I'll be gone. I ain't complainin'. I'm happy to go."

Tod, listening in the background, sniffled audibly.

The parson went on: "That is, I'll be glad to go, providin' this thing ain't left undone. Before I die, I want you and Boone to come before me, each takin' the other's hand . . . like two lovers with their whole lives and this great new country spread before 'em . . . and let me jine you forever. There won't be no preachers in Bannack where you're goin', child. And no book of God's word. The only book there will be the Devil's book of fifty-two pages, and the only god will be Mammon."

Nora's eyes cast about like a trapped animal's. Her free hand clutched convulsively at her shawl. She tried to put his mind on other things: "No, Parson, not now. You must sleep, then you'll feel better. You just have a touch of chills and fever."

"Nope, I'm a goner sure as shootin'. In my Father's house there are many mansions, and I'll soon be tradin' this here ornery old prairie schooner for one of 'em. Tod . . . ?"

"Yes, Parson."

"You'd better run out and fetch Boone."

Tod ran to do the parson's bidding

Nora paled. "But we can't be married now. My dress . . . and Father buried only yesterday. . . ."

"Child, buckskin is as honorable as snow-white linen. And as for your paw . . . well, I know he'd be wantin' it thisaway."

The parson made a move to sit up, but he dropped back to the bunk. "Pshaw, I forgot the witnesses. Who would you want? Prudence and Tom?"

"After a while . . . but you must rest now."

But the parson would have none of resting. Not even an hour's delay would he tolerate.

Boone Logan, handsome, broad of shoulder, stepped through the door followed by Tod. A few snowflakes glistened for a second on his jacket. He leaned over and took Nora's hand, squeezed it, but she avoided his eyes. On the parson he looked with studied solemnity. "How are you, Parson?" he asked.

"Poorly. I'm about to pass over the great divide, Boone, and I don't mean Lemhi, neither. So, as a last act, I'm hankerin' to jine you two young folks in the bonds of wedlock."

Logan looked at Nora. "Do you want to?" he asked.

For a moment she was silent, studying the parson's brown, dehydrated hand that lay in hers. But her eyes did not see the hand. Her eyes saw Wils Fleming—as she remembered him, tall, with something of the whiplash about him, handsome with that devil-may-care way of sitting his horse with long-stirrups Indian-style. But Wils was gone, already to Bannack, perhaps. And Wils had killed her father. Her eyes found the parson's. In them was such a depth of pleading she could not refuse.

"You will?" Boone asked softly.

"Yes," she said.

"Fetch the witnesses!" cried Parson Joe.

Nora said quickly: "No. Give me . . . just an hour."

"Fiddlesticks! Why wait? A woman can waste more time!"

Boone said magnanimously: "An hour isn't long, Parson."

"All right," said the old man, resigned. "One hour." He heaved a great, satisfied sigh. "My dyin' day, and the happiest day in my life. . . ."

VI

That very morning Bogey had declared his back cured—or practically so. He drove the team until the train stopped that noon, and, while the scene just recounted was taking place, he was out hobbling horses. Coming back to the wagon, he was hopeful that Prudence would reward his activity with a cup of coffee. The door to the wagon was ajar, so he walked in. Prudence was speaking to Nora.

"But why today? It's foolishness. There's no need for such a hurry. Marriage can wait till you get to Bannack."

Bogey cut in: "Marriage! Who's gettin' married?"

Nora dropped her eyes.

"You figurin' on gettin, married?" he pursued.

"Yes, Bogey."

"To Boone?"

She nodded.

Prudence, now aided by Bogey's presence, spoke firmly: "But not today."

"It will have to be today. Parson Joe's . . . going to die."

Prudence promptly exploded: "Die! He's been headed for the Great Beyond ever since I first laid eyes on him five years ago. Look at last winter. He said he was a goner then. Why, that time he even gave instructions for buildin' his coffin! He ain't that far yet."

"He's really sick. He's telling the truth."

"Well, so be it. But you needn't get married to please some old decrepit sky pilot."

"I'm sorry. It's no use arguing. I'm going to be married in an hour . . . half an hour now. I've promised."

Bogey asked: "You wouldn't keep your promise if it meant marrying the man that planned your father's murder, would you?"

"No, of course I wouldn't."

Without saying more, Bogey turned and left the wagon. He found Ceiver's wagon, now deserted. This time, somehow, he must find the bullet. He worked systematically. First he climbed atop a low stool at the front with his head on a level with the aperture through which the bullet had been fired. He sighted at the spot where Ebbert had most likely stood. Fired at this angle, the bullet would strike the wall about eight inches above the floor. But the wall and floor were unscarred—he knew that from his search the other day. Obviously something was wrong. Had some other object stopped the bullet's flight, an object subsequently moved?

"Let's see," he muttered. "Ebbert stood here. Turned, fell here. Wils must have been here. Then he jumped through this tear. Hello. . . ." The old family table of the Ceivers now stood before the rent in the canvas. "He couldn't have jumped the table. It must have been put there since."

He had examined the table before, but he slid it in the only possible direction—toward the back—and again sighted from the aperture. One table leg near the wall was now in the path of fire. On hands and knees he scrutinized it. The leg was of mossy oak, large enough to stop a bullet, but it was un-marked. He looked closely—then, in surprise, more closely still. What occupied his attention was not a bullet hole—it was a fresh crack that split apart the time-honored varnish to expose the wood's white heart.

"Funny what would cause a crack like that," he muttered. "Look's like some pressure is holdin' it apart from inside."

He shook the leg—it was loose. It twisted in his fingers, and, as it turned, there was exposed a gaping bullet hole. It was large, a hole made from the slug of a Navy pistol. Working feverishly, he started to dig at the bullet with his Bowie. He thought better of it. Instead, he twisted the leg from the table, leaving the table teetering there while he ran for Ebbert's wagon.

Gleefully he hammered on the door. Silence! He looked in. The wagon was deserted. "Parson's wagon," he muttered.

He ran outside. But which wagon was it? They stretched at intervals for half a mile along the edge of the park. He ran north, caught sight of a man gathering dry twigs beneath a clump of fir trees.

"Where's the parson's wagon?" he panted.

The man's mouth fell agape at sight of Bogey's standing there with the mossy table leg over his shoulder like some Brobdignagian ball-bat.

"Where's Parson Joe's, you idjit?" Bogey screamed.

"Back thar." The man pointed south.

Bogey turned, raced away. There were four wagons around the grove of quaking asp at which the man had pointed. Bogey hammered at the first one. The man who answered was small, freckled, had suspicious eyes.

"Where's Parson Joe's?" Bogey asked.

"What you want with the parson?"

Bogey gave up, ran to the next wagon, opened the flap without knocking, and glanced inside. There, with joined hands and facing Parson Joe's bunk, stood Boone and Nora. At their right and left were Prudence and Tom Ceiver. All looked startled at Bogey and his table leg.

"Stop this foolishness!" cried Bogey.

His words, and the impetuousness of his appearance, shocked them all to silence. Parson Joe let fall the shaky hand that held the Bible. With an unusual effort, he sat upright in his bunk. "This is no foolishness," he quavered. "This here is a sacred ceremony you're interruptin'."

"Maybe you won't be so durned anxious to go on with it when you hear what I got to say." Bogey pointed toward Logan with a finger that trembled with excitement. "Miss Nora, there's the man what plotted your father's murder!"

Logan spun on Bogey. He loomed over the elder man with fists clenched. But Ceiver stepped between them. "Calm down, Boone," he said. Then, to Bogey: "Get out of here! And be gone from the wagon train in five minutes. If you think you'll stop this wedding, you're wrong. You can't, because the wedding is all over."

"All over?" Bogey glanced at Nora. With an inclination of her head she indicated Ceiver was telling the truth. "Too late," Bogey said in a hollow voice. Then he seemed to grasp his resolve. He was still not beaten. "By thunder, it's not either too late!"

He spun away from Ceiver, pistol in hand, and might have fired, but Prudence grasped his wrist, forced him tightly against the wall by superior weight. Bogey struggled impotently in her grasp.

She whispered: "Put that gun away, you fool. Want to spoil everything? Let me handle this."

Bogey relaxed. Freed, he reluctantly dropped back the pistol in its holster.

Prudence turned on Logan and her husband. "Get out of here," she commanded.

Logan glowered. "Get out! Me get out?"

"Yes. Both of you."

Logan hesitated, finally said: "Very well. Come, Nora."

"No. Nora stays."

"Listen, I don't know what's on your mind . . . but Nora is my wife, and she goes with me."

Prudence stood her ground. She took Nora by the shoulders, and drew her close. "I said . . . get out. Haven't you any feeling in your hide for this poor girl?"

"What's goin' on here?" Parson Joe wailed, but no one heeded him.

Logan turned abruptly and clomped through the flap door. It slapped shut behind him.

"What's in your head, Prudence?" asked Ceiver.

"Never mind. You go, too."

"You don't put store in what Bogey says, do you?"

"Never mind, just git."

Tom Ceiver did as he was told.

A moment of quiet followed. Parson Joe sighed; he relaxed, supinely peaceful with hands folded across his chest, his eyes closed. A smile relaxed his lips.

Prudence said: "Let's see that table leg."

Bogey triumphantly handed it over. She examined the hole and nodded her satisfaction. "It's from a big-bore gun, right enough. How come we didn't find it the other day?"

"The leg was loose. The force of the bullet striking it must have turned it around so the bullet hole couldn't be seen."

"What does it all mean?" Nora asked.

"This is the bullet that killed your paw," Bogey explained. "But it never came from Wils's gun. Wils's gun don't throw a slug more'n half this size."

Prudence dug out the ball with a butcher knife and dropped it in Nora's hand.

She looked at it for a moment. "No, this isn't from Wils's gun."

Bogey thought of something. "Miss Nora, you remember the day he shot at those men back on Birch Creek?"

"Of course."

"How many times did he shoot?"

"Only once."

"Did he reload the empty cylinder while he was with you?"

"No."

"And he didn't reload in camp that night, either. I remember Comanche John puttin' cap and ball in his pistol, but not Wils."

Prudence demanded: "What you gettin' at?"

"Just this. Wils likely never did reload that cylinder. And if he didn't, he couldn't show his pistol to be examined. . . ."

"Glory be," breathed Prudence.

Nora's eyes flashed. "Then it *was* someone else."

Bogey responded: "Sure it was. And I don't have to guess much as to who, either. I could have spit on him not three minutes ago."

"But it couldn't have been Boone."

"Couldn't have, hey? Well, he was Johnny on the spot to accuse Wils by time the shot quit echoing."

Prudence shook her head. "Boone was at that meetin' in Donovan's wagon when the shot was heard. A dozen men can prove that."

"How about his men?"

Prudence stepped to the door, thrust out her head, and bellowed: "Ceiver!"

Her husband was sitting on the steps at her feet. "What do you want?"

"Come in here. Ceiver, were all of Logan's scouts in Donovan's wagon at the time Ebbert was shot?"

"All but Mex. He was hobbling horses."

"Mex, hey? So it was him!"

"What about him? You mean he killed Ebbert?"

"That's right."

Nora sank to a chair. Her lips were drawn in a tight line. Her hands clenched until the knuckles were bloodless. Prudence thrust out her jaw and looked belligerent. Bogey fingered the pistol at his belt. An expression of doubt had even found its way to Tom Ceiver's face. But in the bunk, oblivious to the scene just enacted, Parson Joe sighed in deep contentment. He muttered: "The happiest day of my life, jining these two happy young folk in the bonds of wedlock."

VII

That afternoon Bogey pointed his horse up the trail toward the pass.

"Don't come back without Wils," Prudence admonished.

"I'll bring him back. You watch over Nora."

"Don't worry. I'll see to it that Logan scoundrel don't take his nuptials too seriously."

It was heavy going through the wet snow. Bogey didn't press his horse, for he knew all its strength might be needed before the trip ended.

Near nightfall he sighted two riders approaching from up the trail. They proved to be Indians—a buck and his squaw. Bogey pulled his horse across the trail, held up his hand, palm forward, in signal of friendship. The Indian pulled up, returned the signal.

"How!" said Bogey.

"How!" the Indian answered. He was old, had a parchment face wrinkled by many seasons. His squaw was young—he must be a man of importance in his tribe, Bogey thought.

"How far to Lemhi Pass?" Bogey asked.

The Indian shook his head.

Bogey repeated the question in the dialect of the Crows, but the Indian still responded in the negative. He was probably a Shoshone, or a Bannack. Bogey thereupon motioned toward the mountains at the east and with a zigzag gesture indicated a trail. The buck nodded and, without speaking, but with eloquent use of his fingers, pointed to the peak ahead, held up two fingers, motioned north with his thumb, spread fore and middle fingers, then gestured east with both hands. After this he proudly expended his entire fund of English: "Fort Benton, four sleeps."

These directions satisfied Bogey. He was to pass this and the next mountain, go east when the trail forked. The Indian, who supposed him headed for Fort Benton, estimated the distance at four days' travel.

Bogey dipped into his pouch for a fragment of blackstrap tobacco and three rifle balls that he proffered as a gift. In exchange, the Indian drew forth a once gaudy, but now bedraggled, fragment of calico; this he presented in return. They parted with a sign of friendship.

A day had passed by the time Wils Fleming gained the foot of the steep ascent of Lemhi Pass. Here he must decide his course: would he do the sensible thing—continue on to Bannack, or would he wait to fight it out with Logan and his henchmen? It was not an easy decision. He pondered at length, the while allowing his horse to pick its leisurely way up the steepening trail. They proceeded thus, without destination, for five or six miles.

A voice sounded a few yards to his rear: "Waal, if it ain't Wils."

Comanche John was emerging from a clump of jack pine near the trail. He led his horse and was just returning a pistol to its holster.

"Comanche John! I thought you'd be in Bannack by now."

"Reckon I would be." John aimed a spurt of tobacco juice at a white quartzite boulder. "Reckon I would, only certain

169

things held me up . . . or t'other way around." He winked, drew the back of his hand across his disreputable black whiskers. "You see, I been doin' a little minin' right here in the pass. Likely spot."

"Mining?" Wils looked doubtfully at the inhospitable cliffs, and down at the torrent that frothed over jagged boulders in the gulch.

"Yep!" To prove his assertion, John drew from his saddlebag two weighty buckskin pokes. "Gold," he said, hefting them expertly. "That Bannack must be a right rich spot. Leastwise, the pilgrims comin' out has a powerful lot more'n the ones goin' in."

Wils made no question of John's mining methods. In the Northwest of 1862 it was neither polite nor healthful to question another's line of business.

"Business is good, Wils, better jine me."

"Sorry, John, it's not my line."

"Well, every man for his principles, I say. But share and share alike is my motto." In proof of this philosophy, he held out one of the bags of gold. "Take it. There's plenty where this came from."

Wils shook his head. So, with a resigned gesture, John put the gold back in the saddlebag. "You run into all kinds on a gold rush," he muttered. "Headin' for Bannack?"

Wils shook his head doubtfully. Then he told of Ebbert's murder and of his own escape.

"I don't reckon I'd worry much more about 'em," John said.

"I wouldn't . . . except for Bogey and those two women."

"Ah-ha." John sagely nodded his head.

"And I believe Logan has some scheme."

"Maybe. That fellow's a rattler, right enough."

"The train should heave in sight tomorrow. I think I'll

keep an eye on it."

Wils turned back down the trail. Without question, Co-manche John did likewise. John said: "Thanks for cuttin' me loose t'other night. Looked like I'd staked claim on one of them Californy collars for sure."

"Me cut you loose?" And Wils gave his version of John's escape, of his own approach to the wagon, of the dark form that had appeared, and finally of the unexpected turn of affairs through the discovery of Ceiver's Bowie.

John, marveling, shook his head. "I was just sittin' thar, tied good and snug', tryin' to wear one of the ropes thin on the edge of the bench. Then I heard the sound of cloth being cut right behind my back. I reckoned it was you. I dropped my hands low, and somebody cut the ropes. The knife was put in my hand, so I did the rest . . . snitched Ceiver's guns and lit out. I forgot the knife . . . lucky, too, way it worked out."

Darkness came early, and that night it snowed. All the next day the two watched for the train. At dark, Wils grew worried. "This trifling snow shouldn't hold them up. Suppose they got off the trail?"

Comanche John shrugged. "Tomorrow we'll ride back and have a look-see."

That night the two slept not an hour's travel from where Bogey was camped beneath a spreading evergreen. Dawn came misty and sunless through a sky of lead gray, warning of blizzard. Neither Wils nor John mentioned the weather, but both mutely recognized that wagons that wanted to negotiate Lemhi before spring would have to hurry. They started down the trail. In the distance, a rider approached. It was Bogey.

He took scarcely time for greeting; instead, he gave a rapid account of happenings since Wils's departure. "We got to get back," he concluded. "Nora needs you."

Words seemed to fail Wils for a moment. Finally he burst out: "But she's Logan's wife . . . don't you understand that?"

"Wife! Them few triflin' parson's words ain't so important. . . ."

"Yes, they are, Bogey."

"Then he can annul it."

Comanche John patted a revolver. "I got the best annuller you ever saw, right here. Maybe that girl would appreciate the happy state of widdahood."

"Yes," Wils said after a moment's consideration, "we have to go back. She . . . and Prudence are our friends. We can't abandon them."

They started down the trail, expecting the train with each mile after the first ten, but there was no sign of it. Finally they rode atop a promontory from which a vast area spread beneath their gaze—an area limited only by the purple haze of fall, by the jagged outlines of the Bitterroots, the Salmons, and more distant ranges. The valley itself was visible almost to the Birch Creek divide—but no wagon train was there.

Bogey finally asked: "Think they took the wrong trail?"

Wils answered grimly. "Maybe it's the wrong trail Logan had in mind all along."

"It's likely," John mused. "Blind trail in the mountains . . . Injun attack, say . . . that game's been played before. The provisions on that train would be worth as much as gold in Bannack."

Wils asked Bogey: "Was Logan there when you left?"

"He was, but his men weren't. They left to look for the pass."

Wils cursed under his breath. He looked up and to the south where a light spot in the clouds told the sun's position. It was late morning. Then he cracked his horse sharply with the quirt. "We'll have to hurry," he said through clenched teeth, "and hurry like hell."

Down the hill they went, clattering over stones, paying no heed to branches that snatched at clothing and slapped their faces. In the snow were still the impressions of the hoofs of three horses—Bogey's, and the two Indians he had encountered the day before. At last, on nearing the train's campsite of the previous day, they found the wagon tracks. These had headed across the valley toward a cleft in the foothills backed by precipitous mountain walls. Without comment they turned, urged heir horses to greater speed. From the distance came the rattle of gunfire.

After Bogey departed, Prudence returned to the wagon where Nora was sitting. She went to the corner where the guns were kept and hauled out a big-bore shotgun. From the barrel she dug the wad, and poured out its charge of birdshot. Then, after adding a few grains of powder, she poured in a heavy load of buckshot, rewadded, inserted a fresh cap for good measure, and leaned the gun against the wall within reach of her rocking chair. "Great thing in an emergency," she growled. "If the devil was on my heels and I only had one shot . . . give me buck."

After that, she and Nora waited nervously, but when darkness fell, Logan had not returned. Prudence lit the tallow lamp, but its sad, reddish flare seemed so ineffectual against the gloom that she became reckless and dipped into her hoard of tallow candles, one of which she lighted and placed in a brass holder beneath a chimney. After that, she brewed coffee, and the two felt better.

Tom Ceiver came in, poured a cup of coffee.

"Where's Logan?" his wife asked.

"Out exploring the pass."

"*Humph!* Thought he knew the country so well."

"It's not only the pass. This happens to be Blackfoot country. He and his men are out scouting a raiding party."

At the word Blackfoot the two women became tense. The Blackfoot nation was the scourge of the Northwest. Well they knew the fate of other emigrants who had become the prey of those painted horsemen.

A little later a sharp rap came at the rear of the wagon. Unconsciously Prudence checked the position of the shotgun. She said: "Come in."

The door opened to admit Boone Logan. He didn't glance at Tom or Prudence—his gaze was for Nora. He smiled. But the girl did not lift her eyes; they narrowed and grew hard as she looked at the floor, and her mouth set in a line remindful of her father's.

"May I have coffee?" Boone asked, noticing the pot that still bubbled on the stove.

Prudence answered: "Help yourself."

Ceiver attempted to smooth the atmosphere. "Any Blackfoot signs?"

Logan maintained silence until he had drunk half his coffee, then he answered. "Yes. I don't want to scare anybody, but they're about. I have the men watching them. So we'll get warning before an attack. However, it would be well to start early tomorrow."

He finished his coffee, set down the cup. Then he stepped over and set a hand on Nora's shoulder. His eyes narrowed with a hard glitter when he noticed how she flinched beneath his touch. He appeared to hesitate for a moment, then he said: "My wagon isn't exactly the place I'd want to take a bride. But we'll have a real home . . . in Bannack."

Nora didn't answer. Logan looked at her for a few seconds, then turned his gaze on Prudence. He could not help but read the suspicion on their faces. Without speaking more, he left the wagon. They all breathed more easily when the flap shut behind him.

With the first gray hint of morning the wagoners were out unhobbling their horses, hitching them between traces that each morning grew more stiff with cold. Smoke billowed from some of the stovepipes, but, reading a warning in the leaden sky, most of the travelers ate hurriedly of cold beans or jerky. Nora ran down and called on the parson. Inside his wagon a lamp cut the pre-dawn gloom. The old man sat in his bunk, taking nourishment. "Feel a lot better," he confided a trifle sheepishly. "Reckon I'll get a chance to convert them Bannack heathens, after all."

The parson's good health irked Nora—of course, she wanted to see him recover, but the fact stood out that his chills and fever hadn't been serious, yet because of them she was now Logan's wife. After a few words she returned to her wagon.

The air soon rang with the cries of teamsters, with the sing and pop of long-lash whips. The wheels creaked in the cold, and soon the dozen divisions of the train were in motion northward. Boone Logan rode ahead, tall, erect, his ringed buckskin aflutter. A while later two riders approached from up the trail. Logan galloped ahead to meet them. The teamsters looked to their priming, for these two were Indians, and this was Blackfoot country. But they proved to be only a peaceful old Shoshone and his squaw who sat stoically by the trail and watched as the train rolled by.

A short time later Logan turned abruptly toward the east. He motioned the lead team to follow. He led the way across the valley to a gulch that, in turn, pointed toward what appeared to be a cleft in the mountain wall. "It's Lemhi!" "It's the pass!" These were the words that ran along the line of wagons.

175

It was fair going the first two miles, but as the gulch narrowed, the road became only a wide deer trail that followed sidehills among evergreens. After a long, continuous climb it dropped to the floor of a grassy park, spongy with springs. A herd of twenty deer watched with jet eyes, tame as milk cows, even curiously following a few stiff jumps at a time—but no one shot, for the air bore snow flurries and the idea of haste was uppermost in all minds.

Climbing from the park toward an area of spectacular cliffs, the trail was difficult and rocky. Twice the drivers of the lead team were forced to pry slide rock from the trail that, when freed, went rolling and crashing in a series of leaps only to stop at the gulch's bottom far below. Always, now, the wagon wheels clung precariously to the trail. Some of the more timorous shouted questions to Logan, but he rode ahead, unheeding.

High above a golden eagle veered in small circles, effortlessly, on set pinions. Then with a flap of gathering wings he came to perch on a crag that stood spire-like away from the vertical porphyry cliff.

At last, on reaching a broad sweep of treeless mountainside, Logan signaled a halt. Almost in unison with his gesture a teamster shouted—"Indian!"—and pointed toward a feather-decked figure that appeared atop a large rock two hundred yards above.

A chilling scream rent the air. Guns crashed from all around. Men toppled from several driver's seats. Somebody raced from a wagon, started dragging away a wounded man. A gun spat out from behind a nearby rock. The man sprawled over his wounded comrade.

One frantic driver commenced lashing his horses, turned them downhill in an attempt to escape the way he had come, but the wagon faltered as it turned, swayed, hung for a

176

moment on two wheels, then plunged crashing toward the abyss, the terrified horses squealing with fright, hoofs flying in a horrible tangle. From the wagon's rear a barrel of flour rolled, leaped high in the air, shattered with a cloud of white powder.

Logan ostentatiously found refuge between two rocks, fired at something. He turned, motioned to the driver of the lead team who had hidden in his wagon when the shooting commenced. "They'll get you there!" he shouted. "Come here."

The man hesitated for a moment, then he leaped from the wagon. Bent double, he hopped like a jack rabbit over the slide rock, but a waiting pistol, not thirty feet distant, cut him down. The firing then ceased, the horses became calm, and the silence of the mountain fastness was again complete.

Prudence Ceiver peeped through a rent she had cut in the canvas of the wagon and spotted a glint of gun shine up the hill. She looked down the long barrel of her rifle, waited perhaps a minute. Something dark appeared around the edge of a stone. She squeezed the trigger. A man stumbled into view, pitched face down.

"One," she growled. She dumped another charge of powder down the barrel. But something closer attracted her attention, so she passed the rifle over to Nora and kept watch with the shotgun.

Boone Logan attached a white handkerchief to the barrel of his gun and waved it as if asking for a truce. A feather-decked man appeared briefly to motion, then hid again. Logan climbed down the hill. Soon he emerged from the parley and, still bearing his white flag, advanced along the train.

"They'll let us go, but we'll have to leave the horses and

wagons," he announced along the line. "Get ready and follow me."

When Prudence heard his words, she thrust out her head and bellowed: "Stay hid, you fools, or he'll get us all killed. Don't you see it's his own gang fixed up like Injuns?"

Logan spun on her as if stung by a whiplash. Fury twisted his face. He dropped the kerchief-draped barrel as if to shoot, then thought better of it and forced a smile. "You'd better come!" he shouted. "It's your only chance."

The sound of a different gun cut the air. It came from back on the trail. One of the befeathered men sprang up, then fell. His companions—there were but three left now—leaped to find some place safe from this unexpected attack. But one was knocked down as he sought to escape. Wounded, he crawled desperately on all fours. The head and shoulders of a black-whiskered man in a disreputable slouch hat appeared momentarily over a rock, his pistol bobbed up, cracked, and the wounded man lay still.

Prudence, watching, gasped in surprise: "Comanche John!"

Nora asked: "What's that?"

"Looks like Bogey brung back the whole crew!"

Boone Logan jumped behind the wagon, ran quickly along to enter at the rear. "Come, Nora. We still have time to escape. We can reach my horse along this side. He'll carry us around the mountain to safety."

The girl drew back, an expression of revulsion answering him.

He repeated: "Come!"

"I'll stay here, you . . . murderer."

"You little fool! Call me murderer? I'll tell you who attacked us . . . it was Wils Fleming and those highwaymen friends of his." He took a stride as if to seize Nora and drag her with him.

"Stay where y'are!" It was Prudence's voice that cut the air.

He drew up short, for the shotgun was trained at his heart.

She said: "There's a dozen buck in this bar'l, enough to blow you to the blackest spot in hell, I reckon."

They faced each other a second. He spoke in an icy voice: "You wouldn't dare pull that trigger."

"Don't pass the end of that table," said Prudence.

He laughed through his teeth, commenced a stride.

The gun leaped with a roar in Prudence's hands. The concussion of the charge spun Logan half around. He fell heavily to the floor.

For a few seconds the women stared at him, but with more relief than horror. Then their attention was drawn outside where a perfect fusillade had broken out: the last two of Logan's men had broken and run for it—with disastrous results.

Comanche John, atop his rock, turned to Wils and swore as the last of them went down from the well-directed bullet of a wagoner. "Just my luck! Whenever I get some good wing shootin' stirred up, somebody has to horn in and spile it."

That afternoon the train managed to turn on the dangerous mountain trail and descend. Toward evening the sun broke warm and yellow through a rift in the clouds—assurance that the year's first blizzard was not in the offing, after all. The camp was at the approach to Lemhi. While Wils and his two companions were having supper at Nora's wagon, the flap raised to admit Parson Joe, hale and hearty after his attack of chills and fever.

"I come to apologize for marryin' you off to that varmint, and to congratulate you on bein' a widda."

Nora smiled. "That's all right, Parson."

"But," he went on, looking from her to Wils and back

again, "mebby I'll get to perform another ceremony over in Bannack."

The smiles on Wils's and Nora's lips left him in no doubt.

Over by the kettle, Comanche John sliced off a strip of venison with his keen Bowie. He pondered the parson's words and looked speculatively at the bunk where Tom Ceiver lay with a bullet-shattered arm. "Got a might' good idee to finish off this pesky Ceiver fellow so Prudence and I can make it a double," he said.

Prudence shook her head. "I don't reckon you're the marryin' kind, John. But just the same, I'm right glad I cut you loose the night they was measurin' you for that Pike County cravat."

No Gold on Boothill

Dan Cushman later incorporated scenes from "The Conestoga Pirate" into his novel, NORTH FORK TO HELL (Fawcett Gold Medal, 1964), but Comanche John is not a character in that story. Norman A. Fox, a fellow Montana author of Western fiction who wrote notable novels like TALL MAN RIDING (1951) and NIGHT PASSAGE (1956), both of which were subsequently filmed, was a close friend of Dan Cushman's. Fox frequently commented that the kinds of characters who were villains in his stories somehow seemed heroes in Dan's. There might be some truth in this. Comanche John scarcely embodies many of the qualities one associates with a traditional Western hero, although he is perhaps truer to life and the history of those times.

I

It was noon when young Tim Conners reached the crest of Blacktail Pass. He reined in for a while and sat there, his tall, angular form resting easily in the saddle as he surveyed the vast country that lay below—timber, broken mountains, and off there somewhere the fabulous diggings of Eldorado Bar. One of the pack horses snorted, tossed its head, and looked down the trail. From the deep timber came the regular *clop-clop* of a horse's hoofs. The sound grew steadily. Finally a horse and rider came in sight a few yards below.

The man was of medium build. A thick mass of tangled black whiskers rendered his age indeterminable. A nondescript hat was pulled low over his forehead. He wore a buckskin shirt with the remains of Shoshone beadwork, natural-gray homespun trousers, and scuffed jackboots. Two Navy pistols were carried on cross belts, a sawed-off shotgun stock protruded from a saddlebag, and his small arsenal was completed by a Jager rifle thrust in a Mexican scabbard beneath his saddle. He rode almost to the crest of the pass before he glanced up and saw Tim sitting there. Then he pulled up and shot a quick glance around. The next thing Tim knew he was looking into the muzzle of one of the Navy pistols. The action had been so quick and unexpected that Tim scarcely saw the gun come to the man's hand—a twitch of the shoulder, and there it was. Tim raised his hands.

The black-whiskered one chewed his tobacco in silence for a while and inventoried the outfit. He said: "This here's a toll road, young man, and I got instructions from the gov'nor to collect from each wayfarer. Shell out!"

Tim had little money. A week before he had been working on a big placer mine at Bannack. When stories of the richness of Eldorado Bar reached him, he spent all except a few dollars on the outfit he now had—three horses and a quantity of Utah beans that he intended to dispose of at a profit on reaching Eldorado. He nervously felt through the two pockets of his fringed buckskin pants. All he had was a greenback in the five-dollar denomination and a large two-cent piece.

The road agent looked at this money with contempt. "Is that paper money Union or Confederate?"

"Union."

"Union! Why, that piece of paper won't be worth more'n so much Mex when the war's over." He voice became hard. "I said . . . *shell out!*"

"This is all I have."

The road agent considered for a while. His black-whiskered chin revolved methodically around his cud of tobacco. He sent an accurate spurt of tobacco juice at a nearby pine trunk. "I'm a busy man," he said, "and I just spend so much time with a customer. It so happens that your time is up." He thrust the gun a few inches closer. "I'll count five. If you ain't got your poke out by then, why. . . ." He jiggled the gun significantly. "One . . . two . . . three. . . ."

Tim supposed this minute was his last. But he had no more to give. "Take my outfit. . . ."

"Four. . . ." The road agent hesitated. Then, instead of either saying five or pulling the trigger, he made a gesture of

184

resignation and put back his Navy. "A man gets too soft-hearted at this business," he growled apologetically.

Tim took a deep breath. He looked around. He was still there, sitting in the saddle. His horse reached down to crop some mountain grasses. A bird hopped along a pine branch. He was alive!

The road agent pointed to the hand that still held the greenback and the two-cent piece. "Where you goin' with all that money?" he asked good-humoredly.

"To Eldorado Bar."

"That's a high-priced camp." He thought for a moment, then reached into a saddlebag and brought out a handful of nuggets. "Share and share alike is my motto," he said. "I've had a good day today and won't miss this none."

Tim was already too surprised to allow this unexpected beneficence to surprise him more.

The road agent went on: "I hear tell gold's right plentiful down thar at Eldorado."

"Plentiful! They say it clogs the sluices. It will be bigger than Alder or the Grasshopper."

"Hmm. That sounds a likely spot." The road agent scratched his mat of black whiskers. "Maybe I'll team up with you."

Tim was a little leery about teaming up with a road agent, but it was lonesome traveling alone, and he couldn't hold back a glow of good feeling toward the man who had spared his life and given him nuggets. He said: "Come along. They say there's plenty for everybody. The bar gravel's all located, but there's lots in the gulches 'round about. Everyday there are new discoveries."

"A-course I don't much go in for the gulches," the man admitted. "I more generally specialize in minin' the miner. Sort of sluice out his pockets as it were. But every man for his principles, I say, and the gold is where you find it." Then he repeated through force of habit: "Share and share alike's my motto."

They rode down the rocky trail together. The black-whiskered man thrust out a hand that, while grimy, significantly showed no evidence of toil.

"Comanche John is my handle," he said.

At mid-afternoon they paused beside a clear mountain stream and made a meal out of jerked venison and cold biscuits. They traveled on. The road wound across a level valley floor, then it turned and dropped toward a swift river. Comanche John, who was in the lead, reined in and pointed.

A stagecoach sat in the middle of the stream, one rear wheel gone, and tilted at a precarious angle. Its axles were deep under water. The driver and guard had just unhitched the teams and were driving them to the bank. The coach was crowded with passengers. While Tim and John sat there, one man clambered out, dropped to his waist in the icy water, and started wading to shore.

A handsome, elderly man with china-white hair leaned from the window and shouted: "You! Driver!"

The driver, busy with his horses, did not look around. Perhaps he couldn't hear above the rush of the stream and the hoofs' splashing.

"You! Driver!" The elderly man shook his fine crop of hair angrily. He got his arm out of the window and gestured with his walking stick. "Driver!"

By now the stage driver had reached the bank. "What d'you want?" he bellowed with poor humor.

"You know what I want. You know better than to abandon us in the middle of this torrent. You come back and get my niece to shore this minute. The president of the line will hear about this. There's water running across the floor six inches deep. Do you hear me? I'll notify the governor."

The driver shook water from his bristle of red whiskers and eyed the elderly man with malevolence. "Notify Lincoln, too. Ol' Abe will raise tarnation with us." He started freeing the horses from their harnesses. The coach sat like a derelict, rocking gently in the current, but apparently it was in no danger of being washed away. Comanche John pulled to one side where he was partly concealed among some spindly quaking asps, hung one leg easily around the saddle horn, freshened his chew of blackstrap, and chuckled happily over the stage occupants' discomfiture.

"They've had a full day of it," he said with a wink, the significance of which Tim did not immediately comprehend.

The elderly man kept waving his walking stick while he shouted threats and wailed entreaties. "First we're robbed and next we're nearly drowned. It's high time there was a little law and regulation in this country. I demand that you get my niece out of this coach immediately."

"His niece is right pretty," Comanche John remarked.

Tim hadn't as yet caught sight of her. A moment later she thrust her head from a window at the other side. Indeed, she was pretty. She had dark brown hair and thin, finely cut features. Her smile showed she was not nearly so upset over the inconvenience as her uncle.

The stage driver doffed his hat and said: "We'll be there in a minute, Miss Mayand. Jest as soon as I can get the harnesses off some of these Injun hosses."

She wasn't the kind of a woman Tim was used to seeing in camps along the frontier. She was like one of the girls back home. Acting by impulse, he tossed Comanche John the lead string to his pack horses and set his own mount splashing into the stream. He rode to the upstream door of the coach, leaned over, and opened it.

The girl looked out at him with a surprised expression. He touched the broad brim of his hat and smiled. Tim wasn't handsome at first glance, but he had a way about him that inspired confidence, and a way of smiling that was so honest that she couldn't help smiling in return.

"Won't you share my hoss as far as the shore?" he asked.

She hesitated. She had drawn up her feet and tucked them under her because, as her uncle had said, the floor was inches under water. She might have accepted Tim's invitation, but there was no way she could see of leaving the coach without wetting her feet and perhaps the skirt of her fringed traveling dress as well.

Tim could see the cause of her indecision. He reined his horse close against the door, reached in, picked her up from the seat, and set her down in the saddle in front of him. By her startled expression it was plain that she didn't realize what was happening until she found herself sitting there.

The stream rocks made slippery, difficult footing. The horse slipped, plunging to its haunches. The girl uttered a frightened cry and wrapped her arms tightly around her rescuer's neck. Her cheek felt smooth and warm against his throat. The horse splashed in the shallower water, trotted, dripping, to the bank. For a moment the girl didn't seem to realize they had safely reached the shore. When she did, she pushed herself away, flustered.

"I'll help you down, miss," Tim said.

"Don't bother!" Spurning his assistance, she jumped down—a little awkwardly, for her skirt was not constructed for such gymnastics. He couldn't help seeing how pink her cheeks were. She nervously tucked a stray strand of hair back where it should be. He smiled and that only seemed to make her cheeks become pinker.

"What do you mean, dragging me out of the coach like that? Whenever I need help, I'm perfectly able to ask for it."

Tim could see that her temper was defensive. She knew everyone was looking at them, and she feared she looked ridiculous. Her temper made her all the more ridiculous—she knew that, also, but now it was too late.

"I'm sorry," Tim said, doffing his broad, California hat. "I thought you wanted to get to shore."

"Well, I didn't!"

"You should have told me. I'd have left you there."

Her cheeks became rosier than ever. Should have told him! She knew how she had wrapped her arms around his neck when the horse plunged. She looked around. There stood the driver, his red whiskers parted in the biggest kind of a smile. She felt foolish. It made her furious. And this man on horseback was smiling, too. He made her all the more furious. If she were a man, she would have fought with him.

Tim asked with extreme politeness: "Miss, please, you don't *really* wish you were back in that shipwreck, do you?"

"Yes!"

Before she knew what he was doing, Tim had swung down, grasped her by the waist with his two hands, and lifted her from the ground. And there she was, once more seated in front of him in the saddle. She made a move to push herself away, but the horse was plunging into the water. Again she wrapped her arms around Tim's neck—she didn't want to, she just couldn't help herself.

"Put me down!" she cried, holding tighter than ever.

He pulled the horse to a stop. They were halfway between the coach and the bank. The cold, clear water gurgled around the horse's knees.

"Not here?" he said.

"Of course not, you fool! On the shore."

189

He reined around. The horse splashed again to dry land. He didn't give her the chance to dismount by herself this time. He lifted her from the saddle so lightly one might think she weighed ten instead of one hundred and ten pounds.

During this last portion of the episode, the white-haired man had been shouting at Tim from the coach window. He threatened with his walking stick. "Leave my niece alone, you young fool! You'll have me to deal with, I promise you . . . !" But nobody paid him much attention.

Tim doffed his large hat and sat there, looking down at her, solemn as a preacher at a funeral.

"You think you're awfully smart, don't you?" she sputtered.

Then he smiled. It was such a friendly, genuine smile that she had a hard time staying angry with him. "I'm sorry," he said sincerely. "I guess maybe I haven't been acting like a gentleman."

"I should say you haven't!" Then her eyes traveled to the elderly man who was still leaning from the coach window. "At least you might bring in my uncle."

Tim rode back to the coach. He opened the door.

The uncle demanded: "What do you want now?"

"I came to rescue you," Tim answered.

"Rescue me! Young man, if you think I intend to submit to the kind of treatment my niece got, you're mistaken. And I'm not through with you on that score." He waved a long and extremely white finger warningly. "I'll have you know you're not bullying some common miner. I'm Judge Mayand, and I come to Eldorado Bar by special appointment of the territorial governor. . . ."

"Judge, I only wanted to help. No matter how I went about it, your niece is on shore where it's nice and dry. I think she's better off there than she would be in this coach."

The judge, placated by Tim's tone, cooled off a little. He lifted from the water first one sodden foot, and then the other, but he still made no move to leave the coach.

Tim looked at the tilted vehicle with pretended alarm. "There are rapids below," he said. "I just hope you aren't carried away by the treacherous current."

The judge looked first downstream, and then at the coach with a startled expression. He could feel the vehicle sway in the current, and the steady passage of water gave the illusion of movement. He glanced at the faces of the other passengers. They didn't appear to be alarmed, but, still, the young man might know what he was talking about.

He made up his mind. "Give me a stirrup and I'll get on behind."

The judge took the stirrup and mounted with more agility than one might have expected of him. By the time they were on shore, the driver had completed the unharnessing and was ready to bring in the others.

Tim helped the judge to dismount.

"Here's your uncle, miss. . . . What did you say your name was?"

"I didn't say," the girl answered with some mitigation of her coolness, "but it's Della Mayand."

The judge felt considerably better now that his feet were on dry ground. "Thank you, young man," he said. "Maybe I was a little too sharp with you out there at the coach. An experience like that doesn't help the temper any. I'd be glad to remunerate you, but a road agent robbed us when we were on our way across the pass." He fumbled in the breast pocket of his long black coat. "However, here's a cigar. He didn't find that."

At the word "robbed," Tim looked across at the clump of quaking asps, but Comanche John was not there.

"I didn't expect to be paid," he assured the judge. "I hope the road agent didn't get too much from you."

"He got enough," the elderly man answered cantankerously. "It wasn't the money so much I hated losing, but he took my watch. It was an heirloom. Belonged to my father. A green and yellow gold case with a diamond, a ruby, and an emerald mounted in its back." The judge grimaced at the recollection. "Share and share alike, indeed!"

Tim tried to smile at Della, but her eyes avoided him.

"At least we're lucky in one thing," the judge went on. "We're almost to Eldorado, so we won't have to spend the night on this riverbank."

"I have a couple of extra horses," Tim said eagerly, more to Della than her uncle. "You can ride my horse, miss, and the judge and I can do with the others."

"I think I've ridden your horse once too often this afternoon. Besides, the guard has already started in for saddle horses."

Tim considered her words for a few seconds. Then, without saying more, he turned to mount. As for Della, she evidently regretted her sharpness. She started to say something, but just then several riders came galloping from the direction of Eldorado.

The leading horse almost slid to its haunches when the rider hauled back on the reins. He sprang from the saddle, graceful as a circus equestrian. A dashing picture he made in fine Spanish boots, silver spurs, silver and pearl gun butts against the fine black serge of his trousers.

"I understand Judge Mayand is here. . . ." His eyes fell on the judge. He stopped abruptly, stared. The judge, too, was startled. They stood facing each other in surprised silence for a moment—perhaps a couple of seconds—then the newcomer got control of himself. "Are you Judge Mayand?" he asked.

The judge tried to speak, but the words hung in his throat. After a couple of starts, he managed to squeeze out: "I am."

The newcomer thrust out his hand. A smile of welcome spread across his sharp, handsome face. He gracefully swept off his beaver hat, and his eyes dwelt appraisingly on Della.

"I'm Rodger Splain, deputy U.S. marshal. The governor has informed me of your appointment, Judge Mayand. May I say we are honored to have such a distinguished jurist sent us. Further, the governor has instructed me to render all possible assistance to you, both in your duties as recorder and judge." He looked again at Della. "And I suppose this is your niece?"

Tim had started to go, but he paused a moment to watch. He didn't like this Marshal Splain. He didn't like the close-clipped, confident way he spoke—like a man reading from a book. He didn't like the man's dash and sparkle. Most of all, he didn't like the way Splain was looking at the girl. He wondered why Splain and Judge Mayand pretended to be strangers. They weren't. He knew that. They recognized each other that first moment. It must be there was something off-color in their old relationship. Titles like judge and marshal didn't mean much. A man could be as dishonest with such a title as without.

Tim started across the ford.

"Wait!"

He pulled up. He recognized Della's voice.

She was coming toward him. She smiled. "I'm sorry I spoke so mean just a minute ago. I really *do* appreciate your taking me off that coach. And thanks for offering the horses, too, but Mister Splain seems to have provided for us. Perhaps I'll see you in Eldorado."

Tim immediately vowed that she would. He watched from the far bank of the river until Della and the rest disappeared beyond a turn in the trail. Then he looked around for Comanche John, but he was gone, and the two pack horses were gone with him. Suddenly fearful for his outfit, Tim rode up and down the bank. It was then he heard John call to him.

"Here I be. Up the hill."

Even after hearing the voice, Tim had a hard time locating him. At last he caught sight of him in a thick clump of junipers.

"Distance is a good thing at times," John explained. "It might not be wise for them folks to get too close a squint at me, one reason or t'other. You was right heroic with that gal. Who was them people, anyhow?"

"Judge Mayand and his niece, Della."

"Judge?" John chuckled.

"Yes. I gathered he'd been appointed judge and recorder at Eldorado."

"What was that dashin' fellow what rode up?"

"He was the law."

Tim expected Comanche John to show some concern over the nearness of the law, but that worthy flicked not an eyelash. He aimed a stream of tobacco juice at a small boulder and grunted with satisfaction when he hit it dead center.

"The law?" he asked. "Son, one of them pewter badges ain't the law." He slapped the Navy on his right hip. "That's the law up yere in the Northwest. These judges can haul in stat-choots by the wagonload, but the real law is carried on the hip, and the quickest wrist and the closest eye is what enforces it. It's impartial. It applies equal to human, Chinese, or Injun. There ain't no writs nor no hung juries. No appeals. No, sir. She has six sections, and, when she executes sentence, it's downright permanent."

II

The placer diggings at Eldorado Bar were scattered along three or four miles of terraces facing the river. Rich gravel had also been discovered here and there in the narrow gulches that cut through the rugged hill country nearby.

The first houses of the boom camp were less than a mile from the ford. These were small, brush-roofed cabins clustered in a little clearing. Beyond them, the road wound through thick forest, then another clearing and more houses. A flume, passing over the road, dripped water on them. Two mules hitched to a scraper hauled gravel to the head box of a sluice. A hundred yards farther on, the same work was being performed by a dozen Chinese laborers. Up a low hillside, a crow-bait pinto horse walked in a weary circle turning the crude mechanism of an arrastre that slowly pulverized rich quartz from a lode location.

The forest fell away and the main portion of the camp lay before them. It was aimless and planless, a city of log cabins, of brush wickiups, canvas-topped emigrant wagons, one of them still bearing an ancient slogan: **Pike's Peak or Bust**. Some men lived in dugouts with pole and sod roofs, and many in tattered tents and skin lodges.

The main business district was a mile farther on. These buildings were no less disreputable than the houses—they were only larger. Gambling, dancing, saloons, a store, then more saloons and more saloons. The main street was jammed with freight wagons, mules, oxen, and cursing drivers. **Assaying done Hear**, a sign read, and another **The Lucky Dog Gaming Palace** next to it. **Snake River Joe's**, then **Katie's—20 Beautiful Partners.**

"Shoot me for a Blackfoot," roared Comanche John, "look thar!"

A low, log building was set between Katie's and the Bird Cage Opera House, and across its front hung a banner on which were emblazoned the words: **Repent Ye, while ye have the time.**

"Ain't it beatin' how them sky pilots git around?" John marveled. Prompted by curiosity, he rode his horse up over the pole sidewalk, leaned in his saddle, and cupped his eyes to peer through the building's one window. He caught sight of something inside that made him yip with pleasure. "Why, it's the parson!"

"The who?"

"The parson. Blamed old graybeard of a sky pilot I hove into Bannack with, a year or two ago. He's an ornery old parrot, but not so bad, either, seein' he's a preacher." Comanche John swung from his saddle, clomped across the walk, and tied his mount to a post. He motioned for Tim to follow. "C'mon in. We'll see how he's doin' with the sinners."

John flung open the door and peered into the gloomy interior. "Hello, Reverend, how ye be?" he shouted.

"Comanche John!" came the response. The voice was high, quavery, and had a cracked quality that did remind Tim of a parrot. "Why, John, I heered the Orofino Vigilance Committee caught up with you months ago."

John hee-hawed and clomped on in. "They did talk some

about fittin' me up with one of them Californy collars," he admitted, "but I snuck out on 'em." He marched down between the two rows of split-log benches and pumped the parson's hand. "Likely lookin' mission you got fixed up yere."

The parson, a gaunt scarecrow of a man, grunted without enthusiasm.

"What's wrong?"

"The mission's all right, I suppose, but missionaryin' is toler'ble poor. Only fetched five converts all week, and three of them was drunk. A-course, I been doin' a brisk business in funerals, but a funeral's a mite late place to save a man's soul, to my way of thinkin'."

John noticed that the parson was packing away his religious tracts and ratty old hymn books in a frayed carpetbag. "You ain't quittin', are you?"

"I ain't doin' nothin' else," the parson growled, tossing in the last of the hymn books with more force than was necessary. "Bogey and me has gone to minin'. You remember old Bogey?"

"That varmint? Sure, I remember him. So you've gone to minin'! Have you turned the color?"

"We've turned her," the parson stated with satisfaction. "You bet we've turned her!" His tone caused John to arch his eyebrows. "We ain't said a heap about it yet. We've been keepin' it a sort of secret until the new recorder came so we could get it down legal. There's been a heap of claim jumpin' of late. . . ." He noticed Tim. "Who's this?"

"This is Tim . . . ," John said, turning toward Tim. "What'd you say the rest of that handle was?"

"Conners," Tim said. "Tim Conners."

"He's square," John assured the parson. "We're teamed up together. Lookin' for gold ourselves, one way or t'other."

The parson appeared to be satisfied. "Yep. This camp is

wicked to shame Gomorrah, but murder and gun robbery ain't the only crimes. There's a heap of smooth claim jumpin', too. It ain't healthy to make big strikes around Eldorado. You can't do much ag'in' a gang, 'specially when the gang works with some of our so-called *best citizens.* A man makes a find, the news leaks out, then he comes home and finds his claim jumped. Then, if he makes a fight for it. . . ." The parson tossed up his hands. "That's the last you ever hear of him."

John was scandalized. "Why, the dirty robbers! Ain't you got no miner's court here in Eldorado?"

"Sure, and a vigilance committee and a deputy U.S. marshal, too, but none of 'em appear to do much good. Oh, if you're one of the first discoverers, one of the old-timers that came in the spring and have a claim here on the bar, they'll give you protection. But us Johnny-come-latelys don't get protection. That is, we didn't up to now. We're finally safe, though. The gov'nor sent us a recorder, Judge Mayand. He'll bring things to time. All he'll have to do is snap his fingers, and the gov'nor will send troops. Bogey is down at the recordin' office now to get our claim on the dotted line."

"Will we need troops with the marshal here?" Tim asked.

"That Marshal Splain?" The parson might have been speaking about some rattlesnake judging by the face he made. "He dresses too fancy to be an honest man, accordin' to my way of thinkin'. Fact is, there's some talk that Splain is in pretty close with the claim jumpers."

"You must have quite a rich piece of gravel up thar," John said with a certain craftiness in his tone.

"You bet we have," expanded the parson. "Why, there's more gold to the yard up on our claim than anywhere down here on the bar. A-course, we ain't got so much gravel, but it's the richest thing anybody's struck here yet." The parson glanced cautiously around to make sure no one had come in and, perhaps, concealed himself among the pews. Then he drew from his jeans' pocket a nugget the size of a pistol ball. "Picked this up at the bottom of a test hole only yestiddy."

John's eyelids drooped when he took the nugget and allowed it to roll around in his palm. There was more than usual weight to his words when he spoke. "Reckon there must be more gold up on that ground than a couple of old varmints like you and Bogey would know what to do with, ain't they? And in case of trouble, four men can fight a heap better'n two. A-course, I ain't hankerin' to horn in whar I ain't wanted, but if I made a big strike, I'd deal cards to you boys." He rubbed his right palm significantly across the butt of one Navy. "Share and share alike is my motto."

The parson waved a bony finger. "You don't need to go rubbin' that pistol butt. I ain't scared of your guns." Then he cooled down. "But now you mention it, I suppose there is more up on that claim than would be good for Bogey and me. And there's more gravel open for location up the gulch."

John winked at Tim gleefully. "See? Didn't I say he was agreeable for a preacher? Maybe I'll go in for real bedrock minin', after all."

At that moment, a short, grizzled man clomped in.

"Well, she's did," the newcomer announced. "I was his first customer. The judge didn't want to set up shop until after supper, but I convinced him of how important it was. Told him we'd put off tellin' anybody about it on account of claim jumpers." His eyes became accustomed to the murky interior, and he recognized Comanche John. "Why, John! I never expected to see *you* ag'in. I heard you was hung over in Orofino." He pumped John's hand for the better part of a minute.

John slapped the grizzled man across his thick shoulders,

called him Bogey, and also a number of strong names that the parson agreeably overlooked. Tim liked this man from his first glance.

John took Bogey's arm and turned him around. "Bogey, this here is Tim Conners, my pardner. He's an honest lad jest come in from somewheres lookin' for his fortune."

Bogey greeted Tim warmly. "Your fortune? Stick around with us and like's not you'll find it."

John said: "The parson's already offered us a share in your claim, and we accepted. I hope you don't object."

Bogey didn't. "Sure. We'd like to have you dig gold with us. There's more'n enough for all." He looked respectfully at John's two Navies. "Wouldn't mind havin' you around in case of jumpers."

The parson, gathering up the last of his belongings, went beyond earshot, and Bogey confided: "It gets all-around tiresome when you're shacked up with a preacher. Take the parson, thar . . . he's all right in his way, but all he wants to talk about is Moses and them old smooth-bores." He explained, Tim thought, a little proudly: "Moses is in the Bible. When he was a little shaver, the daughter of some gambler named Faro found him in the bulrushes. Later on he growed up and got at the head of a bunch of sheepherders, but they all stampeded on a gold rush while he was up a mountain, and, when he clumb down, they was after a golden calf. Believe me, if I seen a nugget the size of a calf, I'd go for it, too."

"Amen!" said Comanche John.

The sun had disappeared beyond the horizon by the time the parson finished packing and the four were headed away from Eldorado Bar. Comanche John rode ahead with Bogey, while Tim and the parson followed with the pack horses. As he rode, Tim's mind roved back across the day, perhaps the most momentous of his twenty-odd years. A road agent had spared his life and given him a handful of nuggets; he had met the most beautiful girl he'd ever seen—yes, more, known the thrill of her cheek against his throat; and now, to furnish a most gratifying climax, he had been given a share in the richest claim at Eldorado Bar.

The trail left town and wandered among the growing heaps of boulders and gravel tailings thrown out by the placer mines. It passed beneath a flume, then took a branch trail up a narrow gulch. In this gulch, too, placer mines were throwing out long heaps of washed gravel and carving long trenches to the bedrock. A few months before, the stream at its bottom had no doubt been diamond clear, but now it was milky with silt. The grade of the gulch increased, and the placer mines suddenly played out. Here and there was a little prospect hole—that was all. They turned up a feeder gulch. In a minute they caught sight of a cabin, faintly visible in the settling dusk.

"Thar she is," said Bogey. "The Golden Leaf placer mine. Richest strike at Eldorado. All entered on the books and ourn for sure."

"Hold back!" Comanche John pulled in and looked suspiciously at the cabin. "I jest saw somebody come out that door."

"That? Probably just Henry the Chinaman. He's our hired man."

John grunted, but his eyes were still narrow slits of doubt. They rode on. It was almost dark where evergreens branched over the trail. A man leaped up from a spot of concealment among some junipers.

" 'Lo! Wait up, quick!"

Bogey started with surprise. "Why, that's Henry the Chinaman! What the thunder!"

The tall Chinaman came bounding down the hillside, leaping from rock to rock, his long queue waving behind. "Man up there," he panted. "Thlee, floor, maybe twelve, I don't know." His eyes were wild when they roved from face to face. "Just come maybe flive minute." He made a movement in imitation of men drawing pistols from holsters. "Bang! Bang! I run like hell, hide. Maybe-so claim jumper, hey?"

Bogey's usually good-humored face seemed to freeze. "Maybe so! Maybe they are claim jumpers. But how would they know we made a strike up here? We never breathed a word of it until the claim was recorded with the judge this afternoon."

They were all thinking the same thing. It was a gold-mad country, the Northwest, and men of all stations abandoned the ways of honesty when the fever got them. To Tim's mind came the recollection of that moment, out at the river crossing, when Judge Mayand first stood face to face with Splain. They had met before, yet there was something about that previous meeting that prevented either man from admitting it in public—and Splain, according to the parson, was already suspected of complicity with the claim jumpers.

Bogey came to a decision. He started his horse up the trail at a sharp trot.

"Hold on, you idjit!" John called to him.

When Bogey didn't stop, the others hurried after him.

Suddenly a man appeared in the trail. He threw a sawed-off shotgun to his shoulder, aimed. Bogey reined in so hard his horse almost went to its haunches.

"Stop where you are!" the man shouted in a voice Tim could hear over the clatter of hoofs. Then the man paused to size them up. "What are you doing on this claim?" he demanded.

"What are we doing on it?" Bogey spluttered. "This is my

claim. *Our* claim. We been workin' it for a month or more. We recorded it this very afternoon."

The man grunted. He kept the sawed-off shotgun pointed without a waver. "Don't get no foxy ideas with your guns," he cautioned. "I ain't holdin' this ground alone. There's some partners of mine back in the trees a bit, and they might have itchy trigger fingers."

But Bogey showed a fine disregard for the shotgun. "You're a gang of sneakin' claim jumpers, that's what you are. This is our location, and we can prove it."

The man laughed—an unpleasant, edgy laugh.

"Laugh! Go ahead and laugh! But you jumpers are licked this time. Yes sir, you've come to the end of your rope. There's a law in this camp now, in case you don't know it. We got through enterin' this claim on the books of the new recorder, Judge Mayand, and, if you try to stand in the way of justice, he'll have the soldiers up here in short order."

The claim jumper seemed to be impressed. "You say Judge Mayand is here?"

"You bet he is, and this claim was the first one he entered on his books. I seen him do it with my own eyes. So you might just as well move on."

"Not so fast." The jumper seemed to be doing some thinking. "If the judge is in Eldorado like you say, we're perfectly willin' to let him decide it. All fair, square, face up on the table top, that's us. If the judge says this ground is yours, we'll clear out. Seems to me that's fair enough."

To Tim, there was something familiar about this man. It wasn't his voice—he'd never heard that before. It was more the way he stood there, the way he moved. He rode a little closer. The man looked up. Tim recognized him then—he was one of the riders who had come out to the coach with Marshal Splain. The truth was obvious. Splain was at the head of the jumpers, just as the parson suggested. And where did that place the judge?

Without considering the consequences, Tim burst out: "Don't fall for it, Bogey. That fellow rode out with Splain to meet the judge this afternoon. He knew the judge was here. They're all in together. . . ."

The man cursed. He wheeled with the shotgun. For an eternal split second, Tim stared into its twin barrels. He had no chance to go for his own gun—no time to move.

Twin reports shattered the air, right past his ear to the right. They were so close as to be almost a single sound. His horse reared, turned, bolted. The trees blurred past. There was a fury of shots—red streaks of gun flame. A bullet *whanged* the ground right under him, droned off into the darkness.

As he rode, a picture of the scene was frozen in the retinas of his eyes: there was the jumper, shotgun slipping from his fingers while his body slumped forward in the trail—Comanche John, holding two smoking Navies—the blur of moving, startled horses. The others were close on Tim's heels—some of them, anyway. He could hear the drum and clatter of hoofs. The bullets that followed were wild, for aim was impossible among the trees, so near nightfall.

Tim decided he was out of range. He pulled up. The parson was there a second later. Then Bogey and Comanche John.

John seemed gratified with the excitement. He chuckled and slapped his leg. "Did you see me fetch him? Best shot I made since I picked the guard off that Yuba coach."

Bogey was not so cheerful. "The rattlers!" he fumed. "They're all in cahoots. The judge and all of 'em. The only way we'll ever get 'em off the ground is to shoot 'em off. We'll get our rights, maybe, but it will be with a pistol, not through some tinhorn judge."

"Now don't be too hasty," the parson cautioned. "I ain't favored well toward shootin'. And I don't think we have a right to be too rough on the judge. We haven't got reason to condemn him . . . not yet, anyhow."

"We haven't!" Even in the twilight Tim could see the blood mounting to Bogey's forehead. "Why, you Bible-shoutin' old buzzard, how else could they find out we made a strike out here if the judge didn't tell 'em? He's the only one that knew, aside from John here, and the young chap . . . and they ain't been outta our sight." He turned to Tim. "Didn't you just a second ago say that Splain and that jumper back thar were out to meet the judge when he came?"

Tim nodded.

"Then that's proof aplenty for me. Nobody in Eldorado needs to be told where Splain stands on the claim jumpers. He's in with 'em like salt in biscuits."

"Maybe, but it still ain't a fit reason to condemn the judge." The parson had set his mind on this, and, when he set his mind, he was hard to change. "Chances are he don't know a thing about Splain's doings. Splain is the marshal here, and the judge would naturally expect him to be honest. The judge would be anxious to co-operate with him."

"Co-operate?" fumed Bogey.

The parson was a little nettled. "Yes, co-operate. And we'll have to co-operate a bit, too, if you want my judgment. We won't get far buckin' law and order. Personally, I'm for law and order one hunnert per cent."

John said: "You say you know the marshal is in with the jumpers . . . why don't you do somethin' about him?"

"What can we do?" wailed the parson. "We're just common miners."

"What can you do? Shoot him." John tried to reason with

the old man. "Shoot him and you've settled the question permanent. And if you suspect the judge, why shoot him, too. Then if he's in the same pot with the jumpers, or if he ain't, it don't make no never mind. You got him, either way."

The parson waved a bony finger under Comanche John's nose, his long, gray hair escaping from his hat and waving wildly when he shook his head for emphasis. "No matter where I run onto you, it's the same . . . violence, violence, violence! It ain't accordin' to the Good Book. You'll come to destruction by it, mark my words. Them which live by the sword shall die by the sword, that's how it was writ in the days of Solomon. . . ."

John chuckled and aimed a stream of tobacco juice at a shadowy pine trunk. "You're barkin' up the wrong tree, Parson. I ain't ever owned a sword in my life."

"Anyhow, thar won't be killin' on this claim while I have a say."

John pointed back up the trail. "How about that bucko up yonder? You goin' to make me take my bullets back and bring him to life again?"

"That was necessary," the parson conceded. "What I meant was there should be no *unnecessary* killin's."

John slapped the pommel of his saddle and roared. "Then we see eye to eye. Keep talking thataway and you'll have a convert out of me."

In the heat of the dispute they failed to detect the sounds of riders approaching from the direction of Eldorado. Suddenly there they were only a few yards away. Instantly all except the parson drew pistols.

"Who's thar?" demanded Bogey.

The riders came to a halt. They were shadowy forms off in the near darkness. Tim counted six of them, and then he spied two more at a greater distance.

"What was that shooting?"

The sound of the voice, sharp and ringing, was like a knife blade thrust in Tim's middle—the shock of recognition made him jump—Marshal Splain!

At sound of Splain's voice, the claim jumpers came down the trail from their hiding places. There were three of them. The one in the lead spoke up.

"These four men murdered Jack Donlin. Now they're tryin' to jump our claim."

"That's a lie!" Bogey's voice lashed back. "We been on this yere ground for more'n a month. I can show anybody a month's work in prospect holes. It took time to build that dam up the gulch yonder where we aimed to store water for the dry end of the season. I can prove to any miner's court that we been workin' the ground. Besides, we recorded the claim with Judge Mayand just this afternoon." He rode closer to Splain. "But what good does it do to tell *you?* This is your own gang. Everybody in Eldorado knows you're in with the jumpers."

Tim could sense the contraction of Splain's muscles. His palms rested on his gun butts. His companions became very quiet. Comanche John tried to edge a little farther into the shadow. The night silence seemed to ring. It was a tense, breathless moment.

The parson spoke out with a reasoning tone: "Hold on now, Bogey. You ain't got proof of what you're sayin'. I say, stick to law and order and you'll always be further ahead in the long run."

The parson's words snapped the tension. Everyone breathed easier. Splain sat back a little in his saddle. It occurred to Tim that the parson's words saved some of their lives—maybe *all* their lives, for they were outnumbered three to one.

Splain said: "If this is your claim, as you say it is, and, if it has been properly recorded with the judge, my deputies and I will run these fellows off. I promise that. All we need do is look at the judge's record. If it's there in your name, that settles it."

"That's fair enough," said the parson.

Bogey glanced at Tim and Comanche John. "What do you think?"

"Right honorable," John said piously.

This was the smart way, Tim knew. The odds were too heavily against them. Best to play along and act innocent. "I think Splain's suggestion is fair enough," he said.

Bogey gave in. "All right, I'm willin' to see just how much this law and order amounts to. If the judge is on the level, we'll prove it quick enough who the ground belongs to." He pointed at the three jumpers. "But make them fellows come along, too."

"We'll stay with the claim," one of them growled. "It's ours, staked and legal. 'Tain't our duty to prove our right. That's up to you. We're not givin' up possession till the judge says we have to."

Tim spoke to Bogey on the side: "Take it easy. Act like we're playing along. They have the drop on us."

Bogey nodded. He could see it, now that he got his wits about him.

One of the jumpers led out his horse and mounted. He was going along to present their side to the judge.

"Let's get moving," Splain said in his sharp, commanding voice.

They had covered almost a mile before Tim noticed that Comanche John was not with them.

"Where's John?" he asked the parson.

He shrugged. "Fetched if I know. Up to some deviltry, I suppose."

★ ★ ★ ★ ★

Eldorado looked larger by night than day. Its lights twinkled across wide benches and along the river front. Saloons, gambling houses, and dance halls blazed from the flames of oil lamps and grease-dips, and the placer mines worked on by the ruddy flares of pitch torches.

They turned down the crooked main street. The whine of concertinas, scrape of fiddles, and the wail of a lone clarinet mingled discordantly in the clear mountain air. The street was the same welter of mules and lurching wagons it had been that afternoon.

They threaded their way slowly until a side street led them to a rocky knoll on which set a new log house.

"The judge's mansion," growled Bogey.

Tim wondered, nervously, whether Della Mayand would be there. He couldn't prevent a little thrill of expectation. He should dislike the girl, knowing what he thought he knew about her uncle, but he didn't.

Splain leaped lightly from his horse and strode to the door. His boots gleamed in the light of Eldorado's lamps and torches. He rapped sharply, waited. In a few seconds the door opened. Tim expected it to be Della, or the judge, but it was a Chinese servant. Splain went inside first, then he reappeared.

"All right, the judge will see you now," he said sharply.

The Chinese servant led the way down a short hall. He opened a door. All the other doors Tim had seen in Eldorado were homemade affairs, but this one must have been brought in from Salt Lake City. It was walnut with lots of carved leaves and flowers—the camp had certainly gone first class in providing for its new judge and recorder. Tim wondered if he deserved it.

The interior was bright with the flames of three reflector lamps. There sat the judge, tall, white-haired, dignified, behind a table. He nodded coolly to each man as he entered, but he started a little when his eyes fell on Tim.

"Well," he said with a quick, suspicious glance, "so we meet again." He extended his graceful hand. "I'm glad the circumstances are more pleasant." Then his eyes roved from one grim face to the next. "Or are they?"

Bogey spoke up. "Judge, don't you recognize me? I was your first customer."

The question seemed to have an unnerving effect on the judge. His thin lips tightened, and his long fingers fumbled with a quill pen. He glanced at Splain, then back at Bogey.

"Sure," he finally said. "Sure, I remember you. Sorry. This poor light. . . . You registered a mining claim." His laugh was colorless. "I've registered so many this evening."

Bogey went on. "Well, right after you recorded ours, we rode out and found a pack of claim jumpers sittin' on it. I want you to fetch out that big book of yourn and show who's the real owner."

The judge opened a large book on his desk. Tim noticed that his hand trembled a little when he turned the leaves. He paused to scrutinize a page, then leafed on. Finding the page he sought, he polished the glasses that hung on a silk ribbon and placed them on the bridge of his nose.

"The Golden Leaf placer claim," he read. He paused, glanced quickly at Splain. Splain was inscrutable. "Is that it?"

"That's her!" answered Bogey.

The judge read on. "Its southern boundary one hundred paces from the mouth of Red Rock Gulch. . . ."

"Hold on. Look again, that reads one *thousand* paces."

"No. One hundred paces." The judge became more nervous than ever. "You can see it written right here. And there's your name signed right below."

"I never signed that paper. I signed one that read one

thousand paces." Bogey turned away form the judge to face Splain. "So that's your game. It's just as I said. You think you can bring this high-grader of a judge in and get all the best diggings in the palm of your hand. . . ."

One of the silver-mounted guns flashed from Splain's holster. "You keep a civil tongue in your head, miner. I don't have to take insults. One more from you and you're a dead man."

"Splain," the judge remonstrated weakly.

The marshal paid no heed to the judge. He faced Bogey for a second or two, then he motioned toward the door with the gun barrel. "Get going, all of you. I think we've settled who the claim belongs to."

Bogey started to say more, but Tim pulled him out the door. Halfway down the hall he turned his head and shouted. "All right, Splain. You win this turn. But we'll meet sometime when you ain't got the drop."

The marshal laughed and thrust his pistol back in its holster.

"That's what your law and order amounts to," fumed Bogey. "Why, the belly-crawlin'. . . ." He stopped abruptly. " 'Scuse me, miss," he mumbled.

Della was standing there, facing them. She had just stepped from a door that evidently led to the living quarters. Tim fumbled with his hat.

She favored him with her best smile. "How do you do? I didn't think we'd meet again so soon."

"We came to see the judge."

"Oh, business again. It's been a steady stream of it ever since we got here. Miners, I guess, and all of them with claims to record."

Bogey growled on his way out. "They'll be here with a rope one of these days if he don't change his system."

This statement shocked the words out of her for a few seconds. "What does he mean?" she finally asked.

Tim was certain now that Della knew nothing about her uncle's shady activities. Further, he was certain that the judge was only a tool in Splain's hands. He had no good reason for believing this—he just did. He tried to pass off Bogey's words lightly. "Just his way of joking, I guess."

"I don't think it was very funny."

Tim wanted to hurry after his friends, but he wanted to stay here and talk to Della, too. It wasn't just because she was young and beautiful, although he found nothing objectionable in these qualities; it was because through conversation he might get some line on the judge's previous scene of activities. Past histories followed men and tripped them up, even on the frontier. "Did you come up from California?"

"I did. I met my uncle in Bannack."

"I thought he was from California, too."

"He is, originally. He hasn't been there for the past year."

"Oh, he's been in Bannack since."

"No. Some place over in Oregon, I think. I'm not sure what the name of that town is. He told me, but I've forgotten."

The door to the office opened and Splain stepped out. His eyes narrowed when he glimpsed Tim talking to Della. He nodded to Tim, then gave Della a flashing smile.

"Ready to go?"

Della hesitated and glanced at Tim. Then she made haste to explain. "The marshal has offered to drive uncle and me around the placer mines. I understand they're quite beautiful at night." Turning to Splain: "Perhaps your carriage has room for one more passenger."

Splain bowed to Tim with every appearance of cordiality. "I'd be pleased to have you, Mister Conners."

Resolving not to be outdone, Tim answered with a bow that was even deeper than the marshal's. "I'm honored," he said, "but my friends are waiting for me. Thank you just the same." Then, hardly realizing what he was going to say, he turned to Della: "Perhaps you would ride with me tomorrow night."

He shouldn't have asked her. Certainly she'd refuse. But to his amazement she smiled with genuine pleasure.

"I'd like to!"

He felt a trifle dizzy when he left the house. Down below he could make out the parson and Bogey, mounted and waiting. He seemed to float more than walk down the rocky pathway.

III

Eldorado had only one real street. Branching from this were numerous crooked roadways that wound around through its vast skelter of cabins, tents, and wickiups. In leaving the judge's mansion, the three men chose one of these wandering roads that approximately paralleled the main street and so took them to the edge of the camp and the road leading up Red Rock Gulch. The parson pulled up there and turned to Bogey: "What do you aim to do?" he asked.

"Aim? I aim to get our claim back."

The parson was thoughtful. "You don't suppose it would do us any good to appeal to the gov'nor."

Bogey snorted. "While we was foolin' around between here and Virginia City, the jumpers would sluice out all the best gravel. Then we could have the claim and welcome. No, sir! No more lawin' for me. I'm goin' out thar and shoot them buzzards out. If you fellows are with me, come along. If not, I reckon I'll have to tackle the job alone."

"I'm with you," said Tim.

"I ain't even got a gun," the parson wailed, "and I wouldn't know how to use it if I did. But I'm with you. I ain't no quitter."

They soon left the camp behind. The last of Eldorado's lights blinked out around a turn in the gulch they followed.

The moon had not yet risen above the steep hills, and it was quite dark. Nobody spoke. The only sounds were the clatter of hoofs on the rocky trail and the regular *squeak-squeak* of saddle leather. They made the turn in the direction of the claim. Here the overhanging pines and Douglas spruce made it darker than ever. The horses moved at a slow walk.

A hand grasped Tim's bridle. It was Bogey. Although he was not a yard away, it was so dark there among the trees that Tim could barely make out the outline of his face. Bogey's arm was pointing. Up ahead was a dim-glowing rectangle of light—an oiled paper window. "They must be inside." Tim could hear Bogey dismount. "Or maybe they ain't. Let's go on afoot."

Bogey struck out among the trees, Tim and the parson following closely behind. They seemed to be on a narrow, climbing deer trail. Bogey had to know the country well in order to follow a trail like this—either that, or he had eyes like a night-prowling cougar. A soft coating of pine needles carpeted the rocks. They made no more sound than one walking on a featherbed. The night was clear and sharp, but to Tim it had become oppressive. Sweat streaked down from under his sombrero.

It seemed that they were going aimlessly. They must be far behind the cabin by this time. The window was no longer in sight—hadn't been for a long time. Surely they'd covered at least a mile. He stumbled into Bogey.

Bogey took his shoulder and turned him a quarter of the way around. "The cabin's right down yonder," he whispered.

Tim looked. Slowly the outline of a roof and chimney emerged from the blackness.

Bogey went on: "You sneak down. They ain't a trail, so be careful. You wait by that northwest corner. I'll move around and have a look-see through an open chink I know about.

Chances are they ain't both inside, so walk quiet. I'll hunt you up when I see how she lays." And a final admonition: "Keep your pistol handy."

"How about me?" asked the parson.

"You stay back here and do the prayin'," Bogey growled. "Chances are we'll be needin' it."

Tim started slowly down the sharp decline. The trees grew close. Dead branches reached out to snag his clothes. He bent the branches gently while he moved along. One of them snapped. In the tense silence it seemed as loud as a pistol shot. He stopped, silent. He scarcely breathed. The only sound was the steady rush of blood through his ears—no sound of the jumpers, no sound of Bogey, or of anyone. He crept on. Several times his hand went reassuringly to the butt of his long-barreled Navy six.

Suddenly he was against the rear of the cabin. The un-peeled log wall was rough against his palms as he felt along to the northwest corner. He waited. A few little sounds came from inside—a tiny thump, a voice mumbling. It seemed like ten minutes must have passed with him standing there, but more likely it was only two or three.

Someone stepped among some dead twigs no more than a dozen feet away. Tim clung to the wall, tense, pistol ready. It was a dim, crouching form. Tim almost jumped from his clothes when the man spoke. It took him a second or two to realize it was Bogey.

"Waal, I'll be fetched." He chuckled.

Bogey was on hands and knees looking through a crack where the mud chinking had dropped from between the logs. He moved over to make way for Tim.

Tim looked. Two men sat at the corner of a table playing cards. The red flame of a grease dip lit their faces—Comanche John and Henry the Chinaman.

216

Tim's shoulder bumped a log. Instantly John was on his feet. His pistol seemed to leap up to meet his hands.

"It's only us," Tim assured him.

John thrust back the pistols and roared out: "Waal, come on in! Don't stay out thar in the cold. My heathen friend's got a pan of biscuits on the fire, and we was just waitin' for the parson to say grace before we et 'em."

At sound of the voices, the parson came crashing down through the trees.

"What kept you so long?" John wanted to know when they were all inside.

"Legal matters," Bogey answered.

"The judge was a whizzer, wasn't he? Waal, I figured it all along. But I'm glad you satisfied yourselves. Now we know right whar we stand. Everything fair, square, on the table top, and the quickest pistol wins the pot . . . that's the way she ought to be."

The parson thought of something. He fastened Comanche John with his ancient, gimlet eyes. "Whar's them men which was here?"

John looked surprised. "Which men?"

"You know which men."

John shook his head. "Ain't been no men here recent. In fact, it's been well onto hours." He fumbled at a massive gold chain that dangled from the pocket of his homespuns, and pulled out a watch of green and yellow gold. A diamond, ruby, and emerald set in the back glittered in the lamp flame. John scrutinized the face of the watch. "Yep! Well onto hours." Then in an attempt to change the subject: "Did you boys see my watch? This is an extra fine timepiece. You wind her at this end, and she ticks in the middle. The man I . . . er . . . *bought* this watch from tried to tell me it was a hair loom." He snorted. "As if I didn't know a *watch* when I seen one!"

217

"Don't try to change the subject. What happened to them men?"

"You mean the claim jumpers?" John scratched his thick whiskers. "Waal, now! We held a little term o' court up yere, and, after I read 'em two sections of my own personal statchoots, they up and vamoosed. Yes, sir, vamoosed." John accurately aimed a shot of tobacco juice at the glowing wood coals an inch or two below the pan of biscuits that Henry had browning in the stone fireplace. "Vamoosed permanent," he added.

Nobody spoke for a second. The tobacco juice hissed itself out among the yellow coals. Unexpectedly Henry the Chinaman shook his queue and uttered a high-pitched laugh. "Sure. John shoot bang! bang! Like toblacco juice dead clenter alla time." He ran a rueful hand over his pocket. "Play good euchre, too."

Pay dirt at the Golden Leaf lay in the narrow gulch bottom. The width of the gravel was seldom more than four or five yards, and, as with most placers, the surface was almost barren—the heavy gold, through the course of centuries, having settled to bedrock. Aside from a sprinkling of prospect holes, the chief piece of development on the claim consisted of a high log dam that had been built up the gulch a hundred yards for the purpose of storing water for late summer and fall. Because of heavier-than-usual rains, the reservoir had quickly filled, forming a small but deep pond.

In the morning Comanche John, armed with his Jager rifle and two Navies, climbed to a high rock that overlooked the gulch, there to keep watch while the others fell to work constructing a sluice. The day passed without incident.

"Maybe they learnt their lesson," the parson said hopefully.

But Bogey was doubtful. "Not them. That Splain fellow is plumb determined. Chances are they're just waitin' for us to build the sluice so we'll save them the work."

"By Henry's! I hope they do come back," John said, filling his mouth to capacity with biscuit and stewed venison. "It gets long tiresome atop that rock with no excitement."

Tim ate in silence. He was thinking about the appointment he had made to take Della Mayand driving. He had no rig, of course, and his casual questioning of Bogey and the parson during the afternoon revealed that there was only one in camp—the one belonging to Marshal Splain. So there was but one way for it—he'd have to lead in a horse and take her riding instead. Provided, of course, she'd go with him.

It was dark by the time he'd completed the trip through Eldorado and was at the foot of the knoll where the judge's house stood. He tied his horses and climbed the path. The Chinese servant opened the door.

He asked for Miss Mayand. The Chinese led him to a sitting room.

"Have chair, please," the Oriental said. He padded out on his soft shoes.

Tim waited uncomfortably. He wondered what kind of a reception he would receive. Who knew what yarn the judge or Splain had given her?

He could hear something like the swish of a woman's gown. A door opened, and there she was, looking at him.

She smiled: "Good evening, Mister Conners."

Tim was a trifle embarrassed. He wasn't exactly sure why. He noticed she wore a floor-length gown of some silky material. It wasn't the sort of dress women wore for horseback riding. He confessed: "I couldn't find a rig. But I brought a horse, and a livery man over in camp lent me a sidesaddle."

She didn't act as though she heard what he said. She just

stood there, looking at him. Tim had forgotten how beautiful she was, and her honest, straightforward expression—how could such a girl have an uncle like the judge?

"I understand you and your partners have been threatening violence as a result of a decision my uncle made about your claim." She seemed to be requesting a denial.

Tim shifted uneasily to the other foot. Threatening violence! It had gone much further than threats. Didn't she know what had happened to the three claim jumpers? But maybe Splain had not seen fit to tell her. "There were some words," he conceded.

"I would hardly expect you to defy my uncle and then have the audacity to expect to take me riding. Still, I suppose I shouldn't be surprised after the way you acted yesterday."

But he could tell that she wasn't really angry. She looked hurt more than anything, and her eyes asked for a denial.

"I'm sorry," he said. "Maybe there was some misunderstanding. Maybe your uncle wasn't aware of all the facts. You see, two of my partners . . . Bogey and the parson . . . located the ground. They discovered it. They developed it according to law. Now the judge wants them to get off and turn it over to some claim jumpers."

Her eyes blazed: "You mean to imply that my uncle is dishonest."

"My partners think he is," he answered with simple directness. "Personally I believe in law . . . as long as the law means justice."

"You mean by that you're determined to fight it out."

"That's about it."

"You're making it very difficult for my uncle. You say you believe in law. If you really do, you'll settle the dispute by legal means."

"What do you want me to do?"

"The judge wants to be fair. He's willing to review the case tomorrow. If you'll bring your partners to the office. . . ."

"All of them?"

"Why, yes."

The request came as a jolt. He could see the reason behind it. While the case was being reviewed, the jumpers could take the ground without opposition. He studied Della's face. Was she in with them? He was no longer certain. "Did the judge know I was calling on you tonight?"

She shot him a startled glance. "Yes."

"And he told you to ask me that?"

"What difference does it make? Why shouldn't he?" It was her turn to be nervous. She twisted her fragile lace handkerchief into a tiny ball.

"I'm sorry. We haven't any new proof to offer. A review of the case would only be a waste of time."

"Uncle suggested a compromise."

"I'm afraid not."

"Then you refuse?"

He nodded.

"Very well. It was only for your own good. It doesn't really make any difference to me."

Her tone made it evident that their meeting was at an end. He inclined his head with all the polite gravity he could command. "I'm sorry."

"I'm sorry, too."

When Tim left the living room, he glanced down the hall toward the judge's office. The door was open an inch or two, and he imagined he could see the shadow of a man who stood there, watching.

During the next days, Tim worked hard at the claim. He swung pick and hammer willingly through long hours trying to drive the girl from his mind. Over and over he told himself that she knew quite well what her uncle was doing. But she haunted him. All day, as he worked, her words would keep running over his mind. And at night, when he took his turn as watchman, he could think of little else.

One day, while they were lining the log frame of the sluice with a quantity of sawed lumber from Eldorado's new mill, they heard John shout. "Ho! Down thar."

This was something unusual. When anyone came suspiciously close, it was John's custom to let whang with his Jager, fanning a bullet near enough to the trespasser's nose to inform him of his mistake. Always, up to now, one bullet was sufficient. Hence the three at work on the sluice were surprised at this change in John's tactics.

They listened. The *clip-clop* of a horse could be heard down the trail. A few seconds later a girl rode in sight. With a shock Tim realized it was Della.

She seemed to be embarrassed and had a hard time meeting his gaze. "I'm really sorry for the way I treated you the other night," was the first thing she said. "I guess you thought I was trying to lure you away from your claim. I wasn't. Not intentionally. I only wanted to do the right thing."

"That's all right." Tim forgave her with all his heart. "I guess I said a little more than I intended."

She was anxious to get on another subject. "I'd be glad to go for that ride this afternoon."

While he was catching a saddle horse, Bogey spoke to him on the quiet. "You goin' ridin' with that gal?"

"Sure."

"It's you for it," he said, "but she has the judge's business up her sleeve." He considered for a while. "Reckon maybe it would be a good idea to go ridin' with her at that. Might get a line on their plans. But take my warning . . . don't go in the direction she wants. *You* pick the trail."

The suggestion that she might lead him into an ambush at first seemed ridiculous. But, once mentioned, it stuck. They rode to the lower boundary of the claim before either spoke.

He was relieved when she turned and said: "You lead the way. I can't tell one direction from another in these mountains."

They rode far back among the hills to a high divide from which great, unexplored areas of timbered country were visible. Neither had much to say. Della seemed to be thoughtful, troubled. Something was bothering her. Several times she seemed to be on the point of saying something, of asking some question, but each time she changed her mind.

It was evening when they rode back to Eldorado. He bid her good night at the front step of the judge's house.

Splain caused no more trouble. The parson insisted that the jumpers had given up the Golden Leaf as a lost proposition. But Bogey and Comanche John were suspicious.

"Wait till we turn the water in the sluice. That's when they'll ride in on us," Bogey warned.

Soon the water was turned in, and the first wheelbarrow of gravel went rolling through. Comanche John sat on his pinnacle, keeping closer watch than ever. But nothing unforeseen occurred. That evening they removed the riffles and took out several bucketsful of black sand, garnet, and gold. Bogey panned this concentrate. The resulting heap of coarse gold and nuggets exceeded their most optimistic anticipations. The yellow light from the grease dip glittered on the heap of it, and on the eyes of its beholders.

"This beats preachin', don't it, Parson?" Comanche John asked, rubbing his palms.

The parson was inclined to agree.

Bogey gloated: "Three hundred feet of gulch like that and we'll be able to tour Chiney in our own carriage. Just keep them jumpers off for a month more, that's all I ask. We'll skin the cream by then, and they're welcome to the leavin's."

But later that evening, after the gold had been swept into a buckskin bag and secreted beneath a loose stone of the fireplace, Bogey became thoughtful. He seemed to be listening for some sound outside. Although the parson was standing guard, he blew out the light and went to the door to listen.

"He's gettin' a mite spooky." John winked at Tim.

In the morning, Bogey rolled out several kegs of blasting powder. He explained: "I wouldn't be surprised if the marshal and that judge would try some of their tricks now that we've started to take out the metal. But I got an idee that will cut 'em short if they put us in a tight spot." He pointed up the gulch toward the high log dam. "Thar's a respectable lake a-hind that dam. If she was to come down all at once, it would wash away sluice, jumpers, and all. Then I don't reckon they could work our gravel until the crick rose next spring. Let's load her with powder."

They placed the charge beneath one of the key logs of the dam and primed it with a quarter-inch fuse. When it was done, they resumed sluicing with more confidence. They arranged a signal. In case of trouble, one of them was to station himself by the fuse and touch it off on receiving a signal from the others.

Several days passed in smooth succession. They worked at the sluice from dawn until dark. The pay streak was narrow but extremely rich, and each night they cleaned up and panned the concentrate. One small buckskin bag after another became heavy with yellow metal and was stored under the hearth's loose stone.

One afternoon they sent Henry the Chinaman to Eldorado for provisions. At sundown he came home in a great hurry. They watched his approach with alarm. Out of breath, he dropped his bag of groceries by the head box and handed a note to the parson.

"For *me?*" asked the parson incredulously. He looked at the folded paper with suspicion and at a distance. It was the edge torn from a page of the *Eldorado Nugget*. A message was scrawled on it, evidently with a pistol ball.

"Who sent it?" the parson wanted to know.

"Man I don't know. Man yell, say . . . 'Here, Chinaboy, take this note all same pleacher man.'"

The parson unfolded the long strip of paper and spelled out the badly scrawled words: **If you're troubled with legal claim jumping let the sheriff of Rocky Gulch know that Robins and the lawyer are here.**

That was all. No name signed. They pondered the note for quite a while. Henry the Chinaman had never seen the man before. The man had just handed him the note and walked on. No doubt he wanted to avoid getting in trouble with Splain's gang. A person couldn't blame him for that.

To Tim, this accounted for the year's lapse between the judge's California career and his arrival in Montana Territory. He and Splain had been up to something shady at the camp of Rocky Gulch, over in Oregon, and no doubt they had left just a jump ahead of the sheriff. Robins, that must be Splain, and the lawyer was Judge Mayand. But, refreshing though the information was, Tim doubted that the sheriff of Rocky Gulch would travel this far.

"We'll write him a letter," said the parson. "We got Pony Express now. That's mighty quick."

Bogey snorted. "Write a letter for some Pony Express

225

rider to cook his coffee over? No, sir. One of us better go over thar in person."

Rocky Gulch, however, was a six-day stage trip—south to Fort Hall, around the loop of the Snake River, and then north.

"I never put much stock in sheriffs," Comanche John grumbled. "But if we have to send somebody, let it be Henry the Chinaman. He don't do much shootin'. We're likely to need all the guns we got right here on the ground."

That night the parson composed a letter with descriptions of the judge and the marshal. He sealed it, addressed it, and deposited it in Henry's waiting hand together with a generous poke of dust. The Chinaman left on the early morning stage.

Days passed. Tim went riding again with Della Mayand. It was evening, and they sat for a long time on a hillside overlooking Eldorado while the pitch torches flared to life near and far across the vast sweep of bars, benches, and terraces, until, in the settling darkness, it seemed almost the equal of the firmament overhead.

Neither of them had spoken for many minutes. Then Tim asked: "Did your uncle live in a camp called Rocky Gulch?" Sometimes questions slip out when a man doesn't intend them to.

She seemed to catch her breath. She didn't look at him; she kept staring out across the wide spread of lights. At the foot of the hill a torch lit the side of her face and at her throat a tiny scrap of lace. He could see the lace move rapidly, regularly from her quickened pulse. The lace gave him all the answer he needed.

"Why do you ask?" She found her voice, but it trembled a little.

He acted casual. "Oh, nothing. Wondered how the color

lay there. I thought he said something about Rocky Gulch that first day we met."

It was the following afternoon that things really started to happen. Tim, Bogey, and the parson were sweating in the white-hot mountain sun, when suddenly the air was ripped by the concussion of a rifle. A little haze of gunsmoke drifted above the junipers where Comanche John sat. A few seconds later John fired again. Like an echo, a gun answered from down the gulch.

The three men hurtled from the diggings, grabbed their guns. Even the parson was going armed these days. They listened. Hoofs clattered rocks, became distant, died away.

A minute later Comanche John stalked down from his rocks. "Them was the marshal's boys, I reckon. They was fixin' to nail some paper to a tree when I stirred 'em up. I 'spect it's one of the judge's legal card tricks." He chewed rapidly for a few seconds and aimed a shot of tobacco at a fragment of white quartz—and missed. "See thar? This minin's gettin' me jumpy. Settin' around waitin' for t'other fellow to move ain't my style o' coat. Person'ly I'd like to ride down, knock off the marshal and the judge, and be done."

"And get Kentucky Smith and his vigilance committee after us, I suppose." The parson glared.

After suitably expressing his contempt for Kentucky Smith and all others of similar ilk, John climbed back to his post. A few minutes later, gravel was once more rolling over the pole riffles, but the men worked apprehensively, frequently pausing to look over the nearby mountainsides.

In the evening, Tim said: "Seems to me we're getting a little too much gold here for comfort. If the claim doesn't lure the jumpers, the gold is likely to bring us some road agents. What do you say we take it to camp, sort of on the quiet, and place it with the express company for shipment?"

So they removed the stone from the hearth and took out their hoard of gold—twelve small, but amazingly heavy, buckskin sacks. It was a small fortune. They placed it in saddlebags, and Bogey and Tim set out for Eldorado.

The camp was growing. Main Street stretched a third again as far as on Tim's first visit. They guided their horses in and out to avoid the usual conglomeration of jerkline ox and mule outfits with profane drivers. The same fiddles fiddled, and the same concertinas wailed from door after door as they passed.

The express office was at the far end of the street. They rode up and glanced in, but the Last Chance coach had just rolled up and was disgorging its passengers. Without dismounting, Tim and Bogey rode on up the street. They returned ten minutes later. A couple of men were inside talking to the express agent. In a few minutes the men left. The agent, a grayish little man with bushy eyebrows, opened his ledger and began making entries in it with a long quill pen.

Neither Tim nor Bogey noticed the man who stood in the shadow between two buildings and watched them as they dismounted, unfastened their heavy saddlebags, and went inside.

The agent glanced up, nodded automatically, and returned to his writing. The delicate point of his quill pen hissed softly.

"We have some gold for shipment," Tim said.

The agent lifted his bushy eyebrows a trifle when he glimpsed the heavy bags. But shipments, even large amounts such as this, were too common in Eldorado to cause him much surprise. He carefully wiped the quill on a scrap of flannel. "Bring it to the back room, boys, and we'll weigh it up."

At the moment they were following the agent to the back room, the man who had been observing them emerged from the shadow of the two buildings and started at a swift pace in the direction of the judge's house.

It took about five minutes to weigh the dust. The agent placed it in company containers and started filling out a form. He explained: "We have to keep track of all shipments . . . two ounces or a million. Company rules. Your names?"

They told him.

"Name of the claim?"

"The Golden Leaf."

"Location?"

Before they could answer, the door of the room was flung open. There stood Marshal Splain, both guns drawn. Behind him were three of his deputies.

"We meet again." Splain's voice was crisp. He inclined his head a fraction of an inch and smiled in a way that showed he was well satisfied with himself. He indicated the gold with the muzzle of his right-hand gun. "I take it that gold is from the Golden Leaf."

No one answered.

"Is it from the Golden Leaf?" Splain asked the agent.

"Yes."

"Well! That must be a rich claim. No wonder it's in litigation."

"Litigation!" exclaimed the agent.

Tim knew there was no use arguing. Splain was the law, and he had the drop. But Bogey had less control over his temper.

"What is this, a robbery?"

The marshal seemed to be hurt by the word. "Robbery? Certainly not! My men and I are here merely to enforce a court order."

Tim asked: "You're here to take the gold?"

"I'm here on orders of Judge Mayand to attach this shipment of gold."

"You're going to take it with you?"

Splain hesitated. Perhaps he hadn't decided just what he was going to do with the gold. "You have it ready for shipment?" he asked the agent.

"Yes."

"Very well. We'll ship it, but ship it under the name of Judge Mayand. The credit will be held until his office decides on the title of the claim. Then it will be turned over to the rightful owners. The decision of the court will be available in a. . . ."

"Decision of the court!" Bogey fumed derisively. "You and your fixed judge. But you won't get away with it forever. We'll go to Kentucky Smith and his vigilantes. . . ."

"Go ahead." Splain smiled.

Watching Splain's face, Tim added quietly: "Maybe the vigilantes from Rocky Gulch."

The stab struck Splain in a vital spot. He winced, then controlled himself. "What do you mean by that?" he asked in a voice so even it was colorless.

Bogey had noted with satisfaction the effect of Tim's remark about Rocky Gulch. "You bet," he bluffed, "We know aplenty about you and your judge. . . ."

Splain leaped forward like a spring had released him. He rammed the muzzle of one pistol like a fighter driving his fist. Struck in the stomach, Bogey doubled and almost went down. He gasped for breath.

Splain's words came like the snarl of a vicious animal. "Keep that mouth shut or you're a dead man."

He meant it. Tim knew he meant it. Another word and the man would kill, express agent or not. Tim grabbed Bogey by the arm and pulled him to the door. The older man pulled back, still gasping for breath, but Tim took him anyway.

All the way out, Splain's eyes were on them, hard as knife steel.

"Robbed! Robbed at the point of a gun in the name of the law!" In his wrath, Bogey waved his head so violently that his long gray hair escaped from under his hat and fell in tangled wisps to his shoulders. "I'm goin' to look up Kentucky Smith. If his vigilance committee amounts to a hoot, he'll do somethin' about these robbers."

IV

Kentucky Smith was a giant. He was deep-chested, black-whiskered, with a broad head whose conformation made him in some respects resemble a buffalo. On his belt was an old-time double-barreled pistol that went well with his size. Stories had been told that Kentucky could split a two-inch pine plank with a blow of his fist, and that he had lifted the entire rear ends of freight wagons from the chuck holes of Eldorado's streets. Tim didn't doubt the stories once he laid his eyes on the man.

Kentucky seemed to overcrowd the little, low room of his cabin, while he stood there, listening to what Bogey had to say. He was calm until Bogey expressed doubt of Judge Mayand's integrity.

"The judge is no crook!" Kentucky bellowed, thrusting out his black whiskers aggressively. "I won't stand by and hear the judge called a claim jumper. He's honest as a Baptist bishop. He was sent over here by the gov'nor, and anybody the gov'nor sends is aces on the table with me."

Tim cut in: "Then you really *know* the judge?"

"Sure, I know him."

"For how long?"

"Ever since he came."

"But nothing about him before?"

"I'd heered about him. He was well-known down in Californy. Frisco."

"Where was he last year?"

"I don't know what you're getting at," Kentucky said suspiciously.

"I just wondered if he ever mentioned being at Rocky Gulch over in Oregon."

"If he was, or if he wasn't, I don't see what it mounts up to."

Tim wasn't sure what it mounted up to either. But he didn't give hint of that in his manner. He acted like he knew a great deal. He saw with satisfaction that a doubt had been placed in Kentucky's mind.

Tim went on: "Maybe when you know about Rocky Gulch, you won't like your judge and marshal quite so much." He plucked Bogey's sleeve. "We'd better get back to the mine and tell the boys what's up."

"Hold on!" Kentucky had come down considerably. "Tell me about this Rocky Gulch."

Tim only smiled. "I don't expect you'd believe that any quicker than you did the story about our claim being jumped."

They left him standing there in the middle of the room wearing an expression like a baffled buffalo's.

When they were beyond earshot, Tim remarked: "If he gets curious enough, maybe he'll dig out something. And if he does, I have an idea you could comb the territory and not find enough men to stop him."

Comanche John was surprisingly calm when he heard about the gold. Not so the parson. He reared up and did everything but curse the marshal, the judge, Eldorado's vigilance committee, and he even went so far as to drop in an insinuation adverse to law and order in general.

When finally the parson ran down, John hee-hawed and whacked his leg. "By jingoes, it's worth losin' the color just to hear the parson cut loose. Next thing he'll be packin' hisself a Navy and actin' plumb human."

"I don't believe in violence in principle," the parson cooled off long enough to say. "But there are times. . . ."

"Yep, there's times," John agreed. "Tim, what time did you say that shipment was to go?"

"It was billed for the three a.m. coach."

John ostentatiously pulled out his watch and held it, dangling on its chain, at arm's length. Its jewels glittered as it swung from side to side. He asked: "What time is she when the short arm's straight up and the long one's nor'-nor'-east?"

"Five after twelve."

John grunted satisfaction. Then he heisted his feet off the table, stretched himself, and started out on a minute inspection of his two Navy pistols. The load in one cylinder failed to please him, so he dug out ball, wad, and powder and inserted a fresh charge. He dropped the pistols in their holsters, placed his sawed-off shotgun in the crook of his arm, paused by the door. "Reckon I'll drop in and see what's doin' down in camp. I'll be back in time for biscuits tomorrow mornin'."

Bogey hopped up and started to buckle on his gun belts. "Hold on. If you're figgerin' on gettin' the marshal and judge, I'm comin' along. I'll do my share of the fightin'. . . ."

John waved him back. "Nope. Reckon I been lone-wolfin' it too long to change my habits. You boys would only get in my way."

When Tim opened his eyes next morning, the first thing he saw were several leather containers that had been dumped onto the table. On the one nearest him, he could see the express company's brand. Balanced atop the heap was a sawed-off shotgun. He rubbed the sleep from his eyes and noticed that John was sitting there on a stool, shoulders propped against the wall, dusty boots on the edge of the table. His slouch hat was pulled low over his eyes, and he snored regularly.

A board squeaked when Tim moved in his bunk, and John was awake with a start. Seeing who it was, he put back the pistol that a reflex move of his hand had brought from the holster.

"What's that?" Tim asked, nodding to the express containers. He knew quite well what they were.

"This?" John looked at the containers like he had never seen them before. "Oh, *these!* Waal, I'll tell you. I was out last night, sort of ridin' along, enjoyin' the night air, when on a sudden I come to a coach which was mighty heavy loaded. Mighty heavy. In fact, it was so heavy loaded I knew for certain she'd never pull the ford. So, bein' a good Christian, like the parson has made me, I decided to relieve 'em of some extra weight. I debated for a while, then, seein' as gold was the heaviest thing they had aboard, I took that. And you know, I wouldn't be surprised if some of that gold didn't come first off from this Golden Leaf claim of ourn."

Awakened, the parson hopped from his bunk. "*Some* of it!" He hefted the bags. "This is plenty more gold than we had." He stood there like a scarecrow, bony legs protruding from his short, tarlatan nightgown. "You should have took only what belonged to us. This is robbery, and I won't stand. . . ."

"You won't!" John looked offended and took his feet off the table. "Why, Parson, you wouldn't have had me stop with just *our* gold. That would have been selfish."

Bogey, who suffered few of the parson's scruples, slapped his leg gleefully. "Look at her, will ye? Serves 'em right. Attachment! Attachments is somethin' can work both ways, I reckon. And as for getting' a little more'n we started with . . . well, bankers get interest."

John gestured lavishly. "Divide her up, boys. Interest and all."

"I won't touch stolen money!" the parson yelped.

John shrugged with a complacency that even further exasperated the old man. "All right. Every man for his principles, I say, but. . . ."

"But share and share alike is your motto," concluded the parson.

John looked surprised. "Now *there's* a right Christian fee-lo-sophee."

The browned biscuits had just been taken from the oven and the crisp salt pork was still sizzling when a horse clattered on the stones outside.

Comanche John whipped out a pistol. His eyes went shifty and hard. "Hide that gold," he commanded.

Tim buckled on his gun and stepped outside. A horse slid to a stop. The animal blew from exertion. A girl jumped to the ground. It was Della. A flush brightened her cheek bones, but her lips were drawn so tightly they were colorless.

Her first words were: "They're coming for you."

He couldn't move from the surprise of seeing her. He stood there, staring, jaw still thoughtlessly masticating a fragment of salt pork.

"Don't just stand there." Her eyes flamed up. "I tell you they're coming for you . . . all of you. You'll have to get away, quick."

"Who's coming?"

"The marshal, Kentucky Smith, the vigilantes . . . everybody."

So it had finally come to a showdown. But he had figured only on Splain and his gang. It hadn't occurred to him that the vigilantes would come, too. But then he hadn't figured on being warned by Della Mayand, either—and that surprised him most of all. He wondered why she had come. Was it for the reason he hoped—was it because of him, or because of something she'd found out about her uncle? He looked at her thoughtfully.

"You'll have to hurry," her voice rose to plead. "They were ready to start when I left. I had to sneak out the back way, and that took me longer. They can't be five minutes behind."

The others were outside by now. Bogey said: "Don't pay any attention to her. She's in with 'em. It's just a plan to get us off the ground so the jumpers can take over."

"It's not a plan!" Her sudden intensity took Bogey back a little. "And I'm not in with anybody." She stood there for a moment, looking from one to the other, then, with a gesture that indicated her exasperation, she swung back to the saddle. "All right, stay here and be hanged. I've done all I can."

John took her horse's bridle. "Why are they comin'? On account of the claim, or . . . ?"

"That, yes. But the vigilantes have some fool idea about one of you being a coach robber."

"You don't say!" John wore a shocked expression.

"We ain't quittin' the ground," fumed Bogey. "Let 'em come! We'll stand 'em off. This is our claim, and I aim to hold it."

"You're fools . . . all of you." In spite of her words, there was admiration in Della's eyes. "Go while you have the chance. There are twenty of them."

Tim didn't hear her. His ears had picked up the sound of approaching hoofs. He watched the trail narrowly. There was a sinking sensation in the pit of his stomach he could not repress. The parson licked his lips nervously. John dashed inside. A few seconds later he reappeared with two leather containers that he hurled in some thick junipers up the gulch side.

"Then you're not going?" Della's voice was a final plea.

Tim shook his head. "Guess that would be pretty much like admitting we *were* claim jumpers."

"But you haven't a chance. Not the shadow of a chance."

"You mean, not a chance whether we're guilty or not?"

She bit her lip but looked him square in the eye. "That's what I mean. Guilty or not." The horses were approaching. "I have to go," she said. "I can't let them see me here."

She glanced around. The trail seemed to end at the cabin. Only a rocky pathway led on up the gulch toward the log dam. The gulch sides rose steeply on each side. It suddenly occurred to her that she might be trapped. But Tim seized her bridle.

"Up there. It's steep, but you can make it. No trail . . . just keep among the trees." He pointed to the heavy-timbered gulch side in the direction of Eldorado.

She lashed with her quirt. The horse went splashing through the trickle of water in the gulch bottom, dug in frantically to climb the steep bank, and, a moment later, both horse and rider were lost from view among the evergreens.

"The dam!" John shouted. "Somebody get ready to blow the dam!"

Bogey ran from the door with a smoking faggot. He called over his shoulder: "I'm goin' to post myself up thar! If she looks bad, remember the signal. Wave something white overhead three times . . . then look out for the deluge because she'll be a rip-snortin' dandy."

He had scarcely disappeared when three riders came in view down the gulch. They pulled up and sat watching the gulch. Tim thought they were three of Splain's deputies. John, a gun in each hand, dropped behind a boulder. Tim stepped in the door, but the parson remained in full view.

"Get inside, you blamed idjit!" John shouted. "Get inside or they'll snipe you like a sage chicken."

At the same instant, the lead man lifted his rifle from the pommel of his saddle, tossed it up. The parson jumped for the house. A bullet whanged past, scattering stones a rod or two beyond.

John bobbed up briefly, beaded, squeezed the trigger. The gun came to life in his hand. The deputy dropped his rifle and slumped down the side of his horse. His boot twisted, hung in the stirrup. Frightened, his horse bolted, dragging the rider behind.

"One!" John, pleased with himself, crouched back down. "I was a-feared all the minin' I been doin' was gettin' my shootin' eye off or. . . ."

"Throw up your hands!"

They were taken by complete surprise. Kentucky Smith and three others stood there, guns drawn, not ten paces away. They had circled in from behind, approached unseen around the cabin. Evidently the men down the gulch had been intended as decoys.

Tim, the parson, and Comanche John unhesitatingly obeyed the command.

Kentucky Smith was in the lead. He strode up, huge, shaggy-bearded. His large, double-barreled pistol was in his hand, and he kept swinging it back and forth as though he wanted to aim at all of them at once. "Jig's up, boys," he said.

"You've jumped your last coach. This is the day of reckonin'." He glowered at Tim. "You and your smooth talk about Rocky Gulch . . . and that other old goat's talk about claim jumpers. Thought you'd get me off the scent! Waal, here's one coon hound which don't quit his trail for no rabbits." He made a high sweeping gesture with his pistol.

Seven or eight riders came in sight from down the trail. Then some others came crashing down from the hillside. In a minute the ground seemed to swarm with men and horses.

Splain was there, conspicuous, the early sun reflecting from his fine silver trappings. He swung down from his horse daintily, with a precise movement of his pointed Spanish boot. He smiled coldly in Tim's direction but did not speak. Apparently he was willing to let Kentucky take the lead.

This the huge man did. He strode around talking in a loud voice. "Tried to turn me ag'in' the judge. Tried to say other folks was claim jumpers to hide their own tricks . . . but they couldn't put their pig in my kitchen. Naw, sir! I was too wise for 'em. I pretty quick smelled out their game." He glared at Tim. "Rocky Gulch!"

"I suppose the marshal there told you all about his affairs at Rocky Gulch."

"He was never even thar, he nor the judge. Neither of 'em. I went around last night and asked 'em."

"When the sheriff of Rocky Gulch gets here, you may hear a different story."

"You ain't worryin' me with your lies."

Maybe not Kentucky—he had no worries—but Splain moved uncomfortably.

All through this, Comanche John took his ease against the cabin and looked on with an expression of amused tolerance. He brought his twist of blackjack from the pocket of his homespuns, clamped hold with his teeth, and gnawed and pulled until he secured a cheekful. "That sheriff will be here before nightfall," he said confidently. "You may be the smartest man in Eldorado today, Kentucky, but you'll be huntin' your hole tomorrow."

Kentucky was not alarmed. "Mebby," he countered, "but unless I'm off on my mountain justice, you won't be here to enjoy it."

Splain appreciated this joke. He smoothed his neat mustache and laughed.

Kentucky bellowed. "Enough of this jawin'! We didn't come up here to talk. We come to get things done." He pointed to the cabin door. "Get in thar and search the place. See if you can locate the gold they lifted from the coach last night. And if we do. . . ." He arched his eyebrows significantly. "Well, coach robbin' is a serious offense."

Splain's voice cracked out: "They just shot down one of my deputies, don't forget that. Murder is a serious offense, too."

"Not like coach robbin' it ain't," Kentucky answered with the aggressive tone he always used when he thought someone was disagreeing with him. "I wisht I had every coach robber in the Nor'west in that cabin thar. I'd touch the tinder to her and burn 'em like bedbugs."

"Why, that's cruel!" John seemed offended. "Glad I ain't no coach robber."

Inside, the men were ransacking the cabin. They tipped everything upside down, tore the ticks from the bunks, strewed the floor with kettles, dug into bags of beans and flour. One man sounded along the logs next to the dirt floor; another braved the heat of the fire to peer up the chimney. After that he knelt to examine the stones at the front of the fireplace. One seemed to catch his attention. He lifted it, put it back. Lifted another. At last they gave up the search.

"Probably buried it outside some place," Kentucky growled. He stood there, looking from one of his prisoners to the other. His eyes lit on the parson. "Who are you?"

"Me? I'm the Reverend . . . the Reverend. . . ." It had been so long since the parson had been called any name but "Parson" that he momentarily forgot what his real name was.

"Reverend! Don't try givin' me a story like that. I ain't one that's took in easy. Reverends wear long black coats, like gamblers."

"I am too a reverend," the parson brayed at him. "A-course I wouldn't expect *you* to know it, but I run a mission right down on Main street in Eldorado. It was in that log buildin' betwixt Katie's and the Bird Cage Opry."

"It's a dance hall thar now."

"Hallelujah," said Comanche John.

Kentucky looked over the parson with dark suspicion. "Waal, if you're a reverend, like you say, how come you're shacked up with road agents and claim jumpers?"

The parson fixed him with his Old Testament eyes. "They's claim jumpers here, true enough, but it ain't us." He pointed to Splain. "Thar's the claim-jumper-in-chief. . . ."

"Shut up!" barked Splain.

The parson was not bullied. "I'll have you know. . . ."

With a quick movement, Splain raked the pistol from his right-hand holster, brought down the barrel with brutal force across the parson's forehead. The old man tossed his arms like he was drowning and sprawled to the ground. He lay there quite still. A little stream of blood rolled down across a couple of stones. Splain re-holstered his gun with evident satisfaction. "That's how I deal with men who insult me," he swaggered.

"That's pretty rough, seein' he's such a harmless critter," remarked Comanche John.

"Keep your mouth closed or you'll get the same."

Splain's action didn't go well with Kentucky. The big man started to say something, then he changed his mind. "Let's get on with the trial," he boomed.

Tim watched until the parson showed some signs of life. Then he sat him up against the cabin. Afterward he sought a few private words with John.

"Looks bad, doesn't it?"

"A bit on the tight side."

"Suppose we should signal Bogey?"

"To blow her up? Not yet. 'Twon't do us much good unless we get 'em all bunched down in the gulch. Let's sort of keep that flood for an ace in the sleeve."

The trial took place in front of the cabin. Tim, Comanche John, and the parson, the latter shaky but still defiant, were lined up against the log front. Kentucky Smith presided. He took a gargantuan chaw of tobacco and sat on the rough tree-trunk bench that had been brought from inside.

"Court'll come to order," he announced, slapping his palms. "These men are accused of claim jumpin' and highway robbery, chiefly the latter. Let's have testimony."

Splain then came forward, escorting a small, meek-looking man dressed in city clothes. How such a one came to be in a remote mining camp like Eldorado, Tim couldn't guess. Perhaps he was a drummer or a musician. Whoever he was, he was noticeably ill at east among the rough, gun-toting vigilantes and deputies.

Kentucky suspiciously eyed his starched white collar and cuffs. "Who are you?"

"Hector Smith."

"Smith!" It was plain to see that Kentucky Smith cared little about this insignificant person having the same name.

"Yes, sir."

"Well, say what you got to say."

The little man stammered for words, so Splain came to his rescue. "He was on the robbed coach last night, and he came here to identify. . . ."

"Let him tell about it."

"Yes, I was on the coach, as the marshal says." Hector Smith talked rapidly from excitement. "We were riding along through the trees when all of a sudden the coach stopped. It was pretty dark, although there was some moon. Nobody could tell what was going on. But pretty soon the driver opened the door and said the coach had sprung a spoke and we'd all have to climb down. We didn't know it was a robbery until we were all outside. Then a masked man stepped out with a sawed-off shotgun. I guess he'd dropped on top of the coach from a limb and. . . ."

"Do you see that man here?" Splain interrupted.

"Yes. It's that fellow right there." He pointed at Comanche John.

"What?" John bellowed in a voice that made Hector Smith contract a full inch. "*Me,* a road agent?" He rolled his eyes like a Christian martyr. "Why, I'm as innocent as a babe unborn."

Tim asked casually: "You say he was masked?"

"Yes. He wore a white handkerchief with eyeholes."

"And you say it was dark?"

"Well, there was a little moon."

"It was *dark,*" Tim insisted.

"Yes."

"But in spite of it being dark and the robber masked, you're able to identify this man. By the way, Smith, do you know what vigilance committees in this territory do to witnesses who stretch the truth . . . ?"

"Here! Keep your mouth shut," Splain cut in.

"I'm runnin' this court," Kentucky bellowed. "And I intend to run a fair, square trial. Anybody can say what he damned pleases." He nodded to Tim. "Have your say."

"Do you know what is done to perjurers?"

The meek man shook his head.

"Tell him, Kentucky."

"We hang 'em."

The small man gasped. He began to hedge. "I'm not *sure*. I'm not sure at all."

Splain made an impatient gesture. "Don't let him talk you out of it. Of course, you're sure. Tell them so."

Kentucky wasn't sure now, either. After all, they hadn't found the gold. What real proof was there? Besides, he was edgy toward Splain for rapping the parson, and he didn't like this scissorbill witness being called Smith. He glanced around at his men. Like Kentucky, they were for the most part honest miners who were out to stop robbery rather than hang innocent men.

"We can't hang a man on that kind of testimony," Kentucky growled.

Tim's heart leaped. Splain's idea might fizzle, after all. The judge and marshal had little power without the backing of the vigilantes.

Splain was looking at something. His expression caught Tim's attention. He was staring with fixed interest at something Comanche John was carrying. The hair prickled up along the back of his neck when Tim saw what it was.

"What's that chain?" the marshal demanded, pointing to a few heavy gold links that hung from the pocket of John's homespuns.

John's eyes became narrow slits. "What chain?"

Splain pointed.

"It's on my watch."

Splain jerked out the watch and held it dangling. His voice leaped exultantly. "Look! A watch with a diamond, ruby, and emerald in its back. This is the judge's watch." He turned to Kentucky. "You remember the judge saying his watch was stolen by a road agent on his trip over? Remember he described it to you? And look here!" He pointed to an inscription on its back. "There's his father's name . . . Ebram W. Mayand."

Kentucky grabbed the watch and examined it. His eyes became baleful. "I reckon that about settles it," he said. "This means hangin'. Get the rope ready."

"Get *three* ropes ready," Splain corrected.

Kentucky considered. "No, we only got one road agent."

Splain fumed. "They're all shacked up together, aren't they? If one is guilty, they all are. Certainly, hang them all. Isn't that right, men?"

His deputies chorused their approval, but the vigilantes were more hesitant. Several of them shook their heads.

Kentucky thoughtfully scratched his whiskers. "I been shacked up with a road agent or two in my time, through no fault of my own," he admitted, "and I ain't hankerin' to get hung."

Tim's eye caught a movement on the mountainside. It was near the spot where Della had disappeared among the trees. A stone clattered, rolled, leaped high in its tumbling descent, splashed in the trickle beneath the sluice. Hoofs clattered rocks. Briefly a horse and rider flashed among the trees.

"It's that other one . . . the old fellow!" Splain shouted. "Shoot him!"

Guns flew from holsters. Every eye watched for the next opportunity.

Tim ran out, waving arms: "Don't shoot! It's a woman. It's. . . ." But he dared not give her away. If she would only remain hidden a few more yards! Fifty yards more and she would be out of range. But a second later she was in full view crossing a break in the timber. From below, dressed in broad hat and riding skirt, she looked like a man.

The guns seemed to crash in unison—deafening. Then she was gone, still riding. The rain of lead must have spattered all around her.

"Some shootin'," John chuckled. "I've seen Chinee do better in a tong war."

V

Directly below the cabin, near the head box of the sluice, stood an ancient, long-needled pine with heavy, gnarled branches. The lowest of these branches swayed down to within a dozen feet of the ground. This convenient branch was chosen for the hanging that was ordered to take place without delay. Just what disposal would be made of Tim and the parson would be decided later.

One of the tallest vigilantes rode beneath the limb and, carefully balancing himself, stood on his saddle and fastened the rope. Then, with a dexterity that hinted at experience, he wound up just the correct amount of its loose end in a hangman's knot. Everyone was silent for a few seconds while they looked at the rope with its fatal loop swinging there in the early sunshine.

Comanche John calmly chewed his tobacco. Tim noticed his eyes were quicker than usual, and several times he glanced in the direction of the dam.

Tim came close. "Should we send the signal?"

"Not yet. Wait till these stranglers are all in the bottom of the gulch. That way, they'll be too busy savin' their own hides to worry about me. But it has to be before they tie my hands. I'd as soon be hung as drownded. Say! You got anything white to signal with?"

"The parson has. He's got that white linen handkerchief he lays over his hand whenever he picks up the Bible."

Tim could sense the contraction of John's muscles. "No, he ain't. I took that handkerchief last night. Cut eyeholes in her and then threw it away."

"He carries one in his pocket. I'll ask him. . . ."

"Stop that talking," Splain barked.

Kentucky was not excited. "I don't guess their talkin' can be harmful."

Tim was at trifle giddy from excitement when he sidled over by the parson. Everything had to work just right. What if a mistake of *his* should bungle it?

"Got a white handkerchief to signal Bogey?"

The parson felt of his pocket. The lines of his face were tight. "I ain't got it! It's beneath the Bible."

"John took the one under the Bible. Used it for a mask and threw it away."

"That's all right. I know of somethin'." He started for the door. A deputy stopped him.

"Where do you think you're going?"

"Inside."

"What for?"

"For my Bible."

The deputy laughed. "Listen to him! He wants his Bible!"

Splain sneered. "I suppose you want to read a few verses to Comanche John."

"That's exactly what I want to do."

Somebody said: "Fat lot of good it would do *him*."

The parson waggled a long finger. The wound on his forehead went scarlet in his excitement. "It's every man's right to have a prayer said to comfort him durin' his last moments. . . ."

Splain's voice cracked like a lash. "Tie his hands!" He was

pointing to John. "Get that rope around his neck. I haven't had breakfast, and most of the others haven't, either. Are we going to stand around here and go hungry while this so-called reverend says prayers? Probably he's trying to kill time. Perhaps that fellow who rode up the mountain is going for help. How do we know but what he has a gang somewhere?"

Kentucky was not excited over the possibility of help. Sensing his sympathy, the parson turned to him. "Ain't it true a man's supposed to have a chance to ready his soul afore he's hung?"

"We ain't been doin' it in the past," Kentucky grumbled. "But I'm not one to stand in the way of a man's conscience. It ain't an easy thing to die. Not even for a road agent. If a man has a last request, we aim to carry it out for him. So, if the prisoner is hankerin' for a prayer, he can have it." He glanced at John. "But maybe you don't want one."

"Me? I sure do want one!"

"Tie his hands," insisted Splain. "Put the rope around his neck. Get him on the rear of the horse, ready for the drop. Let him have his prayer that way."

John objected. "A man can't pray with his hands tied." He pressed his palms together and pointed them downward. "I always pray thisaway, don't I, Parson?"

"That's right!"

Kentucky commanded: "Say your prayer."

"I can't say it without my Bible." Once more the parson started for the door, but the same deputy shoved him back.

Kentucky was suspicious. "Why do you have to have a Bible? You say you're a reverend, but you don't even know a prayer!"

"I know prayers aplenty, but they got more power when the Book's open."

"That's right," Comanche John chimed in. "I want her,

250

Bible and all. I only 'spect to get hung once, and I want her done up proper."

Kentucky motioned to one of his men: "Clark, get the Bible." The man hurried into the cabin.

"You need a handkerchief," Tim whispered. But the parson looked complacent. John led the way to the gulch bottom. He stood beneath the dangling noose, palms pointed skyward, apparently resigned to fate.

Clark hurried out with the Bible and put it in the parson's hands. The parson walked down to where John was standing, shot a furtive glance up the gulch, then opened the Book.

"Gather around, please." He waited. The men drew close.

Then, with a wide, sweeping motion of his arm, the parson waved his Bible, white leaves toward the dam, three times overhead. "That drives off the devil," he explained.

After a moment of silence, the parson started to read. His voice quavered a little, like the words were unwilling to come and he had to force them. John was like a cat ready to spring. Tim didn't breathe. He stared at the Bible to keep from looking toward the dam. The time crept. It was supposed to be a quarter minute fuse. Only a quarter minute, and a minute must have passed already. Maybe Bogey hadn't seen the signal. The parson stopped reading. A-tremble, he started the signal again. . . .

"What's he doing?" Splain demanded with sudden suspicion. "Driving off the devil . . . he's signaling. . . ."

His words were rent by an earth-shattering explosion, the crash of flying rocks and logs through timber, then a roar.

"Water!" a man shouted. "They've blown the dam out. Run, for God's sake!"

Tim fled up the gulch side. The parson was a few steps behind. Suddenly he realized he was running in the wrong direction, for most of the others were headed the same way. But it was too late to turn back.

Down there the gulch was a swirl of water. First a pointed, racing tongue of it, a foot or two deep, then a huge wave. A horse's whinny raised to a scream as it was carried off in the current. Men fled up the rocks, clung to trees, a couple hung to floating débris.

Tim momentarily glimpsed Comanche John, clinging to the hangman's rope. One of Splain's deputies made a grab for the rope, too. John seemed to be helping him—but he only wanted the deputy's guns. He snatched them, then kicked the struggling man back into the swirl of water. Tim took in all this in a couple of glances over his shoulder. The parson was crashing up behind him. He had fallen. Tim leaped back, helped the old man up. Kentucky's voice was shouting. Something seemed to explode in Tim's brain. Then a whirl of blackness.

Tim opened his eyes. He started to sit up. Pain knifed down from his skull. He dropped back, ran his hand gently over his skull. It was sore, swollen. His hair was matted with drying blood. He looked around, trying not to turn his head more than a few degrees.

He was lying on the ground near where the cabin had stood. It was gone now, and nothing except the fireplace remained. The bottom of the gulch was swept clean. But there was the hangman's tree, its rope still dangling. The parson sat near, gloomily staring at the ground. No sign of Comanche John.

Kentucky Smith, noticing his eyes open, walked over to glower. He was still trailing water. His black whiskers bristled. "Your pardner, the coach robber, got away, but it will go all the harder for you. We'll find use for that rope. We'll use it twice. And no prayin', neither!" He bellowed to one of his men. "Toss another rope over yonder limb. And hurry it. We got to run down that road agent."

The tall man once again rode beneath the limb, stood in his saddle, and tied on a rope. While he was winding the knot, two men tied Tim's and then the parson's hands. Then they were shoved roughly down the slope.

They stood under the limb. The two nooses dangled over their heads. Tim was still a little giddy from the blow he had received. He wondered if all this was not some particularly realistic nightmare. Maybe he would wake up and find himself inside the cabin. He thought this, hoped this, with half his brain, but the other half knew it was no dream. The other half knew it was cold reality. Clammy reality. He was going to die. In a minute they would put one of those nooses around his neck, and he would die. His stomach was bottomless, and beads of sweat felt cold on his forehead. He glanced at the parson. The old man stood there, straight and tall, eyes closed, lips moving silently.

Two horses were led forward. Kentucky said: "Boys, we'll make it as easy on you as we can. Do as we say and we'll see you get a good drop." He looked around to see if all was in readiness. "All right. Help them up behind the saddles."

A couple of vigilantes came forward to do his bidding. Splain stood at one side, enjoying the scene. Tim could feel the vigilante's hands at his armpits. But then the hands relaxed. The man and all the others were listening. Hoof beats! Hoof beats speeding recklessly up the gulch.

A wild idea came to Tim's mind—the sheriff from Rocky Gulch! But it wasn't. A tall, familiar man was in the lead. Hatless, his long white hair blew behind. Following him was a girl. It was Judge Mayand and Della.

The judge pulled in a few feet from the tree, sat there, looking from one face to the other. He was gripping the reins so tightly the flesh of his thin hands looked bloodless.

Kentucky swallowed his surprise. "Judge! What are you doin' here? And Miss Mayand. . . ."

The judge started to speak, but only a whisper came from his lips. He glanced at Della. Sight of her seemed to give him strength. "Stop this hanging," he commanded.

"What's that? Stop it? Why, these here claim jumpers. . . ."

"Yes, stop it! These men aren't claim jumpers. They are honest men. The real claim jumpers are right here in your own posse."

Kentucky's jaw sagged. He glanced doubtfully at his men.

The judge went on: "I'll tell you how things really stand. I came here to Eldorado, intending to be an honest recorder. But I haven't been. I've been the tool of a band of claim jumpers. I've been trapped by my past. Last night Kentucky Smith there asked me about Rocky Gulch. I told him I'd never been there, and Splain said the same. We both lied. We both left Rocky Gulch one jump ahead of two ropes like those hanging from that limb."

Splain had stepped away from the group. His guns were out. The judge, seeing him, was struck silent.

Splain's voice rang out: "Yes, the judge and I hail from Rocky Gulch." He glanced at Tim. "Your guess was right, wasn't it? And now I suppose you think you're winning. You're not. Hear that? You're not. In fact, you're practically a dead man. And you, Judge, you, too."

He brought the guns level, hammers back.

Overhead, in the thick branches of the pine tree, there was a movement that no one noticed. A gun crashed. Splain took a step, guns limp. Then, as he fell, one of them fired, but the bullet glanced harmlessly away among the trees.

For a stunned second there was silence. Then a man swung down to the limb from which the ropes hung, plopped

254

to the saddle of one of the waiting horses. It was Comanche John.

On his descent, he had holstered his two Navies—the two he had taken from the deputy during the flood—but he no quicker touched saddle leather than they were in his hands again.

One of Splain's men was concealed by the tree. His hands were at his gun butts. But a voice from a nearby clump of junipers froze his action.

"Keep your hands innocent down thar!" It was Bogey. They could hear him chuckle. "Why, we had you boys surrounded all the time."

Comanche John calmly looked at the gathering. He said: "Guess this settles the question of the claim, but I don't estimate you stranglers have developed much love for *me*. And they ain't got much love for you, Judge, either. 'Course, you might get by *this* committee, but how about the one from Rocky Gulch? I wouldn't wonder if the trail was the healthiest place for both of us. What say we team up?"

The judge shot an uneasy glance at the vigilantes. His eyes fell on the waiting ropes. The ropes seemed to settle the matter. He nudged his horse and rode over beside Comanche John.

"Yep, Judge, I reckon we'd make a tolerable team. Me do the rough work and you give her class. And don't worry about your niece." He winked broadly at Tim. "I wouldn't wonder if she and some young man had a job for the parson one of these days. He's been hankerin' all along for a weddin'."

John remembered something, dismounted and, without ever taking his eyes entirely from the group near the tree, strode to where the cabin had stood, raised a stone from the hearth, and lifted from the concealed cavity a generous half of its contents. Two of the heavy bags he dropped in the pockets of the judge's long, black coat. They weighted it like two flat-irons.

"Thar! You're sort of spare in the ribs, and I expect that'll help you hang your horse better over the rough country." He cast a hand lavishly. "It's gold, and she's yourn to keep. You won't find me a selfish man to travel with, Judge. No, sir! Every man for his principles, I say, but share and share alike is my motto."

He was still laughing when their horses turned to run.

About the Author

Dan Cushman was born in Osceola, Michigan, and grew up on the Cree Indian Reservation in Montana. He graduated from the University of Montana with a Bachelor of Science degree in 1934 and pursued a career in mining as a prospector, assayer, and geologist before turning to journalism. In the early 1940s his novelette-length stories began appearing regularly in such Fiction House magazines as *North-West Romances* and *Frontier Stories*. Later in the decade his North-Western and Western stories as well as fiction set in the Far East and Africa began appearing in *Action Stories*, *Adventure*, and *Short Stories*. STAY AWAY, JOE, which first appeared in 1953, is an amusing novel about the mixture, and occasional collision, of Indian culture and Anglo-American culture among the Métis (French Indians) living on a reservation in Montana. The novel became a bestseller and remains a classic to this day, greatly loved especially by Indian peoples for its truthfulness and humor. Yet, while humor became Cushman's hallmark in such later novels as THE OLD COPPER COLLAR (1957) and GOOD BYE, OLD DRY (1959), he also produced significant historical fiction in THE SILVER MOUNTAIN (1957), concerned with the mining and politics of silver in Montana in the 1890s. This novel won a Spur Award from the Western Writers of America. His fiction remains notable for its breadth, ranging all the way from a story of the cattle frontier in TALL WYOMING (1957) to a poignant and memorable portrait of small-town life in Michigan just before the Great War in THE GRAND AND THE GLORIOUS (1963). THE ADVENTURES OF COMANCHE JOHN will be his next **Five Star Western**.